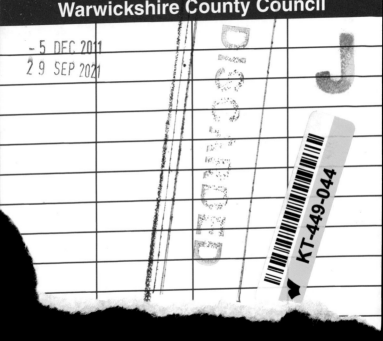

# Praise for the Faire Folk Trilogy

## The Tree Shepherd's Daughter

"The constant action, both magical and otherwise,
will keep [readers] interested in Keelie's fate."
—*School Library Journal*

"One of those remarkable tales in which the reader
becomes completely immersed … It will be enjoyed not
only in its own right, but also will have readers eagerly
anticipating books two and three in the promised trilogy."
—*KLIATT*

## Into the Wildewood

"Compelling and beautifully written … a great
follow-up to an already breathtaking first novel.
Fans of the series will be very satisfied."
—TeensReadToo.com

"*Into the Wildewood* brings a fresh perspective to the
genre with a crackerjack plot and razor sharp writing."
—*ForeWord Magazine*

## The Secret of the Dread Forest

"The pleasant mix of fairy dust and romance—hallmarks of
the previous two books—is still present in *The Secret of the
Dread Forest*. The book zips along—fans of the series will not
be disappointed."
—*VOYA*

"New and old characters combine in a breakneck plot that
will have readers turning pages in class
and long after bedtime."

# Shadows
of the
# Redwood

*To all of the two-legged and four-legged children that make life endlessly amusing, frustrating, and delightful. Biscuits and chew-chews to all.*

THE FAIRE FOLK SAGA: TRILOGY II

# Shadows
## of the
# Redwood

## GILLIAN SUMMERS

### THE SCIONS OF SHADOW TRILOGY

Woodbury, Minnesota

First Edition
First Printing, 2010

Book design by Steffani Sawyer
Cover design by Kevin R. Brown
Cover illustration by Derek Lea

Flux, an imprint of Llewellyn Worldwide Ltd.

This is a work of fiction. Names, characters, places, and incidents are either the product of the author's imagination or are used fictitiously, and any resemblance to actual persons, living or dead, business establishments, events, or locales is entirely coincidental. Cover model used for illustrative purposes only and may not endorse or represent the book's subject.

**Library of Congress Cataloging-in-Publication Data**
Summers, Gillian.
  Shadows of the redwood / Gillian Summers ; [cover illustration by Derek Lea].—1st ed.
    p. cm.—(The scions of shadow trilogy ; 1)
  The faire folk saga: trilogy II."
  Summary: Sixteen-year-old half-elf Keelie, her cat Knot, and her grandmother, also an elf, travel to California to help a redwood forest that is missing its tree shepherd, and with the help of the handsome Sean and a former apprentice of her father's, plus a mysterious coyote, Keelie tries to discover the deadly secret of the bloodroot tree in time to save the forest.
  ISBN 978-0-7387-1552-0
  [1. Elves—Fiction. 2. Magic—Fiction. 3. Trees—Fiction.
4. California—Fiction.]  I. Title.
PZ7.S953987Sh 2010
  [Fic]—dc22
                                        2010002353

Flux
Llewellyn Worldwide Ltd.
2143 Wooddale Drive
Woodbury, MN 55125-2989
www.fluxnow.com

Printed in the United States of America

## Acknowledgments

Much of the research for this book was done online. However, huge thanks to Dexter Henry for walking the big woods and shaking the redbark dust from his hiking boots, giving us a timely addition to our redwood knowledge, and, as ever, to Wendy Davis of the National Park Service, our tree-huggin' muse. Special thanks to our agent Richard Curtis, and to our creative and patient editors Brian Farrey and Sandy Sullivan, our enthusiastic publicist Marissa Pederson, and to Amy Martin, the queen of back-cover blurbs. And much Ren Faire love to Kevin Brown for blessing us with his gorgeous covers. Keelie is ever so grateful.

*Trees [are] like silent witnesses to history as it goes by.*

—LOREENA MCKENNITT, NPR INTERVIEW

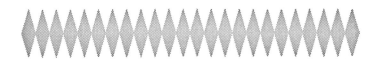

# one

The spring air was brisk and smelled of green buds and rising sap. Keelie Heartwood buttoned her acorn-embroidered
sweater as she closed the post office door and stepped out
onto Edgewood's breezy Main Street. She held five enve-
lopes in her left hand, and one very special envelope in her
right.

It was a normal-looking paper rectangle, except for the
black embossed return address that read Talbot and Talbot.
Her mom's law firm, the one that had sent an attorney to
personally escort her to her father at the High Mountain
Renaissance Faire last year, after her mother died. That day,

Keelie thought her world had ended, and it was true in a way. Gone was the spoiled California mall brat. And though she still missed her mom terribly, now she had a father she adored and a totally different lifestyle. So different that her Los Angeles friends would never recognize her.

For one thing, she was an elf. Well, a half-elf. She'd always been one, of course, but it took living with her elven dad and learning that her tree allergy was really a sensitivity to magic to change her forever.

Now, though, that old life had come roaring back. She hadn't been able to resist opening the letter then and there, and she was still reeling from the news. Mom's house, *her* house, the one she'd grown up in, had been sold. Talbot and Talbot was happy to announce how much money would now go to her trust fund, but Keelie's brain had stopped at the word "sale."

The house was empty, of course. The lawyers had arranged to send her belongings here, to the Dread Forest in Oregon, and the furniture and Mom's things were in storage. Keelie's gut clenched at the thought of her life with Mom in some darkened, airless warehouse space in plain brown boxes. She'd be able to open them again one day, but the house, the gardens, the neighborhood would soon be a memory beyond her reach.

She wished she could go back once more to say goodbye. As long as her house was there, a window was open to her past. She could hear it slamming shut.

The wind picked up, showering Keelie with sweet white blossoms from the pear trees that lined the street. She brushed flowers from her sweater and absently thanked the trees for their gift. They meant well.

*May your leaves shine brightly, Daughter of the Forest,* they answered in tree speak, the telepathic language of the trees. Since she was a tree shepherd, like her father, Keelie could hear them. No other elves could.

Ahead, a glowing neon sign flashed "Magic Forest Tattoo," her friend Zabrina's tattoo and piercing shop. Keelie hurried toward it, eager to tell her friend about the letter and maybe score a cup of coffee. Dad was not a coffee drinker, and this seriously cramped Keelie's mornings.

She pulled open the door, jingling the bell that dangled from the knob on a silk cord, and then slowed, disappointed to see that Zabrina had customers—a group of college students in "I survived the Okanogan Rapids" T-shirts. The one sitting in the dentist's chair Zabrina used for her work looked pale. Zabrina's brilliant purple hair shadowed the area where she was working on his bicep.

A huge pumpkin-colored cat snored at her feet, ignoring the sounds around him. He twisted to look when the bell jingled, and Zabrina looked up.

"Hey, Keelie. How's that belly button ring working?"

Keelie touched her stomach. "It's okay. Perfectly normal." She emphasized the word "normal." Her first belly button ring had been wooden, and her increasing magic had made it come to life, sprouting leaves and threatening to turn into a tree branch sticking out of her belly. Scary. This one was silver and, so far, inert.

"Good to hear," Zabrina said. Her little smile said much

more. She wore a long-sleeved peasant blouse today that covered Molly, the fairy tattoo on her shoulder that sometimes came to life and flitted around the shop like Tinker Bell's shadow. "Need anything?"

"No, you're busy. I'll just grab my cat." Keelie looked at the orange behemoth. "Come on, Knot, time to go home."

In typical cat fashion, Knot ignored her, turning his green eyes toward the wall that was covered in framed pictures of tattoos. Knot wasn't really a cat—he was a fairy, just as Zabrina was, and he liked to hang around with her.

"Take him with you, Keelie. He's been chasing Molly." Zabrina widened her eyes and jerked her chin toward her tattooed shoulder.

Keelie glared at the cat. "You are so evil." He purred, as she knew he would. "You shouldn't stay where you aren't wanted." She knew better than to drag him out, but he'd come along in a minute. He just didn't want her to think he was a pushover. Keelie waved at the bedraggled, tired-looking white water rafters who'd come in for their souvenir tats. A few waved back, and she ducked out of the shop.

She headed south, hoping to see Barrow the dwarf at his parents' hardware store, since she was dying to talk to someone about the letter. She crossed the street in front of the diner. A fuzzy orange blur beat her to it. Keelie knew Knot couldn't resist seeing what she was up to.

Loud banging rang from the narrow old warehouse that occupied the space next to the hardware store, its mellow bricks covered in ivy. Barrow was in his sculpture workshop. His metal sculptures decorated many of the lawns around town, and were popular with the tourists and white water rafters.

She tugged open one of the sagging white doors (pine, from the river's shore), and stepped into the gloom. "Barrow, you here?"

"Back here, Keelie."

She turned toward his voice, but didn't move until her eyes had adjusted to the dark. Barrow's family lived underground, and this was normal lighting for him.

Her vision cleared slowly, until she saw the dwarf at the other end of the warehouse next to a wide kiddie pool, his welding torch and tanks behind him. Keelie's eyes widened when she saw that the pool held the water sprite who lived in the stream in the Dread Forest. The little fishlike sprite was sitting on a rock in the center of the pool, her tail fins splashing lightly and her head thrown back so that her long, green, yarnlike hair flowed down to the water behind her. Barrow had a serious crush on the sprite.

"Keelie, you remember Plu, don't you?"

Plu? She'd never learned the sprite's name, but the bubbly sounding word fit her. "Hi, Plu. Nice to see you again."

The sprite opened her large lavender eyes and then smiled when she saw Keelie. "I wondered who it was that could see me."

Knot rubbed against the side of the kiddie pool.

"I'm doing her portrait," Barrow explained. The dwarf seemed to be about Keelie's age, even though at three feet tall he was the same height as her father's friend, Sir Davey. Keelie had met Barrow last fall Under-the-Hill, which was the underground land where the dwarves lived (the fae had once lived there too, although in recent years only the darkest fae, such as trolls and Red Caps, remained). Dad and Grandmother had been surprised to hear of the existence of this subterranean homeland; the elves had lived atop it for centuries without ever knowing it. The trees, whose roots delved deep, had kept the secret.

Keelie drew closer and looked over Barrow's shoulder. So far, the portrait consisted of three battered steel cutouts welded together.

"I'm just starting." Barrow must have noticed her expression. "I'm going to curl steel ribbons for her hair." The sprite laughed and Barrow blushed. He had it bad.

"It sounds great," Keelie said, still not sure how it would work out. She was no artist. "I got a letter from my mom's lawyers. They sold our house."

"The one in the city?" Barrow pulled a heavy leather hood over his head, then dropped a thick metal shield with a tiny, thick glass window in its center over his face. "Step back and don't look at the flame."

Keelie backed away and turned from the slight "whump," which was followed by the hissing roar of the welding torch. "I'd better leave you to it. See you later."

Barrow motioned absently, his attention on his work. As she was leaving he yelled out, "Let's have lunch before you leave for the High Mountain Faire."

"Sure," Keelie called. She couldn't talk to him until that torch was extinguished. "See you later. Bye, Plu."

She trudged back to where she'd parked her father's battered pickup truck. No one had time for her today. Keelie didn't want to whine to Dad about the sale of the house, as if she was yearning for the life she'd had before, and Grandmother wouldn't understand. She climbed into the truck, waiting for Knot to take his usual seat beside her, paws on the dashboard so that he could watch the road ahead. She started the truck up and headed through town, then turned left at the first crossroad and started up the mountain.

Keelie shivered as she passed the tall trees that marked the beginning of the Dread Forest, and grasped the rose quartz crystal that she kept clipped to her belt loop. The Dread, as it was called, was a powerful magic that the elves had laid upon the forest long ago, to make humans feel a powerful, unfocused terror and run away as fast as possible. By successfully keeping humans out with the Dread, the elves had kept the forest pristine for centuries. As a half-human, Keelie was not as affected by the Dread as a full human would be, but it still made her nauseated and afraid. So, as Sir Davey had taught her, she drew on her rose quartz to channel Earth magic, which boosted her other powers and helped her resist the Dread. Without the crystal, she wouldn't be able to live here with her father.

The lessons she'd taken with Lord Elianard, over the winter, had included a section from ancient books on the elven use of Earth magic. Keelie had picked up some tips about Earth magic that even Sir Davey didn't know. Of course, now she was stuck carrying around a huge book of charms and spells that she had to work through, but it was worth it. For one thing, she'd learned to boost the power of the rose quartz with elven magic, so now she could just clip the crystal to her belt and still be covered by its effect. She had also made extra charms and stashed them in the house, the truck, and even around the forest so she'd never be without one.

After a while the Earth magic charm was self-sustaining, and Keelie was able to let the crystal dangle once more from her waist. The woods were beautiful, thick with tall, ancient trees. The high canopy and shadowed floor held all kinds of life, and Keelie felt as if she was an important part of it.

Soon, the gray stone stable of the elven village loomed ahead, and she parked in the graveled lot next to it. The building housed the Silver Bough Jousting Company's horses in the off-season. This was also where supplies and deliveries were dropped off, before the human delivery drivers quickly left, screaming all the way down the mountain.

Keelie walked around the building, which smelled faintly of horses even though all of them had been trucked to California for the start of the Juliet City Shakespeare Festival. Sean, the head jouster and Keelie's sort-of boyfriend, had been so busy preparing for the trip that they'd barely seen each other in weeks.

She batted aside the thought that if he'd really wanted to, he could have made time to be with her. At least he hadn't been with Risa, who had been his fiancé for, like, five minutes last fall. Keelie tried not to think about that either. The curvy elf girl was joining the Ren Faire circuit for the first time this spring, selling handmade herbal products, and she was starting in Juliet City.

Keelie had wanted to go to Juliet as well, mostly so that

she could be closer to Sean, and also to her friend Laurie, who lived in L.A. (although L.A. was not exactly next door, being hundreds of miles to the south). But now that Risa was going to be at the Festival, Keelie had a second reason to go there. And the envelope in her hand made three.

But instead, she was stuck in Oregon, plowing through the Lore Books that Lord Elianard had assigned her, as well as working through the massive and massively boring book of charms and spells, otherwise known as the Compendium of Elven Household Charms. Lord Elianard expected her to have it memorized by the time they rendezvoused in Colorado at the High Mountain Faire. It seemed Keelie's life was happening elsewhere while she was stuck here.

She walked behind the stone and timber homes of the village elves until she reached her house. Zekeliel Heartwood—her dad, master carpenter, tree shepherd, and current Lord of the Forest—had built this two-story craftsman-style house for his bride Katy, Keelie's human mom. Now Keelie called it home. She couldn't imagine living anywhere else ... except for that little house in Hancock Park, Los Angeles, where she'd lived with Mom.

"Dad?" No answer. Knot shot upstairs, and Keelie left the other mail on the kitchen counter and went back out, the folded Talbot and Talbot letter in her pocket. The village was quiet today. Many of the elves had left for the various fairs they worked across the country.

The air smelled sweet and full of life, and under her feet was the hum of living things. Deeper below, she could hear the heartlike thrum of the underworld. Under-the-Hill, just a hundred feet below her.

Keelie passed the circle of ancient oaks called the Grove, which surrounded the green where the village business took place. A giant but new tree rose in the center, its roots emerging from the broken pieces of petrified wood that had formed the Elven Council's meeting place, the Caudex. Someone had made a pavement out of the fragments of the Caudex, and they still resonated with power.

The tree's branches glittered with hanging chains, wind chimes, and bits of crystal. Her name was Alora. She had come from the Wildewood Forest in New York, an acorn in Keelie's pocket. As a treeling she'd loved to wear Keelie's earrings and other shiny jewelry, which she delightedly called "twinkles." But the treeling had grown with magic, and was now the Great Tree of the Dread Forest. Her place on the Caudex had sealed the presence of the Dread in these woods and restored the balance of magic in the forest.

Leaves swished and branches rattled as Keelie approached the ancient trees and Alora. The trees greeted her, some friendly, some with indifference, but the three oaks call the Aunties trilled their delight at her presence, and Alora at their center most of all.

"Did you bring me twinkles?" Alora asked excitedly. She spoke aloud, although no regular elves could hear her. For all her power, she was still very young.

"No, I just went to the post office," Keelie replied. "Dad doesn't let me drive very far, since I just got my license." She pulled the envelope from her pocket. "I got this, though. The house I lived in with my mom has been sold."

Alora's spirit face pushed out of her trunk. "Your root home? Your forest mother?"

"More like the pot she was planted in." Keelie struggled to find another way to make a tree understand what a house meant. "You've been in my bedroom, when you were small. You know what it was like inside."

Alora shuddered. "A pot made from the bones of trees."

That was one way to describe a wooden house. "I was happy there with my mom. And now it'll belong to someone else." Keelie felt tears burn her eyes.

"But your roots are here. Your pot is not your home." Alora looked puzzled.

One of the Aunties interrupted, in tree speak. *I don't understand how a treeling can have more than one pot. This is your pot. We are your forest.*

Keelie sniffed. "Thanks. I love you guys so much. I can't imagine living anyplace else. But I remember living there, and I was happy because I was with my mom."

*What trees were there?* Another of the Aunties chimed in.

"Um, not too many trees. My mom didn't want me to be around them." Immediately she knew she'd said the wrong thing. Branches started to crack overhead as the trees expressed their disapproval.

"Oh, please," Alora said. "Pipe down, Aunties. Her mother died only a ring ago."

*We remember her*, one of the Aunties said. *She had brown leaves like Keelie.*

Keelie tugged at her short, curly hair. Leaves?

"Have you spoken with your father?" Alora asked. "He has much to discuss with you."

"Uh oh. What's up?"

*You're not in trouble, but he has a boon to beg of you,* the Auntie said.

"A boon? A favor, of me? What kind?"

*We can't say,* the Auntie replied.

Alora ran a slender branch across her mouth, as if zipping it up. The older trees rustled their branches at the human-like motion. They thought that hanging around with Keelie had corrupted their Great Tree.

"Okay, if you won't tell me, I'll go find Dad. I'll see you guys later."

"Bring me back some twinkles," Alora called.

"Right. You're already wearing my entire jewelry box."

It was truly weird that her best friend was a tree, and that when she wanted a pair of earrings she had to climb up and dig them out of a branch. Good thing there weren't any magpies in the forest, or her jewelry would be scattered all over Oregon.

Keelie headed back toward the house, wondering where her dad could be at this time of day. With the Ren Faire season coming up, she thought he might be in his woodshop, and sure enough, that's where she found him, finishing up an armchair made of bent willow twigs.

Her dad was wearing a long tunic of fine golden linen, no doubt a gift from one of the elven ladies who followed him around just as human women did at the Ren Faires. Dad was a chick magnet. At least they'd held off a little when she and Dad had first moved back to the Dread Forest; they probably were disconcerted to find him with a teenaged daughter.

"Keelie, right on time. Give me a hand with this." He gave her a cloth and put a bowl of lemon oil polish between them. Keelie dipped the cloth in the oil and started to rub it into the chair while Dad worked on the other side. She pushed away the vision of the shallow stream and dappled forest which came to her as her fingers touched the willow's wood.

"I got a letter from Talbot and Talbot today, Dad."

"Really? Tax stuff?"

"No, they sold Mom's house in Hancock Park."

"Oh, good. Took long enough." Dad scraped at a blemish in the wood with his fingernail.

Keelie bit her lip.

Dad straightened. "I know the house meant a lot to you, but it couldn't sit empty waiting for you. Someday, if you want it again, you can find the owners and make them an offer. It won't be gone forever." He opened his arms and swept her into a hug. "Home is not a house."

Keelie hugged him back, loving the feel of his strength. When Dad had taken her in when Mom died, he'd loved her unconditionally, and Keelie suddenly realized that she was making a big deal out of the house sale. But there was little of her mother in the Dread Forest, and Keelie wanted to feel surrounded by her mother's presence one more time. Somehow, she had to get to Los Angeles.

"Alora said you had something to tell me."

Dad stopped rubbing polish into the wood and straightened. "I do. I, too, have received an important message. Viran, the tree shepherd of the Redwood Forest, is missing. A few of the strongest shepherds are gathering there to help find him. The Redwood Forest is the oldest of the new world's forests, and the shepherd of the sequoias must be very strong, for the trees are so old that their power could drive a weak one mad. We fear for Viran. No one has seen him in weeks."

"Why don't you ask the trees where he is?"

"Good point. But the trees don't know, either. Or they aren't telling."

"What do you mean, not telling? Trees don't lie."

Dad looked grim. "I said the forest is very powerful. Do you know how the trees here can show their faces, and sometimes root walk?"

Keelie nodded. She saw the trees' faces all the time, and root walking was something she'd seen for herself in the Wildewood Forest, and not in a good way. Trees had dragged their roots out of the ground and moved around as if they had feet, a scary sight. It got even more frightening when they attacked.

"Well, in the Redwood forest, the tree spirits can take the form of people, and interact with people. Their spirits walk among the elves."

Keelie stared at him. "You're serious. They can do that?" She pictured tree spirits chasing her around.

Dad nodded. "They're quite powerful. Of course, most humans don't see it. You'll find them wise and independent. Their tree shepherd is most unusual." He started polishing again. "I'm supposed to open the Heartwood shop at the High Mountain Faire the day after tomorrow, and I can't change that commitment. So I want you to go to the redwoods in my stead. While you're there, you can set up a Heartwood shop at the Juliet City Shakespeare Festival. We've never been there, and there's space available."

A million thoughts sped through Keelie's mind. This was perfect! Running a faire shop was a piece of cake for her now, and she could also go see her former home. Would Laurie, her old school friend, drive up and take her to L.A.? But how could she take her father's place, since he'd said that only the strongest tree shepherds could deal with the redwoods? And how was she going to get to Juliet City?

Keelie only voiced some of these thoughts. "How can I drive myself all the way to the redwoods? They're down on the California coast. And do you really think I'm powerful enough to deal with the ancient trees?"

Just at that moment, Grandmother appeared in the woodshop's doorway. "I will attend to the Redwood Forest. Keelie can tend to the festival."

Keelie looked at her grandmother's stern face, which was framed by tightly braided silver hair. Keliatiel Heartwood was dressed in linen robes embroidered with forest motifs, every inch still the Lady of the Forest.

"Your grandmother knows the redwoods of old," Dad explained. "She will deal with the trees and the other tree shepherds. You will learn much from her."

Goodbye, L.A., goodbye, fun. Keelie looked once more at her stuffy, old-school grandmother.

Grandmother's eyes swiveled to meet hers. "I drive."

Life sucked.

Two days later, Keelie stood staring at the skimpy candy selection in the Gas-A-Minute, fifty yards over the California state line. Two kinds of chocolate bar, dusty-looking, foil-wrapped mint patties, and chewing gum brands she'd never heard of. That was it. Not a sour gummy anything.

Keelie stared at the rack, trying to summon up a little appetite. She deserved a treat, and nothing here was treat-worthy.

She glanced outside. No sign of Grandmother, who'd lost every bit of elegance the minute they'd pulled into the gas station parking lot. She'd pushed the driver-side door open and had raced to the ladies' room, leaving Keelie to turn the car off and wait.

At least they were finally in California. The first two stops had been in Oregon.

"You want some chips instead?" The woman sitting behind the counter, reading a magazine, had been watching Keelie.

Keelie considered, then chose a bag of SunChips. "I'll take these, please."

The woman stood to ring up her purchase. "You can quit looking outside. She's still in the restroom."

Keelie bit her lip. Had she been that obvious?

"Older women sometimes have to go a lot," the woman confided, speaking as if she had personal experience with the problem.

"You don't know my grandmother." Keelie paid for the chips and went back outside, holding the metal bells that dangled from the back of the plate glass door so that they were quiet. Their jangle had made her shudder when she'd entered, or maybe it was because the whole building was made of concrete, steel, and glass. Even the counter was plastic.

She let the door close behind her and inhaled the fresh outdoor air. It smelled different from Oregon, and the trees murmured to her of rain and fog. She hadn't noticed a difference in the tree smells before last summer, when the trees had called to her and she'd discovered that she could talk to them, along with all sorts of other strange creatures that lived in forests. Her half-elf blood had gotten her into so much trouble lately.

She was glad for this road trip, even if Grandmother hadn't let her get near the steering wheel even once.

A screen door screeched shut behind her, and Keelie turned to see Grandmother exiting the little wooden bathroom. Keliatiel walked calmly, with dignity, not like an old lady who'd spent fifteen minutes in a gas station bathroom.

Keelie walked toward her, their paths crossing just short of the truck.

"Are you ready?" Grandmother pulled open the truck door and climbed in, her linen trousers barely wrinkled under her long, leaf-embroidered tunic.

"Of course." Keelie took her place next to her and pulled out the road map.

Juliet City, California, was just seventy miles ahead.

An array of colored crystals was arranged on the dashboard. Sir Davey had taught Grandmother to drive using the crystals, and they guided her better than any GPS.

Grandmother ran her hands over the crystals and the truck's engine turned over. Two minutes later they were back on the road south, headed toward the redwoods.

Keelie leaned back in her seat. All she hoped to get out of this journey was a last look at the house she'd shared with Mom, and maybe a glance at her old school.

"You thought the trees in the Dread Forest were old, Keliel, but you have not seen anything like the redwoods," Grandmother said. "They make one feel insignificant."

A roaring echo filled Keelie's ears, and an odd, musky scent filled the car. *Help us,* tree voices chorused. *Help us, Keliel.* Just as suddenly the noise was gone, leaving Keelie's ears ringing with the sudden silence.

She looked quickly at Grandmother, but the old lady drove on, and behind them, Knot snored on his kitty cushion. Keelie had been the only one to receive the message, yet Grandmother was in charge of this mission.

Whatever it had meant, the trees sounded desperate. Keelie was suddenly determined not to let them down.

# two

Grandmother maneuvered the truck into the sandy parking lot of the Juliet City Shakespeare Festival, narrowly missing the plywood cartoon cutout of William Shakespeare holding a wooden scroll that read, "Welcome to the Faire." It wouldn't have been a loss if the truck had demolished the unflattering portrait. The big, bulging eyes and bulbous nose made the Bard of Avon look like a troll.

Huge sequoias surrounded the festival grounds, and the buzz of their conversation was deafening. Keelie touched her rose quartz, then tapped into her elf magic to put the trees on silent. She would make her introductions later, when she had everything for the shop handled. The truck rolled to a stop and Grandmother turned the engine off with a satisfied smile.

Keelie jumped out, shivering from the chill air. She'd shelved her fantasy of sunbathing in her cute little yellow bikini when they'd passed the steep, rocky beach that was crowded with sleek, fat sea lions. No way. But the town of Juliet City was charming, and she couldn't wait to visit it and get familiar with the festival grounds.

Knot was on the back of the bench seat, tail swishing, ready to join her. She shrugged and let him out. He'd find trouble no matter where he was.

"What do we do first?" Grandmother was stretching out the road kinks, leaning against the truck hood.

"Check in with administration." Keelie felt superior because she knew what to do, while Grandmother had never left her woodland home. The Silver Bough Jousting Company's horse hauler was parked on the opposite side of the lot, and seeing it made Keelie's heart quicken with excitement. Sean was here somewhere, with his jousters. Of course, Risa was here too, at her new business called "Green Goddess Herbals."

Things hadn't been so hot between Keelie and Sean by the time he'd left for the festival. He'd seemed distant. Keelie knew that he was busy with the horses and the other jousters, preparing for the trip, but the worst had been the day when he left. Dad had been right there with the rest of the elves, and Sean hadn't kissed her. He'd hugged her briefly and said, "See you in Colorado." That was it. She'd been stuck with the rest of the group, waving goodbye, as if a piece of her heart wasn't going with him. Elves!

What really bothered Keelie was that Risa had been hanging around the barn in the days before the jousters left, bringing late winter apples, helping to feed the horses, and telling everyone that she was happy to be useful. Keelie was sure that she was scoping out the jousters to see who was available, and maybe even checking out Sean, her former betrothed. No one else thought that Risa was strange, since, after all, Risa was one of the two young, pureblood elf girls, and therefore the biggest chance the elves had of increasing their dwindling population. The other pure elf girl was Elia, Keelie's frenemy. She didn't want to think about Elia, even though they weren't actively at war anymore. Or so Elia said. At least Elia wouldn't be hanging around at this festival.

Grandmother had climbed back into the drivers' seat. She rubbed her hands along the rim of the steering wheel, looking like she was very satisfied with herself for having driven them all the way. Then she got back out, holding a leaf-embroidered tote bag, and carefully locked the dilapidated truck's door. "What are you staring at? Let's get on with it."

Keelie shook her head, forcing herself to focus. She looked at the map and notes that Dad had given to her. "It says Admin is on the edge of the parking area." She looked around. This festival was old and the buildings crowded close to the parking lot, with only a short picket fence separating the cars from the village.

Grandmother gestured toward a house that looked like an English thatched cottage. "That might be the one."

Keelie shuddered, remembering Finch, the draconic director of the Wildewood Faire. Luckily, that faire's Admin office didn't have a thatched roof. Finch's salty tongue would have caught it on fire.

Grandmother yawned, then pressed her hand against her mouth to suppress another one. "Let's check in, then go to the campsite. I need to rest. We can check out the festival grounds tomorrow."

"We need to unload all the furniture," Keelie said. Grandmother must have forgotten the huge trailer of wooden furniture for sale, which Dad had sent ahead.

Grandmother sighed, frowning "I suppose you're right, except—"

"Except what?"

"I can't unload it. My back." Grandmother rubbed her spine.

Keelie forced herself not to roll her eyes. She'd once caught sight of her reflection in the hall mirror when Dad had been imparting his usual parental wisdom, and realized that rolling her eyes made her look like a peevish little kid.

She eyed the Silver Bough Jousting Company's horse trailer. Maybe Sean and the other jousters would help her with the furniture. If they wouldn't do it for her, then surely they would do it for Grandmother, who until recently had ruled the elves of the Dread Forest.

Keelie retrieved the registration papers from her messenger bag. "Let's get going, then. I'll figure something out about the furniture."

Grandmother seemed content to forget the unloading.

She stretched her arms wide and swiveled her waist as if she was doing a yoga move. There was a loud pop. "That's better."

Keelie had practiced yoga over the winter with Zabrina, who thought it would help her control her magic, but it was strange to see Granny Elf doing yoga. It was as if leaving the Dread Forest had given Grandmother a whole new mindset, and Keelie wasn't sure what to think of it.

She started up the gravel path that led to the thatched cottage, Grandmother lagging behind, still stretching her arms. Keelie ignored her, choosing to focus on the feeling of efficiency that filled her. This was her third faire, and she knew the routine. She had to find the Heartwood shop and then convince Sean and the other jousters to help unload Dad's beautiful furniture. She'd park Grandmother somewhere to get her out of the way, or maybe put her in charge of setting up the tent.

Wait until Dad heard. He'd be proud of Keelie's business prowess. She would prove to him that she could be trusted as well as any adult. Even though she was only sixteen, Keelie considered herself to be an adult. After all the things she'd been through, she should certainly qualify as one.

"Keliel. Stop." Grandmother's voice held the "obey me now" tone that she used on the elves of the Dread Forest.

Keelie spun around. "Come on. If your back still hurts I'll see if there's a massage shop here. We're late getting to Admin and there's a lot to do. The Festival opens day after tomorrow." Grandmother was cramping Keelie's efficient business plan.

Grandmother held out a hand to silence her, then turned her brilliant green gaze to the tree canopy above them. She looked at Keelie. "Can you hear them?"

Keelie looked up at the impossibly tall trunks of the sequoias and the leafy canopy that towered above them like faraway green umbrellas. She'd been shielding herself from the trees, not wanting to be distracted by their thoughts and chatter.

Fog suddenly swirled between the trees, enveloping them in eddies like a fast-moving river of white smoke. In seconds, it was impossible to see beyond her grandmother and the silhouette of the Admin building.

Great. Keelie had hoped for twenty-four hours of normalcy before she became involved with the local trees. She had been looking forward to seeing the giant redwoods, but she was afraid of them, too. They were so old.

Keelie closed her eyes and saw, in her mind's eye, a golden sparkling light interwoven with dark mist. This was fairy magic, she knew. Strange, because she hadn't seen a single *bhata* or *feithid daoine* anywhere. The forest seemed to be empty of fae. She willed the mist to dissolve, and a bright green light illuminated the landscape of her mind.

A strong jolt like a mental punch almost knocked her over, as the redwoods' thoughts crowded in and around her. A strong and ancient magic flowed through them. Keelie fought for breath and opened her eyes. Faces now pushed out from the bark in the trees, looking at her solemnly. She'd seen the tree faces before in other forests, but usually the tree spirits waited a while to show her.

These guys didn't waste anytime in revealing themselves. Waves of power poured from them, but Keelie pulled on her magic to create a barrier. Finally she breathed easier, as if the oxygen tap had been turned back on.

Grandmother turned in a slow circle, her eyes wide. "O, Ancient Ones, it is our honor to be among you."

*It is our honor, Keliatiel of the northern forest, to see you and your young sapling Keliel, about whom we have heard so much.* The voice seemed to come from everywhere. Keelie couldn't tell which tree had spoken.

Grandmother bowed her head reverently.

"Hi." Keelie finger-waved, determined not to show how stunned she was by their age and power. She centered her magic on her barriers to keep from being overwhelmed.

*We have much to discuss, and are thankful to the northern elves for sparing you to answer our summons.*

Grandmother bowed again, then lifted her palms upwards. "My granddaughter and I are privileged to help the Ancient Ones. We will do whatever is necessary to aid you."

Was the old lady nuts? You couldn't make such open promises to a tree. They took everything literally. Keelie wanted to kick Grandmother so she'd shut up. Dealing with Alora the treeling had taught Keelie that trees did not understand little human problems like prior commitments, or fear of death and dismemberment. Despite their grand majesty, she was sensing more than great power from the redwoods. There was great need as well, and something else. Something familiar, but fleeting.

*Tonight we shall discuss our problem further, and make formal greetings,* the deep voice said in their minds. *Until then, tree shepherds.* The tree faces melted back into the bark.

Keelie waited for the tree magic to grow faint before wheeling around to confront her grandmother. "Why did you promise them that we could help them? We have no idea what the problem is."

Grandmother waved her hand nonchalantly. "I don't think it will be a big deal." She reached for the papers in Keelie's hand. "Why don't we see about registering for the shop and getting the furniture moved out of the truck?"

Stunned, Keelie watched her grandmother stride toward the thatched cottage, all signs of muscle fatigue gone. The old faker was hiding something. What was going on with her? She'd given up being head of the Dread Forest and now Dad had that role, so why was her supposedly exhausted grandmother extending an open-ended offer of help? There was no telling what the redwoods wanted, and it might be something that they couldn't deliver.

Keelie wasn't happy about being tricked, but part of her admired the fact that Grandmother had done something she might have done. Keelie never could resist a cry for help.

Grandmother turned around at the door of the cottage. "Are you coming, or do I have to do everything myself?"

"You are too much." Keelie marched up the steps, but before she could come up with a smartass retort, her grandmother had entered the cottage.

Keelie clenched her fists. Keliatiel was acting like the bossy old elf that Keelie had met late last summer when she'd first arrived in the Dread Forest. She would not let the old woman's elvish snottiness get to her.

Inside the thatched cottage, the man who greeted them had a beaky nose, long dark hair, and a thin beard on a sharp protruding chin. He sat behind a glistening, polished wood desk that was decorated with Shakespearean knickknacks. The Romeo and Juliet kissing bobbleheads were disturbingly cute. A tarnished nameplate read, "Master Oswald, The Lord Mayor."

"Ladies, please do come in." Master Oswald was faking an English accent. Badly.

Two leather wingback chairs were in front of the desk, and their occupants stood up. Sean and Risa.

Keelie stepped back into the doorway and let Grandmother lead so that she'd have a chance to control her expression. How humiliating if they'd seen her joy at spotting Sean turn to anger at the sight of Risa.

Risa smiled at her, eyes flashing, and Keelie knew she'd seen.

Sean bowed. "Good day, Lady Keliatiel. Please take my seat. We were just leaving." His eyes connected with Keelie's.

Keelie gave him a squinty evil look. "Fancy seeing the two of you. Together."

His gaze darkened, and Keelie shivered. She loved that look. Not that she was going to let on.

"So lovely to see you here, Lord Sean," Grandmother purred. She glanced dismissively at Risa. "And you too, of course, Risa my dear." Grandmother's tone was a whole iceberg.

Risa curtseyed, the movement loosening a cascade of red curls that tumbled over her shoulder. Keelie walked behind Grandmother's chair and gripped its back, enjoying a brief vision of tearing out those red curls by the roots.

Risa's smile was as fake as the Lord Mayor's accent. "I'm here with my own business this year. Your family has been so successful with its woodworking, and father and I hope that our herbal remedies will be as popular. We're honored to begin with the Juliet City Shakespeare Festival." She batted her eyes at the mayor, who grinned in appreciation.

Fabulous. Keelie would have to stock up on aspirin.

The Lord Mayor beamed at them. "We're very excited to have Lady Risa selling her wares at our festival, and it's so wonderful that all of you are friends already."

Keelie never thought she'd admit this, but she was actually going to miss Elia.

"Thank you for your time." Risa gave the Lord Mayor a megawatt elf-charm smile. As she glided past Sean, Risa stopped and put a hand on his arm. "Thank *you* for your help."

Keelie's face burned. She stared at Sean, willing him to look at her. She didn't care if she seemed rude. Sean glanced over at her, then turned to Risa. "Your business will be a success, I know it."

"Lord Sean, we're going to be needing your help, along with the other jousters, to unload the furniture into our shop." Grandmother stared pointedly at him.

"Yes, milady." Sean bowed to Grandmother and headed toward the door. "See you later, Keelie."

Risa wrinkled her nose and frowned, but then her expression smoothed and her smile returned, a little forced this time.

Keelie wished she could stare at people and cats and make them do as she willed, a talent her Grandmother wielded effortlessly.

When Risa left, the Lord Mayor turned to them, sighing. "She's quite a lovely woman."

"Do you have our registration information?" Grandmother glared disapprovingly at him. Keelie had been on the receiving end of that look before and knew its scorching effect.

The festival director shook his head as if clearing it. "Yes. Yes. I do."

He strode over to a filing cabinet and pulled open a drawer, retrieving a brown envelope. "Here we go—Heartwood."

The Lord Mayor handed the envelope over to Grandmother. "We're very excited to have you at our festival. I understand you'll be staying in the forest instead of at the players' village."

*In the forest?*

Keelie looked at Grandmother, who made a sideways chopping motion with her hand. Later. Okay, she'd wait, but it had better be for a good reason. All the Faire folk stayed in the players' village, including Sir Davey when he arrived in his massive RV. Keelie had been looking forward to a hot shower and morning lattes and muffins in his luxurious digs. Instead, it sounded like they might be camping.

Grandmother smiled regally and inclined her head slightly.

Keelie realized that Grandmother looked younger as she spoke to the director. She turned her head and looked at Grandmother from the corner of her eyes, which Dad had taught her was the way to see through elven charm, the glamour they cast to fool humans. Same old Grandmother, stern and elegant. Keelie looked at her straight on, and saw that she seemed younger and taller, and her chest was perkier. The old sneak was using elf charm on the director.

The Lord Mayor bowed, and Keelie followed Grandmother outside. She almost knocked down a slender man, in a red and green harlequin suit, carrying a jester hat under his arm. As the door pushed him back, the bells on his hat jangled, making Keelie shiver at the discordant sound. He grinned like a slithery snake, creeping Keelie out. She felt itchy, as if she'd broken out in a rash underneath her skin. The jester bowed and waited until they were outside, then he slipped in.

There was no sign of Sean or Risa anywhere around. Keelie opened the folded festival map and propped it on the rail fence next to the cottage, scratching at her arm as she located Heartwood.

"Risa was impertinent," Grandmother huffed. "She seemed to think Sean would agree to her advances."

"I thought you were all in favor of them getting together? Being full-blooded elves and all." Keelie kept her eyes on the map, but started walking toward the Heartwood shop. Grandmother trailed behind her.

"Don't be smart, Keliel. You know that I was wrong, and

I apologized. You and Sean have feelings for each other." Grandmother walked briskly at Keelie's side.

Grandmother was imagining things. Keelie had never heard an apology, but she didn't want to start a fight at the beginning of their stay. A fight would ruin her chances of getting to L.A.

"That's ancient history." Keelie knew it wasn't, but she didn't want to talk about it any more. "Why are we staying in the forest? Is there a campground there? A civilized one?" She quelled the whine that threatened to creep into her voice.

"There is a campground. Our work is in the forest, and we need to stay close to the trees." Grandmother slowed as they reached the main road. Keelie could see Sean and several of his elven jousters, waiting outside a roomy timber building with a peaked roof pitched high and a heart-shaped sign swinging above the front. Heartwood.

She gave Sean a dirty look and smiled at the other elves as she ran inside. "Grandmother, look at all this room. I can set up the shop any way I want."

Grandmother followed, looking up at the rafters and checking out the little storage area in the back. "I suppose you can do whatever you like. It's not our main mission here."

Keelie returned to the front of the store, which was open to the street and had a long counter. She would put Dad's dollhouses here. They'd sold very well at the Wildewood Faire and she didn't know why he hid them in the back.

The next hours were spent moving back and forth from the trailer in the parking lot to the Heartwood shop, as Sean and several jousters carried Dad's furniture. The jousters left to care for their horses, but Sean stayed to help Keelie and Grandmother move the merchandise around until they were pleased with the effect.

Grandmother was impressed by Keelie's eye for display, and Keelie didn't admit that she'd just copied the way the furniture was arranged at the High Mountain Faire in Colorado. If Sean remembered the way the shop had been laid out there, he didn't give it away.

"I can't believe we're done." Grandmother pushed a strand of silver hair from her forehead. "We'll have plenty of time to clean up before dinner."

Dinner? That would likely be bread and cheese, since Keelie wanted to sleep for a couple of days. But she waved at her grandmother and continued to unpack the business gear that went behind the massive counter. She ran across the velvet bag she'd jammed in at the last moment, filled with extra rose quartz charms. Just in case. She pulled a couple out and put them in her pocket.

Keelie worked steadily until Sean wandered over. He was wearing jeans and a sweatshirt emblazoned with the Silver Bough logo. He rubbed sweat from his face with his forearm. "It gets hot fast when you're working hard."

"I appreciate your help. I know Grandmother kind of forced you to do it, but we couldn't have unpacked everything ourselves."

Sean reached down and grabbed the bottom of his sweatshirt, then pulled it off in a single move. As the sweatshirt came off, it dragged up the T-shirt he wore underneath, giving Keelie a view of smooth skin over tight abs. She gripped her pen tighter.

"I didn't do it for your grandmother." He shook his hair. "I did it for you."

"Thanks." Keelie's voice came out in a hoarse whisper.

Sean ran a hand along the countertop. "When I do this, I feel a kind of buzzing, but the wood doesn't speak to me as it does to you."

Keelie swallowed, recovering her composure. "Dad says that all elves feel magic, but only tree shepherds hear the trees."

"You're more than elf. You're part fae, too, so you're different."

"That's me." Keelie spoke lightly, but inwardly cringed. She'd been "different" all of her life, everywhere she went. She changed the subject. "I love the shop's location, right off the main road. Everyone will have to walk by here when they enter the faire." She leaned over to straighten the staplers, receipt books, and the credit card machine on the shelf under the counter.

"Better call it the festival," Sean advised. "They're sensitive about it. It's highbrow literature here, you know, not just Ren Faire hijinks." He winked at her. "Your father will do good business here." He leaned over the counter, his face close to hers as she straightened.

Keelie didn't move, hoping he wouldn't either. "That's why he let me come with Grandmother. We'll do okay."

"Better than okay." His eyes were on her lips. "You know that there's nothing between Risa and me."

"Prove it." She lifted her chin a tiny bit, moving her mouth closer to his.

"Keelie Heartwood, is that you?" The man's voice was familiar.

They jumped apart. Keelie looked around Sean, irritated at the interruption. She couldn't believe it. Her father's former apprentice, Scott, had entered the shop.

He looked so different. His shoulders were still broad, but now he looked more muscular. Black hair fell rakishly over one eye, and he wore a decent band T-shirt and jeans that fit. Keelie couldn't believe someone could change from a geek to a hunk in less than a year.

"You know him?" Sean asked. He glowered at Scott, who was smiling at Keelie.

"Yes," she replied. "Don't you? This is Scott. He was at the High Mountain Faire, too. He was Dad's apprentice."

Sean frowned, then nodded. "Of course. You've changed."

Scott smiled broadly. "Been working out."

"It shows," Keelie said.

Sean turned his frown toward her.

"What? I'm paying the man a compliment." Keelie gave Sean the "you're not the boss of me" glare.

Scott looked quickly from Keelie to Sean. "Is something wrong? You need help, Keelie?"

"I'm all the help she needs," Sean growled.

This was a possessive side of Sean that Keelie had never seen. She wasn't sure that she liked it.

The two men squared off, with Keelie trapped behind

the counter. She was torn between horror that they might actually fight over her and a hidden "squee!" of delight.

She turned back to Scott, hoping to defuse the situation. "So, where's your woodshop?"

Scott turned to her, deliberately excluding Sean from his sight. "I work at Tudor Turnings." He pointed casually toward the two-story building that leaned crookedly across the road. Its black-and-white, half-timbered second story overshot the first floor, and hung over part of the path like a saggy, out-of-breath old man. Scott grinned at her expression. "It was built that way on purpose."

"You have got to be kidding. It looks dangerous."

Sean seemed to relax as the conversation turned more general.

"I've got the building inspections to prove it's not. Want a tour of the inside?"

Sean's mouth turned down even more. Keelie really wanted to go into the strange building, but she also wanted to kiss Sean, and if she went off with Scott the chances of that happening again might fade. Although she was having second thoughts about kissing Sean after that macho-elf display.

As if summoned by the almost-kiss, Risa appeared on the road outside, wearing a gypsy outfit with a tight corset that showed off her assets as if they were muffin tops on a plate. She was carrying a frosty pewter goblet.

"Lord Sean, I heard you were working hard and thought you might be thirsty." She put her pouty red lips to the goblet's rim and sipped. "Ummm...honeyed mead. I brought it for you, but couldn't resist a taste." She offered the goblet to Sean.

Oh, brother. Could the girl be more obvious?

Sean reached for the goblet, but Scott beat him to it. "I'm thirsty, too, and I appreciate the offer of a drink, milady." His eyes looked her up and down appreciatively, then rested on her chest.

Risa looked startled as Scott grabbed the goblet, but just before he put it to his mouth she shrieked, "No!" and slapped it away. The goblet fell to the path and its contents spilled.

Scott stared, dumbstruck, at Risa. "Geez, I was just going to take a sip. I wasn't going to hog it. Sean could have had some."

Sean was staring at the puddle. Knot ambled over and gave the puddle an inquisitive sniff, then lapped it up. He loved mead.

Keelie's eyes met Sean's, and she knew they were thinking the same thing. Why would Risa bring a drink, taste it, and offer it to Sean, then pitch a fit when Scott jokingly took it? They looked down at Knot, who had consumed most of the spilled mead.

Risa backed away. "I'm sorry. I don't know what came over me. I knew it was hot work, and I wanted to bring Sean a nice drink, and then—" Her eyes fell on the spilled goblet and widened. Then she saw Knot, and her expression softened.

Keelie almost heard a chime as Knot looked up at the elf girl.

"Oh, such soft fur, such big green eyes. You are the loveliest kitty in the world. I love you." Risa reached down toward Knot. The cat arched, and his fur stuck out as he backed away.

"She's bespelled herself," Sean said.

"That was meant for you, you know." Keelie watched Risa stalk Knot farther into the Heartwood shop. "Must have been a love potion." It occurred to her that she could look it up in the Compendium. Yeah, if she had ten years.

Scott shook his head. "Lucky cat. But why isn't Knot in love with her? Are animals immune?"

"No," Sean said, looking at Keelie once more. "But fairies are."

Keelie had to find how long the potion would last, and what else Risa had up her sleeve. Wait until Grandmother found out what the elf girl had done. Using magic against another elf was forbidden. Risa would be in a lot of trouble, once she got over her kitty love.

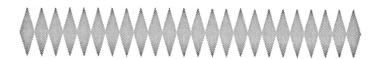

# three

"Keelie, are you ready to go?" Grandmother stepped out from the shadows at the back of the shop, pushing stray strands into her heavy braid. "I'm really tired, and I need to rest. I think we can finish up tomorrow."

"Almost done, Grandmother," Keelie called back.

Grandmother looked behind her. "You would not believe what I just saw. That foolish girl Risa chased Knot out the back door. I've never seen that cat looked frightened before." She chuckled, then turned her piercing glare on Scott. "Who are you, young man?"

"I'm Scott. I'm your neighbor across the street."

"You're our competition?"

"Here at the festival, we like to think of ourselves as an extended family." Scott looked at her curiously.

"He was Zeke's hu…" Sean stopped himself, looking over at Keelie as he tried to control his face. "He was Zeke's assistant, the one who abandoned him before the start of the Wildewood Faire."

Grimacing, Scott turned toward Grandmother. "I had a better job offer, and it was closer to my family. My mother got sick and sent for me."

Keelie reeled with surprise. "Why didn't you say that your mother was sick? You just left a message saying that you had a better job offer in California."

"Because it was a family matter. I wanted to keep it private."

"I understand." Grandmother's glare eased.

Scott's expression was tinged with relief. Grandmother was the type of person whose disapproval you didn't want. A flicker of irritation flashed in Sean's eyes. Keelie didn't know whether to laugh or kick him.

"If you need help with anything at the festival, give a shout out. Like I said, we're all one big family." Scott seemed at ease with the old dragon.

"Thank you. I'm sure we won't need any assistance," Grandmother said. "May I see your shop? I'm curious as to how you arranged your wares in that tiny building."

Scott forced a smile. "Of course. Be my guest." He watched her stalk across the street, then circled around to Keelie. "I'll be seeing you." Lifting his head so that he was eye-to-eye with Sean, he looked at his rival for what seemed a long time before turning to stride back to Tudor Turnings.

Scott had definitely changed. Who knew a geeky wood-carver could transform into such a take-charge guy?

Sean cleared his throat.

Keelie blushed. Sean stared down at her disapprovingly. "You like him."

Indignation gushed through Keelie. "He's a friend." Then an image of Risa popped into her head. "Just like Risa is your friend."

Sean pulled her close. He brought his face to hers, then kissed her full on the lips. "But you're not just a friend." He let her go and stepped back. "I'll see you at the camp to-night." He sauntered away, his walk the one of a man who was totally pleased with himself.

Keelie stood there, stunned by the kiss and by Sean's re-action to Scott. The kiss had been great. But Sean hadn't given her this much attention in weeks, and now, just be-cause a cute guy acted as if he liked her, he decided he was going to act like a boyfriend again. A jealous boyfriend.

"I won't be there," she shouted after him.

Sean turned quickly, eyebrows raised in surprise.

"Grandmother and I are staying in the forest."

His eyes widened and he took a couple of steps back toward her. "At the Redwood Forest elven village?"

"I guess. Is that good?"

"The redwood elves don't let anyone into the deep parts of the forest." Sean seemed impressed, then looked over at Tudor Turnings and laughed. "Guess you won't get to hang around here much after all." He waved to Grandmother, who was walking back toward them, and walked out.

Meow.

Keelie looked down to find Knot at her feet. "Did you ditch your girlfriend?" Knot gagged as if he was about to hack up a hairball.

"Yeah, I figured as much."

"Well, Keelie, I see that you and Sean have mended your rift." Grandmother leaned against one of the Heartwood shop's posts, trying to suppress a smile and looking almost human. "You must be pleased. Are you ready to go?"

Confused, mad, and tired, Keelie decided Grandmother was right. "Yeah, let's go to the camp. I'm starting to crave a shower, something to eat, and bed. Clean sheets, too." Maybe sleep would clear her head, unless she ran into Sean again.

"Knotsie!" Risa's voice drifted from the small stand of trees behind their shop. "Where did you go?"

Knot leaped up onto Keelie's jeans, digging his claws into the denim. His eyes looked up beseechingly.

"Aw, Knotsie. Your girlfriend's looking for you."

The cat did not let go, and Keelie had to walk to the parking lot dragging her right leg behind her, with Knot clinging to it like a dryer sheet on a cactus. She tried not to turn back to stare at the Tudor Turnings shop, in case Scott was watching. Of course, if he was, he would have seen the kiss. She wondered what would happen with Sean if she spent more time with him. More kisses, for sure. The next three weeks were going to be way interesting.

The road to the elven village snaked between and around tall trees. Grandmother guided the truck along the narrow road, occasionally running her hands over the crystals that Sir Davey had attached to the dashboard.

For once, Keelie was glad to be in the passenger seat, because she could concentrate on blocking the strong tree magic that pressed on her from all sides. She patted her pocket, grateful for the spare rose quartz charms. Her shielding power had grown since she'd learned how to use the rose quartz to boost her elf magic—she could now avoid picking up on individual trees, and just felt their collective force—but that collective force still packed a mighty pow. The magical tree energy in this ancient forest could rival a power plant. Keelie rolled down her window and leaned out, looking up into the canopy far above, feeling tiny.

They were deep in the forest now and even farther away from the players' campground, which was near the highway. Dad had told her that the players kept bicycles at their camp, to travel back and forth to the festival. She tried to imagine Sean on a bicycle, but the image refused to come. Maybe because he and his men were housed with the horses, on the other side of the festival.

"This sure is far away."

Grandmother, concentrating on the road ahead, didn't reply.

They drove past the Redwood National Forest sign. The campground registration was located inside the trees.

Grandmother sailed past the registration kiosk and turned right onto a sandy trail that climbed between the giant redwoods. The ground below was filled with ferns and tiny white flowers.

"Are you sure we weren't supposed to stop back there?"

"I'm on the correct road."

Keelie shrugged and leaned out the window, taking deep breaths of the spicy-scented woods. This is what she envisioned when she thought of an elven forest. It had an Old World, fairy-tale feel.

A ranger stepped out of a small hut at the side of the road and Grandmother slowed their truck to a halt. There was something odd about the ranger. As he rounded the truck, Keelie realized that he had long brown hair pulled back over his ears, and that his eyes were the jewel green she was now familiar with. Her own eyes were that color, and she was sure he wore his hair like that to hide his pointed ear tips.

The elven ranger bowed his head to Grandmother. "We're honored by your presence."

"As are we to be here." Grandmother said in the I'm-your-leader tone that Keelie had learned to ignore. Funny, how the other elves jumped when Grandmother used that voice.

*Greetings, Keliel Tree Shepherdess,* a male voice whispered in Keelie's mind. Something had broken through her magical shield. At the same time, she saw fog creep toward them from the depths of the forest. Keelie froze. A vampire. Vampires did the fog thing—she'd seen it back home in the Dread Forest.

*The redwoods are anxious to meet you.*

Keelie shook her head, willing whatever the presence was to leave her mind. She closed her eyes to focus on her magic. She thought about Ariel, the red-tailed hawk she'd rescued and rehabilitated, and her protective magic surged through her. Zabrina had taught Keelie how to fix her mind on someone or something very important, like in meditation, and it helped her to concentrate. If there was a vampire in the forest, Keelie would have to be careful.

The ranger elf handed Grandmother a map. "Follow the road until you feel where to turn."

Grandmother frowned. "We'll feel where to turn? Don't you use the Dread to keep the humans away?"

"We only use the Dread near our village. Out here, we use a charm that Viran created, which holds a hint of Dread. Elves can feel where to turn, whereas humans think the same spot is somewhere they don't want to go. They feel an aversion, a sense of avoidance. Ours is a gentle magic. It doesn't give nightmares."

"That may be part of your problem." Grandmother pursed her lips as if keeping back other words. "Has this magic worked for you?"

The elf leaned in close to the window, his arms perched on the inch of rolled-down glass. "Milady, it's not my place to talk about our policies, but since we're part of the National Park System, we work within the human world. When you arrive in the village, there will be those who will be able to explain our philosophy and our way of life in more detail."

The elf looked past Grandmother and smiled brightly

at Keelie. He seemed young. "It's our pleasure to have you here, Lady Keliel." His gaze widened as he looked at her. "Your eyes—the dark fae magic."

"Yeah, it made these gold circles around my pupils. It hasn't faded yet." Keelie liked him, but she hoped he wouldn't go on and on about dark magic. She'd taken a frightening risk to save Ariel, but it had been worth it. The hawk was flying free and had even met a potential mate, and she had learned that the fae magic could be used for good...although it was risky and hard to control. She smiled back at him. "I look forward to my time here."

"I'm Tavyn."

Knot reached over with his right paw and sank his claws into her thigh through her jeans.

Gritting her teeth, she removed his claws. "Will you stop it? What's wrong with you?"

Tavyn looked awed. "Ah, the infamous Knot. We've heard tales about him and his perilous rescue at the Caudex in the Dread Forest."

Purring echoed impossibly in the truck's cab. Knot wrapped his tail around his legs in a self-satisfied manner.

"Perilous rescue? You mean audacious testimony." Knot had stood before the Council and defended her Uncle Dariel, speaking in front of everyone. She glared at the cat. "He doesn't talk often, but when he does, he can't seem to stop." She moved her legs quickly to ensure Knot wouldn't shred them.

Grandmother shook her head and touched a crystal to shift

into gear. "Thank you, Tavyn. We'll find our way through the forest."

"Yes, milady." Tavyn leaned over and waved. "I'll see you in the village, Lady Keliel."

"Just call me Keelie."

Knot's purring ceased and he was about to sink his claws back into her leg, but Keelie was ready for him. She grabbed his paw. He lifted his big orange head and looked at her with dilated eyes. His ears flattened against his skull. Keelie knew that look. She dropped his paw. "No more. I only have one box of bandage strips with me."

Knot kneaded the upholstery on the truck seat.

Keelie had learned from Zabrina that even though Knot was a fairy, even the fae thought he was unusual. Keelie thought it was a nice way of saying weird. As if picking up on her thoughts, Knot's purr grew louder.

"Whatever." Keelie scooted closer to the door.

The truck reached a crossroads, little more than two deer trails crossing, and Grandmother turned right. Keelie suddenly felt a tingled warning to not go down this road. "Stop!"

Grandmother stomped on the brake. "What's the matter?"

"This feels bad to me. We should go left."

The older woman sighed. "Look deeper, Keelie."

Keelie lowered her defenses a bit and immediately realized that she was feeling the human-deflecting charm. "Oops."

Grandmother accelerated and turned to the right. "I don't

see how they keep humans out. One of my recommendations will be to use the Dread, full blast."

"Still, I think it would be creepy to live out here." Keelie grabbed the truck's door frame to keep from getting jostled.

"The old trees definitely have a presence, and the elves have learned to live with their power. Look at that tree. Look at the circumference of its trunk." Grandmother sighed. "I remember when this land was covered with trees, before the logging. Even in the Dread Forest, we could hear their death cries. Now, to see so few of the Ancient Ones left breaks my heart. I really wish there was a way to time-travel to the past and relive the happiest days of my life."

Keelie straightened. "I understand how you feel." She thought about the letter and wished she could time-travel back to when Mom was alive, to take back the things she said to her before her mother got on the doomed plane.

Blinking back tears, Keelie looked out at the giant redwoods rising to the night sky, majestic and ancient. She couldn't bear to think of these regal trees being logged, especially without a Tree Lorem. She remembered the old ghost forest in the Wildewood, the shades of trees that didn't know they were gone. Shivering, Keelie realized how cold it seemed in the cab of the truck.

Knot hissed.

Keelie asked, "What is your…"

A sharp pain shot through her, a flash of red slicing through her brain, obliterating her magical shield. The tree magic and the fairy magic, threaded closely together within her, began to separate like the rings of a tree being split apart on a cellular level.

Keelie shrieked and grabbed her head.

Grandmother slammed on the brakes. "Keelie, what's wrong?"

As quickly as it had happened, the excruciating pain was gone—the redness, and that sense of being torn apart down to her molecules.

Keelie let her head drop back against the headrest, trying to breathe away the remnants of the pain. She rolled her head toward Grandmother, whose pale face was close, her green eyes wide with worry. She struggled to take a breath, then made herself relax, her hand clenched around the rose quartz charm that dangled from one of her belt loops.

"It's the trees," Keelie gasped. "The redwoods tried to kill me."

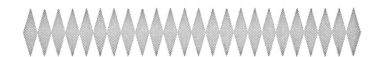

# four

Grandmother scoffed. "You're exaggerating. But you feel it strongly, don't you?"

Keelie pressed her palms to her temples. "It's like a black mark on the magic. It feels sick, like a spot along the edge of the tree magic."

The older elf's bright green gaze was fixed on her. "What do you think it is?"

"You tell me. You're keeping secrets. What is it?" Keelie leaned her cheek against the cool glass of the window, relieved that the pain had eased.

Grandmother stopped the truck, shoving the gearshift into park so that they all were propelled forward.

Instantly, the headache was back.

"You're right." Grandmother stared directly out the windshield.

Okay, Keelie hadn't expected her to agree so quickly. Her headache faded. "What's going on?"

"The Redwood Tree Shepherd sent me a message before the call went out to find him." Grandmother looked at Keelie intently, as if she knew Keelie would understand some kind of secret message in her words.

"You mean he asked you for help before he disappeared? Why didn't you tell Dad?"

"Viran was afraid. You have to understand that Viran is not the fearful sort. He's a steady man, and he values the trees above all. He's been shepherd to the redwoods for almost four hundred years."

"Four hundred years ago the only humans here were the Native Americans, right?"

"That is correct."

"So maybe he's just afraid of change. Too many humans or something. He doesn't like the tourists."

"He's seen more change than many others, Keelie. He said he feared something … dark."

Keelie's stomach sank. Dark. There had been too much dark in her life. What was she, a magnet for the evil gremmies of the world? Redcaps, dark magic books, unicorn killers, vampires, what next? Maybe she'd better not ask.

"There's more, and it may be connected. Soon there will

be a gathering of elves in the Northwoods, where strange things are also happening."

"The Northwoods are in Canada, right?" Elia had said that her mother was from the Northwoods. "So the elves there are organizing?"

Grandmother nodded. "It's unprecedented for the clans to work together."

"Then it's a good thing. More communication. So when did the Redwood Tree Shepherd contact you?"

Sheepishly, Grandmother gave a little half smile, which was very creepy. "To answer your questions in the order you asked them—Viran contacted me because he knew your grandfather, Zaros. He sent for him." Keelie had a vision of an elven Father Time with a long white beard and long white hair. Zaros, her grandfather, had died (or, as the elves said, faded) a century ago.

Yet Keelie sensed there was more that Grandmother wasn't telling her. Maybe having Dad take over as the leader of the Dread Forest had left Grandmother without a job. Some people didn't adjust too well to retirement.

Grandmother reached down to turn the key. Keelie quickly removed it from the ignition. "You're going to tell me what's going on. I want to know what is really happening in the forest. Tell me everything you know, and until you do, we don't go." Keelie dangled the key from her hand.

Anger flashed in Grandmother's eyes. "You're so human sometimes."

"Thanks for not calling me a brat, but back to the subject at hand."

Knot climbed into Grandmother's lap and curled up in a ball.

Grandmother's brow wrinkled in disgust and she pushed the cat away. Knot landed on the floor of the truck with a thump and returned to Keelie's side, satisfied. Annoyed elf: mission accomplished.

"If you must hear it, I'll tell you now, before we get to the village," Grandmother said. "Viran, the Redwood Tree Shepherd, has been here for hundreds of years. When the logging began he tried to stop it, but he was too trusting. He thought that the loggers would hear his plea for the forest with compassion. Instead, he was arrested by the sheriff for disturbing the peace. A small charge, but they kept him locked away while the forest, unprotected, was logged." Grandmother looked out of the window toward the untouched wilderness outside. "The redwood elves discovered that they could only release him by going through the human courts, and thus learned about the importance of integrating themselves into the human world. They helped establish the forest service, and were able to work undisturbed. John Muir stayed with them for a while."

"John Muir? The man who's responsible for the start of the first national parks?"

"Yes. Meanwhile, Viran returned to the Redwood Forest, where he performed a Tree Lorem for each and every tree that was felled. The redwood elves then used magic to sequester part of the forest, hiding it from humans, and that is where the village is located. Viran recovered eventually, but the damage to the forest injured him gravely. He is Lord of the Forest, and you know what that means."

Keelie understood. Grandmother had once been Lady of the Dread Forest. When the Dread had failed last fall and humans had encroached on the forest, the trees were in danger and Grandmother had sickened. Keelie's dad had stepped in, taking on the soul of the forest so that his mother could heal, and only when Keelie and Alora restored the Dread did Grandmother recover. Dad was still Lord of the Forest, and Keelie had assumed that Grandmother was enjoying her new freedom.

"Viran spent many a year up in the treetops," Grandmother continued. "In all weather and even during fires, he stayed with the trees and became more and more like them. Even now he rarely touches the ground."

"Why did he want to contact Zaros?"

"He said the trees were acting strangely."

"It always starts with the trees acting differently." Keelie resisted rolling her eyes.

"He didn't tell me any more, other than he wanted to know how to expand and strengthen the Dread, and that he feared a dark presence. And now he's gone and no one can find him, not even the trees."

Keelie shuddered. She turned to her grandmother. Their eyes met. "I can't save a forest again. It took too much out of me."

"I don't think you're going to be the one to strengthen the Dread. Viran wants to know how to do it."

The tightness that had squeezed Keelie's ribs relaxed.

She'd help Viran as much as she could. She wondered what he looked like, especially if he hadn't left the treetops in hundreds of years.

Grandmother stretched a hand out for the key. "Well, we're here. And we're committed to the festival for the next three weeks."

Keelie handed the truck keys over reluctantly.

Cranking the truck back up, Grandmother seemed almost jovial. She patted Keelie on the shoulder. "I don't think helping the Redwood Tree Shepherd will take that much time or energy."

Foreboding wrapped itself around Keelie like a shroud. This was not what she had planned.

Grandmother had told Dad that she would handle the forest and the missing tree shepherd, but it felt like she had dumped this magical chore on Keelie's lap. Keelie had just wanted an opportunity to relax and run the shop, and to say goodbye to Mom's house. How did one find a missing tree shepherd anyway, when even the trees couldn't find him? She had a mental image of Viran hiding out on the beach. After four hundred years, a dude needed a vacation.

A few moments later, Grandmother drove up to a tiny, beat-up cabin of weathered logs. Keelie couldn't believe that anyone lived here, and she hoped it wouldn't be their home in the elven village.

"Don't dawdle." Grandmother hopped out and quickly walked to the dilapidated door. As her grandmother disappeared into the cabin, resolve steeled Keelie's spine. No way would she use dark magic. She'd felt its presence strongly tonight, even if Grandmother thought she was exaggerating. She had to set boundaries, or else she'd turn into some kind of magical ATM, dispensing energy upon demand. She could relate to the missing tree shepherd and why he might want to ditch his job. Trees, elves, need, need, need. It never stopped.

Keelie stomped across the path and entered the cabin, pushing the door open with a dramatic shove. "We need to talk—"

She stopped.

A tall, silver-haired elf turned to her. He was standing close to Grandmother, holding her hand. He wore robes like Lord Elianard's, but there the resemblance to the stuck-up Lore Master ended. Elianard never smiled. It was disconcerting to see this elegant look-alike beam at her. The silver-haired elf bowed his head toward Keelie.

She managed to slightly tilt hers. Grandmother dropped his hand and stepped away.

This elf's eyes were an icy blue, not woodland green. Keelie had never met an elf with Siberian Husky eyes.

Grandmother cleared her throat. "Keelie, this is Norzan. He is Tree Shepherd of the Northwoods."

"Tree Shepherd of the Northwoods? You're far from your home." Keelie sat down on a dusty, plump-cushioned sofa.

Norzan raised his eyebrows and looked at Grandmother, asking a silent question.

"What's going on?" Keelie looked to Norzan for the answer. Grandmother was dropping tiny clues like crumbs in a forest. Aggravating.

Norzan sat down on the sofa next to Keelie. "This must be overwhelming for you, especially coming into this without any knowledge of the situation."

Keelie was warming to him. "You've got that right." He was talking to her like Sir Davey would. She hoped Grandmother would catch on and treat her like an adult, and with a little kindness. Grandmother would do great in the Northwoods. She was the original Ice Queen.

"The redwood elves summoned help a week ago. Their Council leader, Kalix, sent a request to our leader. As you know, Keelie, things are not well with the Earth. So far, the Redwood Forest has been immune to the changes. Frankly, the fact that the trees themselves cannot find the shepherd tells me that things are more serious than anyone thought. The boundaries between the magical worlds are breaking, and there are those on the dark side wishing to grab power for themselves."

"You think someone took the Redwood Tree Shepherd?"

"We don't know." Grandmother interjected. "The redwoods do not know where he is."

"We can only hope that no dark force is at hand," Norzan said. "Even in the Northwoods, where the boundaries are strongly and magically protected, there is a break between worlds—human, elf, and fairy. But we have always met peacefully, every year, at the Quicksilver Faire. I want to work quickly here and return to my forest before the Faire begins."

"I think you're right, and whatever's out there is very strong," Keelie said. Her head still throbbed from the aftershocks of that psychic attack, whatever it had been. "So what are you guys planning to do about it?"

Silence.

She didn't like the way they were watching her. "Wait a minute. If some dark magical force is kidnapping tree shepherds, why are you here? Aren't you in danger?" Panic rushed through her. "Are we in danger?"

"We don't know," Norzan said. "That is why we must work together, forming a strong bond of magic to protect ourselves."

"We elves can no longer live apart, isolated from one another," Grandmother added. "To my deep regret, I am guilty of separating the Dread Forest from the other clans. We must join forces for all of our sakes."

"And Keelie will be protected at all times," a very deep and beautiful male voice said. A tall elven man walked into the room. His long hair flowed free and loose, which looked odd with the park ranger uniform that he wore. He was followed by Tavyn, the handsome young elf who had been at the ranger booth earlier. Keelie sensed a grounding about these elves, a feeling that was familiar about them, but she couldn't tell what it was.

There sure were a lot of good-looking elves around here. She wondered if they were any different from the Dread Forest elves. She noticed one difference already—at least these guys wanted to protect her.

Grandmother bowed her head, even though Keelie noticed that she pursed her lips. Uh-oh. Granny elf didn't like this tall ranger elf.

"Keliel, this is Kalix. We met his son Tavyn a while ago."

"Nice to meet you."

Kalix smiled at her. "We're honored to meet you, Keliel Tree Talker, Daughter of the Forest." Tavyn bowed to them.

Keelie was dazzled.

"Would you like to see our village?"

"I'd love to."

Kalix motioned with his hand toward the back door, and the group headed out of the cabin. They walked along a small path, and then crossed under an arbor. Keelie felt a tingle flash over her skin as she walked through a veil of magic.

As they stepped off the path to follow Kalix, he motioned toward the ancient woods. Keelie gasped. A scene out of a science fiction movie spread out before them. The lengthening shadows of the day cast the illuminated houses in the treetops into sharp relief. Keelie couldn't believe that people really lived hundreds of feet in the air, but the trees glittered with lamplight from dozens of homes. It was enchanting, and unreal. Her imagination flew up to the treetops, giddy with the thought of spending the next few weeks up there. Her stomach must have been human, though, because she was suddenly queasy.

"How do we get up there? I don't see any elevators."

Kalix walked on. "Follow me. It's easy."

Famous last words, Keelie thought, but she followed eagerly.

# five

They walked through ferns and past tangles of rhododendron until they reached one of the redwood giants. Keelie touched its bark reverently. Even while she was blocking the trees, she could feel her heart lurch as it tried to beat in time with the slow rhythm of centuries.

The platform of the building was hundreds of feet above them.

"Really, how do we get up there?" Keelie asked again.

"We travel the tree sap," Kalix answered.

Keelie had no idea what he meant. Normally she wasn't afraid of heights, but the tree houses were way up there. Her feet were getting clammy at the thought of being that high. Maybe he meant that they had an elevator in the trunk of the tree. That would be cool.

Kalix gestured toward the tree. "Everyone, come closer."

They huddled by the trunk. Knot meowed in a tone that told Keelie he didn't like the idea of going up to the top. She reached down and he climbed onto her shoulder, then sat up, holding onto her head with his paws.

Gold light flowed from the tree and surrounded them.

Keelie felt her internal organs jerk up, and then suddenly they were on a small platform in the high branches.

"Oh my," Grandmother exclaimed.

"How wonderful!" Norzan held on to a nearby limb. "I've heard of sap travel, but have never experienced it." He leaned over the platform and looked down. Just watching him made Keelie nauseous. The deck they stood on was connected to walkways and bridges that spanned the upper canopy. Around each tree the walkways widened, with covered porches and lamplight that shone through windows. The houses were built around the trees.

Maybe if she imagined that the bridges were on water instead of high in the air, she could make it work. Unfortunately, while she knew how to swim, it was harder to imagine surviving a fall from one of the decks.

"Do you always let your cat ride on your head?" Tavyn asked.

Keelie shrugged. "It's hard to discourage him." Knot dug his claws into her shoulder. "Don't worry, furball, I'm not going to let you fall." She stepped carefully off the platform and onto a wide plank staircase that led up to the redwood's trunk.

They entered the tree house, and Kalix motioned to a woman in loosely woven brown pants and a flowy, long-sleeved top in muted colors that showed it was made with natural dyes.

"My lady wife, Sariela." She had long brown hair that curled in waves. She hugged Tavyn and Kalix as they entered, a homey gesture that made Keelie miss Dad and really long for Mom. She thought of the Hancock Park house, but quickly pushed the feelings and images to the back of her mind.

Instead, she studied the interior of the tree house. It was lit by beeswax candles whose sweet honey scent filled the air, mixing with the yummy smell of soup cooking. A tin-punched star hung from the ceiling, casting little pinpoints of light on a huge wooden table. Fresh bread was set out, along with jars of honey and soup bowls. Keelie's stomach rumbled. She hadn't eaten since the SunChips at the Gas-A-Minute, and she was starving.

Kalix put his arm around the woman's waist. "Sariela and I welcome you. My dear, this is Lady Keliatiel, former Lady of the Dread Forest, and her granddaughter Keliel, also a tree shepherdess." Kalix bowed his head toward the other elf. "And Norzan, Tree Shepherd of the Northwoods."

Sariela bowed her head in return. "Welcome, honored guests. Please share our meal as family."

Grandmother smiled graciously. "Keliel and I thank you for inviting us to your home."

Norzan was staring curiously at everything. "Thank you for having us, Lady Sariela. Your home is one in balance with nature and the trees. You are truly blessed." Sariela seemed very pleased with Norzan's compliment.

For some reason, though, Keelie could feel waves of tension come from Grandmother. Was she afraid of heights? Jealous of the nice home? Hungry? Whatever. She would have to get over it. Keelie was starved, and it was nice to be around some happy elves for once. She'd just live in the moment until after the meal.

Dinner was delicious. Keelie asked questions about the treetop settlement as they ate their fill of bread and butternut squash soup, followed by hot mint green tea. Keelie wrapped her hands around the blue earthenware mug, enjoying the warmth that soaked into her hands.

"Are you tired, Keliel?" Norzan peered at her, worried. That caring look made her chest tighten.

She nodded, then glanced over at Grandmother, who was studying the inside of her tea mug, oblivious to Norzan's concern. Grandmother would never have the kind of empathy the Northwoods Tree Shepherd was displaying. Even though she and Keelie had reached an understanding, Grandmother was still her stiff and regal elf self.

Kalix pushed his chair away from the table. "So, my tree shepherd friends. Have the trees spoken to you?"

"It's been a long day." Sariela interrupted, placing her hand on Kalix's arm. "Maybe we can have this discussion another time. Talk to Bella, then let us retire. The child is weary, and she needs her rest."

The "child" actually wanted to hear what the other tree shepherds had felt. Had Norzan felt the dark magic?

Kalix nodded at his wife's words and patted her hand. "I shall be brief, as you suggest, and tomorrow we can discuss our plans and how to proceed." It sounded like this particular "what we're going to do" discussion involved Keelie. She sat up, sleepiness gone.

"As you know, our Tree Shepherd has disappeared, and the trees cannot sense him. It was upon their suggestion that we sought help from the tree shepherds of the two greatest western American forests." Kalix said. "We are grateful for your assistance."

"Could the fae be behind his disappearance?" Grandmother asked.

Norzan nodded. "I would start there. In the Northwoods, we've had discussions with the High Court of the fae. We're working together to strengthen the veils between the worlds."

"I've always disapproved of this unnatural alliance. Beware the Shining Ones," Grandmother said ominously. "The fae have not been friends to the elves."

Norzan frowned. "They approached us first, my lady. We all have to work together. You heard about the Arctic thaw? We must reverse it in order for our ways to survive."

"The fae, as you call them, no longer live in our forest." Kalix's tone was serious. "The trees said it was urgent that we send for you." He turned to Keelie. "Your success in the Dread Forest has been heard far and wide. The trees and the spirits speak the name of Keliel Tree Talker."

She lifted her head. "Me?" Spirits were speaking her name?

"Yes, you." Norzan smiled and his blue eyes twinkled. "You're the first to combine the magic of elf, fae, and Earth. The fairy courts of the Northwoods know you well, and speak of you as one of their own."

Keelie didn't like that. She wanted to be low on the fairy radar. It was one thing to deal with the Dread Forest's fae and *bhata*, but she didn't want to go global. She realized that Kalix was right about the absence of fairies—she'd seen no *bhata* here.

"Why are there no fae in the Redwood Forest?"

Sariela, Kalix, and Tavyn looked at one another as if Keelie had mentioned an unpleasant subject.

Kalix cleared his throat. "They were banished, along with the goblins that sought to overrun this forest."

"Goblins?" Keelie jerked back, almost spilling her hot tea. Just hearing the word "goblin" shot chills through her body. Visions of giant, toad-faced creatures carrying broad-axes flashed in her mind, and she heard again the loud cackling laugh of the Red Cap. She'd come close to death when she'd battled a Red Cap at the High Mountain Faire. The evil little creature had not been easy to kill.

"Do you think that goblins, or other dark fae, are behind the disappearance of the Redwood Tree Shepherd?" Grandmother asked, her face crinkled into worry lines.

"No," Kalix said firmly. "They were vanquished over a hundred and fifty years ago from this forest. The power of the trees prevents them from returning. They're urban creatures now, living like rats in the sewers. We don't use the Dread in the forest, but we may have to. Until now, Viran's charm has kept out strangers. The loss of their shepherd has made the trees fearful."

Sariela made an unhappy sound, then seemed to force herself to relax. She sipped her tea and kept her eyes on the table.

"I thought you won't use the Dread because of the people who visit the parks," Keelie said. "Or at least, that's what I understood from Tavyn."

"That's what the elves would prefer to do. But the trees say differently." Kalix frowned.

"Then what can we do?" Grandmother asked. "Keelie's magic is part fae, and if you have blocked its use we may not be able to help find the missing tree shepherd."

"Keelie can also use Earth magic, and the redwoods insist she can help. We listen to our trees." Kalix's look challenged her.

"It sounds like the trees are telling you what to do." Grandmother sipped her tea and avoided his gaze.

The tree house shook in response. Dishes clattered to the ground.

Keelie leapt to her feet and grabbed Grandmother by the hand. "It's an earthquake." She started toward the door.

Sariela stopped her. "It's just Bella," she said soothingly. "She's close by and she's not happy with Keliatiel's words."

"This tree's name is Bella?" It was an untreelike name.

"No, this tree is Wena. Bella Matera is one of the Ancients."

Foglike tendrils drifted in through the window, and a cold dampness permeated the room. It was the kind of cold that seeped into your skin after walking in a winter rain. Keelie sensed a consciousness in the mist, as if a very old and wise being was here with them. Then the fog swirled clockwise, gold sparkles twinkling in streaks as the mist formed into the shape of a tree inside the room—a tree taller than Kalix and Norzan.

A face formed in the trunk, reminding Keelie of Alora, and then the tree spirit shrank into itself until it was the shape of a woman. Keelie wondered if she was dealing with the ghost spirit of the forest, but she didn't feel like she did when she'd encountered the ghost forest in the Wildewood. The fog was glowing with the silver luminosity of a tall tree wraith. The tree's eyes, green and very human looking, locked directly on Keelie.

A spirit walker. Her father had said that she might encounter one. Keelie felt a tingling in her mind as if someone was trying to read her thoughts, and she clamped down on the invading presence. A smile formed on the tree's specterlike face.

"Good evening, everyone. Keliatiel, Norzan, and Keliel." The tree gestured elegantly with one of her branch-like arms, fingers like long twigs bristling from the ends. "I am Bella Matera. I am the mother tree of this forest."

Keelie looked around as Grandmother and Norzan bowed their heads. Kalix and Sariela followed their gesture, and Keelie knew that they had heard the spirit speak, too.

These were powerful trees indeed, if nonshepherds could hear them. She wondered if humans could as well.

Keelie bowed as she regarded the mother tree. The term was a new one to her. She'd have to call Dad later and ask him about it.

"Wood Mother, we are honored to be in your company." Grandmother's voice rang through the cabin. She really got into the elf rituals. Keelie had studied elf ritual over the winter and had not been impressed. It seemed like a way to keep from having normal relationships.

Bella Matera smiled. "I was most anxious to meet you." The tree's gaze fell on Keelie again.

This was creepy. Keelie had seen trees walk and talk, and she had seen one, Alora, grow from a seedling to a mighty oak queen in just weeks, but she wasn't quite sure what to make of Bella Matera. All forests were different. She just wished there was one rule book that all of the forests followed.

"We have been summoned to the Globe." Bella Matera said this as if it was an invitation to Sunday dinner.

"You mean the Globe Theater on the festival grounds? Aren't you afraid the humans will see you?" Norzan asked.

"It is a customary meeting place for us, ever since the town was founded. We are so inspired by William Shakespeare, who the townspeople revere. We're redwoods, after all, not like the other trees. Since the coming of the humans, they have performed the Shakespeare plays, and we have learned much about humans from them. Now they flourish, and we enjoy watching the performances."

"You leave your tree body"—Keelie couldn't think of what else to call it—"as you have tonight, and then you float into town and watch *A Midsummer Night's Dream*?"

"The humans do not see us. We take the form of fog, and because of the ocean mist, we blend in perfectly. "

"Aren't you afraid of the humans discovering your presence?" Norzan asked.

Bella shook her head. "You know the humans would panic if we took our tree forms. Besides, the fog adds a certain ambiance to the mood of the play. The *Los Angeles Times'* arts critic always complains about it being foggy when he attends. Of course, he seems like an unhappy man and a soul who likes to complain about everything. Master Oswald said so once."

Keelie liked Bella Matera. She seemed like a fun but very smart tree. Who knew? Trees liked Shakespeare.

"Now we must go to the Globe. Bloodroot has called a meeting."

Bloodroot? That was definitely not a tree name. Keelie couldn't shake the sound of the Red Cap's laughter from her thoughts.

"Bloodroot the tree called a meeting. Huh." This was a different kind of place. "The trees in the Dread Forest don't call meetings."

"No, but they attend meetings," Grandmother said. She didn't seem to think there was anything weird about this place.

Bella Matera floated over to Grandmother. She looked

down at Keelie, and her ghostly, sticklike fingers touched Keelie's face.

*The child is tired. Let her sleep.*

Keelie felt warmth, then cold, eddy through her. It was sort of like being filled with hot cocoa, then having a woodsy whip cream sprayed on top. She stared at the tree spirit. Awe and a deep respect for this Ancient One filled her. The tree smiled.

Bella Matera held out her branchlike hand and blew. "May the stars send you dreams and let you hear the songs of the spheres circling the sun."

Keelie could hear a soft melody forming in the back of her mind, along with images of shooting stars and planets swirling around one another like in a planetarium show. It was so lovely; the musical harmonies touched the core of her magic, which sparked, then glowed like a banked fire. Her energy faded, and suddenly she simply wanted to go to sleep.

"I am tired." She tried to suppress a yawn.

Bella Matera began to dissolve into a gaseous mist. The mist floated toward the open window, and a disembodied voice floated in the room. *'Til tomorrow, sleep dreaming of the stars.*

Drowsy, Keelie thought of Grandmother and Norzan meeting with Bloodroot without her. Did Bella Matera want to keep her away? She wanted to see the forest at night. She fought to wake up, feeling the tree's magic around her like a comfy spiderweb. The lovely music faded a little, but held.

"So powerful," she murmured.

Then burning pain slashed across her ankle, and the dreamy moment vanished—leaving only the drone of Knot's purr.

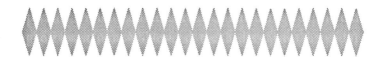

# six

The last sleepy bits of the tree's song lingered as Keelie sat up, screaming. Her ankle bled from two long furrows cut deeply into her skin.

Knot licked his toes delicately, claws out, watching her.

"Thanks, Freddy Krueger Cat. I'll let you know if I need stitches." Keelie stood up. "I'm going to have to buy a whole emergency kit."

"You shook away the tree's blessing." Grandmother's mouth turned down.

Keelie grinned. "Don't want to miss the big tree meeting.

Are you ready to go?" She held back a yawn and limped toward Sariela, who was holding out a wet washcloth.

Kalix frowned, looking at Knot. "The cat takes his role as guardian too far."

"He is dedicated," Grandmother agreed.

Fifteen minutes later, the group was gathered at the base of their tree, Wena, the glow of the sap travel fading. Wena's spirit form stood to one side, watching them but not coming close. The tree's roots were large and went deep into the ground.

Keelie felt the other trees of the forest pressing in and around her, seeking entrance into her mind. A thrum of deep magic surged under her feet, the energy of the Earth. She touched the rose quartz at her belt, using Earth magic to give herself the extra power she needed to block out the redwoods. She shrugged, feeling a little more in control. She was getting better at balancing the magic. But Keelie's head was still reeling from the trip down the tree. She hoped someone would teach her how to travel the sap herself—she couldn't rely on Kalix to be her elevator operator every time she wanted to come or go.

Norzan smiled at her. "Exhilarating, isn't it?"

She swallowed. "If you say so."

Knot was trotting beside Keelie. He seemed to be in a jovial mood, ready for a jaunt in the woods, probably searching for some poor unsuspecting *feithid daoine* as a midnight snack. No such luck. There weren't any here.

The motley crew of elves started walking. Keelie realized she was turned around—she'd thought the highway was in the other direction, but within moments they were in the festival parking lot and Keelie could hear the sea, its waves pounding against the rocky shore on the other side of the highway. The soothing sounds of the waves calmed her unease, and she smiled when she remembered the huge sea lions sunning themselves like sunbathers on the beach.

As they followed the path leading into the festival grounds, the fog thickened and the sounds of the ocean faded. Keelie thought about the water sparkling in the daytime, the tide pools filled with different marine life. The beaches here in Northern California were different from the L.A. beaches, with their swimmers and surfers in the golden California sun. Here, in Juliet City, driftwood was scattered everywhere and huge rocky outcroppings sprouted out of the water.

In the distance, Keelie heard thunder rumbling. A storm was blowing in. She wished she had an umbrella, but Grandmother seemed oblivious to the fact that it might rain. She was acting like this was a field trip, walking fast like a giddy school girl. Around them, sounds of the festival at night rose and fell. The smell of cooking wafted on the sea breeze, along with the faint rhythmic pounding of a drum circle.

The Globe Theater stood alone on the edge of the festival grounds, near the town of Juliet City. The long-ago actors had started performing here when the highway was just a dirt path, and the festival had grown up around it. As the elves walked toward it, more and more tree spirits drifted down to join them. Surrounded by the ghostly figures, Keelie felt uneasy. Once again she could hear the waves crashing on the beach, and she saw a flash of red and green in the distance. Probably some player, still in costume. Some of these guys were in character day and night.

Norzan, with staff in hand, strode with a determined gait and observed all that was going on. Keelie liked him; he reminded her of a wise shaman. Seeing Norzan looking so sage and powerful, she couldn't help but wonder about the missing Redwood Tree Shepherd. How strong was his magic? He must be powerful to deal with these super trees.

The thunder rumbled again. Whatever this meeting was about tonight, Keelie hoped they finished before the storm let loose and they all were soaked to the bone.

They climbed up a tall hill to the Juliet City Globe Theater. It was a circular, two-story, half-timbered building, and looked just like the pictures Keelie had seen of the original Globe Theater in England. But this one was draped with a banner proclaiming "*A Midsummer Night's Dream*, Preview Tomorrow!" You could see it from the road.

Keelie felt like she was living her own version of Shakespeare's play tonight, except hers would be called "A Midnight Promenade of the Redwoods."

A fog seemed to be drifting in. As Keelie watched, a thick patch of ground-level clouds floated in from the sea, merging with the ghostly trees around the Globe. Keelie now knew how the trees were able to camouflage their spirit-walking when among humans. Fog could hide a lot of secrets. She remembered when she'd first seen her Uncle Dariel in the Dread Forest. He'd been a vampire then, and had been able to turn into fog. She shivered and hurried to walk next to

Grandmother, who was strolling serenely, as if they were in a parade.

The Globe was full of humans rehearsing the play. The elves stood by the theater doors, watching Master Oswald in the middle of the action, surrounded by people holding pages in their hands. A woman with glasses resting on top her head was reading something out loud. Keelie picked up on the "thee's" and "thou's." What would they think of the elves showing up to chat with a bunch of tree spirits? She wasn't sure the actors could even see anything, and if they did, they'd probably think it was the mist coming in from the ocean.

Bella Matera appeared, spiraling out of the mist until she was in her pseudo-human form. Her branches looked like real arms, and her hair seemed to be made of leaves.

Other tree spirits appeared and swirled around them. Bella waved her arms in greeting, like a goddess welcoming worshipers. The trees' powerful energy pressed on Keelie's mind, making her head pound. She felt for her rose quartz and pulled on more Earth energy to block them. Grandmother stood close to Keelie, protectively.

Norzan joined them. "This is strange indeed. Even in the lore of tree shepherds, this has never been seen." His voice was cautious but held undertones of wonder.

Surprised, Keelie turned to the Northwoods tree shepherd. "I thought you, of all elves, would know about this."

He shook his head. "Each forest has its own culture and secrets." He pointed his staff toward the tree spirits. "Keelie, now I am certain that all is not as it should be in the Redwood Forest."

"I agree." Grandmother tilted her head upwards and then to the side as a face formed in one of the ephemeral tree shapes.

*Greetings, Shepherds.*

Goose bumps dotted Keelie's arms as a menacing premonition prickled her mind.

As if on cue, the creepy jester wearing the red and green harlequin suit stepped onto center stage. Was he the flash of red and green she'd seen near the beach? Keelie wondered how he'd gotten back here so quickly, if so. With his jangly hat perched at an angle on his head, the jester looked like something you'd see at a medieval circus. He was engaging in a dangerous, Tony Soprano kind of way. All eyes in the theater were riveted on him as he spoke Puck's lines in a hypnotic voice.

"That's Peascod."

Keelie looked up. It was Bella, who was floating above them and pointing toward the stage. "We enjoy his performances and find them inspiring, but sadly we must end tonight's entertainment to prepare for our Lord Bloodroot."

Norzan cut his eyes over to Keelie. Something in his expression told her to be careful.

Bella must have sensed the tension in the air. "Come now, tree shepherds, our shifting can't be that alien to you. Why, Keelie alone is strong enough."

"Milady, I have to be honest. I find it disconcerting."

Norzan leaned on his staff. "Viran never revealed this particular talent you possess."

Bella gave a gossamer laugh, light and airy. "My dear Northwoods Shepherd, we'd hoped you'd find our way enlightening. Although our beloved shepherd is missing, something good has come from our misfortunes. We have met you, and the Ladies Keliatiel and Keliel. We look forward to an exchange of culture and magic."

Norzan nodded, but his bright blue eyes were shadowed. "What do you hope to gain in such an exchange?"

"It may be your gain. I'm sure your trees in the Northwoods can't do this." She gestured. "Nor this." Bella waved her hand once more and the air around them grew heavy, as if green condensation hovered, thickening the atmosphere. Then the air lightened and the wetness evaporated.

All of the actors became silent, their faces vacant. The directors and crew also stood there, motionless and quiet.

Master Oswald suddenly stood up, jerkily. Keelie thought he'd shaken off the spell, but then he waved his paper, his hand flapping like a puppet's. "Good gentles and ladies, our play is over. Now." He left the stage, staggering a little as he went down the stairs to the open pit of the dirt floor.

The other actors began to follow him, silently lining up without jostling, like zombies leaving a baseball game.

Keelie walked down the ramp, toward the stage, looking into the players' faces as they passed her. They were all somewhere else. She tried standing in front of one of the women, but the woman just stepped sideways and continued on as if Keelie had been a wall or a piece of furniture.

No eye contact, no focus, no life. It horrified Keelie that trees could do this. But according to Bella Matera, they did it all the time.

The weird jester dude who played Puck was coming toward her. Again, he made Keelie feel uneasy. As he passed, his eyes flicked toward her and she caught a sinister glint in his gaze. This guy was pretending. He was not under the tree spell, but Keelie didn't want to give him away. What would the trees do if they found out? And what was different about him? If there was anything to be cautious about in the festival, it was this guy. And of course the trees.

"He comes," Bella said in a whispery, scratchy voice.

"Who?" Keelie pulled her gaze away from Peascod.

"Our Lord Bloodroot."

Bella drifted down to center stage and stood with the other tree spirits.

Norzan stepped closer to Keelie. He smiled. "I think we're about to be allowed to see an ancient ritual."

Keelie felt a tingle shimmy up her spine at the thought of seeing an ancient tree ritual. Excitement warred with apprehension at the thought of what she would see. She wondered if Dad had ever witnessed anything like this.

Norzan leaned closer. "We must be careful. I'm very concerned about Viran, but until we find the answers, trust no one, not even the trees and the redwood elves. I think it wise to keep our counsel among ourselves."

Surprised, Keelie nodded. Good advice. She liked Norzan, and she trusted him.

Grandmother joined them, her face transfixed with wonder. "It's not like the real Globe, but it's a very good replica." Keelie knew Grandmother was old, but put in this context...holy cow!

The air suddenly became chilled, and the wind kicked up. Keelie had to push her curls out of her face. Floating toward center stage was a large, dark cloud. All was quiet, as if everyone and every tree was holding their breath, expecting something big to happen.

And it did. A green bolt of lightning flashed in the sky.

Thunder boomed over the Globe, rattling the stage. It was kind of like the special effects at a rock n' roll concert.

A giant tree spirit materialized out of the mist. He was human-looking except for his eyes, which were vertically slitted, like a cat's, and emerald green. He surveyed the stage and the surroundings as if memorizing everything. His trunk and roots, even in the dim light of the lanterns hanging in the Globe, were red like blood. Hence the name, Keelie figured.

And talk about a dramatic entrance. Keelie couldn't help but be mesmerized by Bloodroot's presence. There was something about him that drew her to him.

"Gentle trees, and shepherds who have gathered among us, I bid thee welcome to our forest. May you find peace in our soil." His voice was deep and loamy.

Bloodroot fixed his intimidating gaze on Keelie. Her blood grew cold. He was looking into the core of her essence, and the tree magic within her would soon reveal all her secrets to him. Keelie dug the rose quartz from her pocket and pulled on a strong filament of Earth magic while visualizing a shield. She definitely agreed with Norzan. They were going to have to be careful around such powerful trees.

Grandmother had an enraptured look on her face, as if she'd found tree nirvana. Water droplets sprinkled on Keelie's arms. It was going to rain very soon. She hoped the trees performed their ritual quickly.

"Tonight, we come together to find our shepherd."

There was a deep "om" from the gathered tree spirits.

Bloodroot gestured with his branches toward the sky, and then, as if he'd caught a firefly, he clasped them close together.

There was a unified gasp of awe from the tree spirits.

"We send out an air spirit to seek him." Bloodroot lifted his branches. His twiggy fingers glowed with glacial blue light.

The tree spirits swirled and cheered.

Keelie could barely make out a shape within the glimmering light. It looked like a small humanoid, shimmering like an image on bad TV reception.

"Air spirit, go out in the world, seek the one we have lost," Bloodroot intoned.

Norzan grabbed the back of a chair to help steady himself. "It is impossible for a tree to capture an elemental spirit."

The wind blew again. Lightning blazed like an angry streak of fire in the sky. Thunder roared like a hundred giant lions.

Knot hissed and arched his back.

The trees twirled up into the sky and spun like ethereal

whirling dervishes around Bloodroot and the captured air elemental.

Then a green arc of lightning touched the tips of Bloodroot's branches. Thunder exploded. Keelie covered her head. This was too close for comfort. Bloodroot was a weird evangelist, with a twist of tree wizard. Maybe watching a tree ritual wasn't the safest experience in the world. The tree shepherds could be electrocuted and become elf barbeque.

Then the trees swirled back down to the stage and surrounded Bloodroot. "Go and seek our shepherd," he commanded them. "Do not return until you do."

The air spirit, released, ascended to the sky like a spectral comet.

Keelie followed its trajectory, forgetting to breathe.

More lightning flashed in the sky, and more thunder followed, and the skies released the rain.

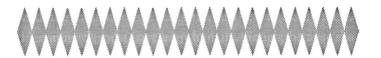

# seven

On the way home, Knot hissed every time a water droplet fell on his fur, which was wet and sticking out in weird points.

"Shut up. You're not the only one getting wet."

A waterlogged Grandmother, Keelie, and Norzan slogged on behind the other elves, each lost in thought.

Keelie heard whispers from smaller trees, which were soon silenced by a green power. But Keelie sensed dark spots in the greenness, and she didn't like it. That same prickly premonition feeling scratched at her brain. She shivered—not from the cold, but from that feeling. When they reached

Wena, Grandmother touched her shoulder and she felt the green glow surround them. Keelie rode the sap without comment, thinking about what she'd seen tonight.

When she woke up the next morning, with a ray of sun shining through the little round window in the guest bedroom of Kalix's treetop condo, something was kneading her hair. A loud purr started up in her ear. Keelie reached out and swatted at Knot.

He purred even louder. She rolled over, quickly rising to her knees, and pulled the pillow out from underneath him.

Knot landed with a thud on the ground, purring even louder. Of all the guardians available in the world of fairy, she'd wound up with the feline version of Puck. That thought reminded her of Peascod, and how he'd been unaffected by Bloodroot's powerful magic last night. Keelie wondered where he worked by day. Probably at one of the festival shops or stages. Maybe he had a charm against the tree magic. If so, she wanted to look at it.

Knot gazed at her, his dilated eyes as black as small hematite stones and ringed in green.

She pointed to the door. He narrowed his eyes.

"Out. It's time to dress, and you have to use the kitty box."

Knot started to wash his tail. Keelie walked over to him, about to throw him out on his rear end, but he hissed and reached out to swat her, missing her bandaged ankle by an inch.

"Missed me."

"Keelie, you're up?" Grandmother asked from the doorway.

Knot shot out of the bedroom like a furry missile on four legs. Grandmother quickly stepped back; otherwise, Knot would've crashed into her. A moment later, the cat came crashing back in, his kitty paws sliding on the polished wood floor. He skidded under the bed and didn't come back out.

Something was different about Grandmother this morning. Normally she would've said something negative by now, but she hadn't even said anything about Knot.

"Do something about your hair. We have company for breakfast."

Okay, that was more like the grandmother she knew.

Then Grandmother frowned, and her lips moved as if she was rehearsing to herself. After a moment her eyes met Keelie's. "It won't be for long, but we'll have to make the best of it." She turned and left, her cryptic words floating in the air between them.

Keelie threw on some jeans and a tank top, pulled a baggy sweater over that and walked out, barefoot. Sariela was at the stove, tending a batch of fragrant pancakes.

The table was set for four. Norzan was eating delicately, as if he'd never seen pancakes before and one might leap up and bite him. Next to him sat Risa, a tidy stack of small round pancakes cooling on her plate. She smiled tightly at Keelie.

"Good morning, Keliel, " she said politely. Her eyes glittered.

"Risa, what a surprise." Keelie looked around, hoping and not hoping to see Sean. He wasn't in the tiny house.

"I've invited Risa to stay with us for a few days," Sariela said. "It's not right for an elven girl to be alone with all the humans."

Unlike a half-elven girl, who had lived among humans for years with no harm done.

"Isn't this a treat for you girls?" Sariela seemed to expect a happy response.

"Oh, joy." Keelie wondered where the elf girl would sleep.

Sariela answered her unspoken question. "Keliel, you and Risa may share that big bed. Lady Keliatiel will have to make do with the little room."

The little private room. The one with no Risa in it. So this was what grandmother had meant when she said it would only be for a little while. Right.

Risa let out a squeal and pointed. Keelie jumped, wondering if Bloodroot had appeared in the kitchen. Knot's head ducked back into the bedroom.

"It's Knotsie! Oh, I'd hoped he was here." Risa jumped up, almost knocking over her chair, and dashed around the end of the table. Norzan watched with his mouth hanging open as she ran into the bedroom in hot pursuit of Knot.

"Love potion gone wrong," Keelie explained. "She and Knot got mixed up."

"Oh, my sweet woods and dales," the tree shepherd said. "How unfortunate."

"Tell me about it." But now it was Knot's problem.

Keelie pulled Risa's pancakes toward her and drowned them in syrup. It was going to be another long day and she may as well fuel up.

"Grandmother, I have some questions about last night. First of all, why did Bella Matera try to put me to sleep last night? Didn't she want me at the ceremony?"

"Nonsense, child. She was being kind."

Keelie remembered the tree touching her face, and then the beautiful music and the dreams about the stars. She'd had her mental guards up to protect herself from the tree probing her thoughts, but a tree using magic to put her to sleep was something new. Although it didn't seem like magic, just beautiful images. She wondered if the zombie humans had seen something like that.

"What kind of magic would bespell a crowd of humans?" Keelie needed to know more. Even though Grandmother said that Bella Matera's motives were kind ones, Keelie was guarded. "It seems like a dangerous kind of magic."

"No elf magic would do such a thing," Grandmother admitted. "Perhaps Viran had access to fae glamour. He's left a lot of mysteries behind."

The back door opened by itself and an orange streak ran out, followed by Risa.

"Gee, I hope she doesn't fall out of the tree," Keelie said. Not.

After a while Knot returned alone, mumbling in a low meow. He looked like a furry porcupine, his fur sticking out in demonic cowlicks, and he smelled like lotion.

"What happened to him?" Grandmother watched as Knot trotted on through to the living room.

Keelie ran a hand through her own tangled hair. "Whatever happened, serves him right." She spoke super loud so the cat could hear her. A loud purr answered her.

"Bloodroot." Keelie contemplated the sound of the name for a few seconds. "Sounds like a tree starring in a horror movie." Looked like one, too.

"Keelie, you must always treat the redwoods with the greatest of honor," Grandmother said, her voice low and her expression shocked. "They're like the ancient sages of the woodland world. They deserve the utmost respect."

"You must be cautious, as well. They are very powerful." Norzan looked at Grandmother as if he would say more, but glanced at Sariela and turned his attention back to his pancakes.

"Finish your breakfast. We need to be at the festival. The Lord Mayor is going to introduce us to the festival players." Grandmother sniffed. "Although I don't know why he feels it is necessary for us to associate with them." Grandmother was sounding more like herself. Keelie didn't know whether to be relieved or to run.

At the shop, the rest of the furniture had been unpacked and the elven jousters were loitering around. Sean was looking very handsome and commanding in a braided leather jerkin that was trimmed in the silver and blue of his jousting troop. He also sported snug leather breeches and tall boots, and looked very much the elven knight.

Keelie thought again of how much Sean had changed

since his father had been punished for using dark magic in the Dread Forest. He was more confident in his role with the Silver Bough Jousting Company, whose leadership he'd now assumed. He'd trained hard and long with the other jousters over the winter, while she'd had her head crammed with elven lore from Elianard. They'd had no time for each other—until now.

Sean smiled at her, crossing his arms over his chest as she walked up to him. The other jousters stood behind him as if waiting for her command. They all looked at her with respect. Maybe they were following Sean's lead. Since restoring the Dread in the Dread forest, Keelie's status as the half-elf daughter of Zekeliel Heartwood had been accepted.

"Lord Sean." Keelie arched an eyebrow, hoping she looked calm and collected. Just looking at him reminded her of the kiss they'd shared, and she was glad she'd remembered to apply deodorant; otherwise, sweat stains would be popping out on the armpits of the white poet's blouse she'd tossed on over her tank top. Keelie knew she looked Ren Faire chic.

A current of energy arced between them as they stared at one another. It was growing stronger, that something they felt for one another. She didn't want to name it with that word, that word that started with an "L," but it shone from Sean's eyes. She wanted Sean to take her away from here, to be somewhere far away, just the two of them, Sean and Keelie, without roles and responsibilities clinging to them. Keelie could only dream of what would happen then.

A loud purr floated up from her feet, and then Knot

rubbed up against her leg. Next would be the sinking of claws into the leather of her boots. She lifted him up with the toe of her boot. His purring increased. She tossed him off her foot. He landed on all fours and gave her his kitty smile.

How did Knot do it? He always showed up at the moments he was least wanted. Moodbuster.

Sean didn't look down at Knot, but the cat's purring indicated the moment of simply Sean and Keelie was over. He was leader of the Silver Bough Jousting Company and she was the tree shepherdess, daughter of the leader of the Dread Forest elves.

"Milady, your realm is ready for final inspection." Sean waved toward the shop. "My men unpacked the rest of your boxes."

"Thank you, Lord Sean." She was touched.

"This is wonderful. Thank you so much." Grandmother had arrived, with Scott close behind her.

"Looks good. You can come work for me anytime." Scott slowly rotated in place as he studied the shop.

Sean stiffened, and then bowed his head to Grandmother. "I was glad to help, Lady Keliatiel."

"Thank you." Grandmother said graciously. Her cheeks were pink with pleasure as she looked around the shop.

Scott stood next to Sean and put a hand on Sean's shoulder. He nodded with appreciation. "If this jousting gig doesn't work out for you, I think you have a future in Ren Faire retail."

Sean shrugged Scott's hand away. "If the woodworking

doesn't work out, come to the jousting ring. We always have a need for squires."

Sean walked away from him and stopped in front of Keelie. He took her hands in his. They were rougher, not as soft as they had been the last time she'd held them. "I'll be practicing this afternoon. I would be delighted to see you at the ring, if you can make it. Come watch us practice."

"Keelie is busy today," Grandmother interjected.

Keelie wanted to kick her grandmother's shins.

"Then I will see you another time." Sean released Keelie's hand.

Her heart panged. She couldn't let him walk away. "Come to dinner tonight."

Sean turned and walked backwards, smiling. "I will."

"Keelie, you didn't clear that with me." Grandmother's tone sounded shocked.

Keelie tore her gaze away from Sean's retreating figure. "I just felt like it was the right thing to do."

"What are you having for dinner?" Scott asked. "I really get tired of macaroni and cheese. It's been a long time since I've had a home-cooked meal."

Grandmother looked at Scott and a smile appeared on her face. "Why don't you join us? We're having an early dinner at the Queen's Alehouse."

Keelie whirled around to protest.

"Thanks, I will." Scott grinned. "Not home-cooked, but the company will make up for it."

Keelie was about to retort, but a sudden darkness filled her. It was like being in the sunlight and then having a storm cloud obliterate the light. She tried to control her breathing, to stop her anxiety as the power filled her. She'd felt this when she'd opened the dark book of fairy magic to heal Ariel. The magic had poured upward, into her.

She stood still and called upon her tree magic, envisioning her feet like roots seeking the nourishing soil of the earth to steady herself. Coolness wrapped her mind, quelling the anxiety.

A loud jangling rent the air. The noise sounded like bells, but horrible, grim bells that made you want to gnash your teeth. She'd heard that noise before. Peascod was somewhere near. What was it with that jester?

The back of her neck itched and she scratched as Grandmother covered her ears, a pained look on her face.

"What a horrible sound," Grandmother said.

"It's Peascod the jester." Keelie put her fingers in her ears. Other shopkeepers were stepping out of their buildings, shaking their heads and looking for the origins of the irritating noise.

Scott scowled. "Not him again. Whatever you do, don't make him mad, because he loves to annoy. He's like a leech— once he latches on, he won't let go."

Keelie felt cold thread its way down her spine. Peascod sounded more dangerous than annoying.

Scott's face was serious. "Funny name, Peascod, but that jester is scary-assed." Scott pointed to his temple.

Grandmother lifted her head as if she was sensing a change in the wind, or possibly picking up a message from the trees. She tilted her face, and suddenly her gaze became riveted on something.

The man in the snug-fitting harlequin outfit and jingly hat was sauntering toward them. The red and green diamonds of his costume seemed to expand and contract with each movement. He looked over at them, and then froze as he and Grandmother locked gazes in an intense stare. Chills coursed through Keelie. The man blinked, and his attention turned to her. She felt as if she was being scanned by an X-Ray machine. Then the jester grinned, revealing small teeth in an oversized mouth. He removed the hat from his head, and bowed gracefully.

He was not attractive. His skin was so pale, it looked as if he had never been out in the sun. His lank hair was pulled back in a ponytail, his nose was hawklike, and for a second, when he blinked, Keelie caught a glimpse of predatory silver in his eyes, as if she had been marked as his prey. He smacked his hat back on his head, setting off another jarring jingle to rip through the air, and jabbed a finger in her direction. Then he whirled around and walked away.

Scott stood behind Keelie. He was so close she could feel the warmth from his body. She felt protected being so near to him.

"Be careful, Keelie. You've fallen onto Peascod's radar."

Just what she needed—another enemy.

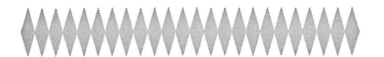

# eight

The next morning, the din of bagpipes that signaled the opening of the Shakespeare Festival was both thrilling and nauseating. It was the only bright sound in the strange, muffled atmosphere of the fog. At least it was much better than the noise the jester had made the day before, Keelie thought as she hurried up the misty path toward the Heartwood shop.

She'd had a good night's sleep despite the fact that it had been cold and Risa was a real blanket hog. The morning was still chilly, and she was grateful for her Rennie boots with the big bone buttons up the sides. They'd cost her dearly, but she would be comfy and warm all day. She'd heard that lots of people took Fridays off to attend the faire, and she was ready for a crowd this weekend.

Her usual Ren Faire garb, of flowy, medieval gowns, was not period for this festival, so Keelie just wore her boots with black pants tucked into them, and a billowy poet's shirt over a bright red tank top. If the Admin guy didn't like it, he was welcome to buy her all-new garb. She was only here for three weeks.

Knot weaved in and out of her legs as if trying to trip her up. She stepped sideways, leaving him in the middle of the path. He meowed, looking sad.

"Faker. At least you have a fur coat." She walked on and soon he was bounding ahead of her, disappearing into the ferns that bordered the paths.

Tree trunks like cathedral columns rose out of the fog all around. She wondered if one of these trees knew where Viran was and wasn't telling. The occasional hurrying figure made her feel as if she was on the set of a spooky film. She strode on, unafraid. Few movies could conjure up some of the real-life creepy sights she'd seen in the past year, and Wednesday night had been one of the scariest.

Grandmother had not been in her bed when Keelie had left the tree house, so Keelie harbored a dim hope that there would be oatmeal and a mug of hot tea waiting for her at Heartwood. They needed to make sure everything was in order before the festival gates opened in an hour.

The thud of hooves sounded behind her, and Keelie stepped off the path to allow the rider to pass. A loud "Good morning Lady Keliel" drifted over the knight's shoulder as he cantered past. One of Sean's men.

It would be nice to meet Sean in the foggy trees. Maybe he'd kiss her again. She paused to lean against the rough bark of the tree and imagined the feel of his lips on hers, his arm around her waist, his hard chest pressing against her. She sighed, and felt the tree stir to wakefulness, eavesdropping on her thoughts.

Keelie didn't care. To her dreamy scenario she added Risa, who would come upon them and growl and gnash her teeth. (What was gnashing, anyway?) Behind her, the tanoak grew warm and gave off a spicy scent. She smiled and stroked its bark. "Back to sleep, old guy. I didn't mean to wake you up."

A green girl with pointed ears trotted past her. Keelie stared, mystified, before realizing that it was a human girl with green makeup and glued-on ears. She stroked her pointed ear tip and hopped back onto the path, hurrying toward the shops. Funny how she'd gone from touching her rounded ear, to reassure herself that she was like everyone else, to touching the pointed one.

The Heartwood shop was empty. Irritated at her grandmother, Keelie yanked on the green cloth curtains, sliding the rings back on the rods, and tied the fabric to the corner posts with a tasseled cord the golden hue of a hawk's eyes.

The furniture was dust-free and in place. She touched a small dresser (cedar from the Northwoods), then looked up, startled, as she saw a pale figure watching her from the back of the shop. Was it a tree spirit or was the place haunted?

Keelie walked quickly toward the back, hiding her apprehension although no one was around to see.

She'd never seen a ghost. Although she'd met enough strange creatures in the world that she shouldn't be surprised to meet the spirit remains of a person, it still was scary. But nothing moved in the back of the shop. She was alone.

Unlocking the safe in the back room, Keelie pulled out the change box and placed it under the carved counter, a close cousin to the one at her father's shop at the High Mountain Renaissance Faire. *Their* shop, she corrected herself, rubbing her palms across the smooth, honey-colored surface of the counter. Carved from a single great oak log, its base looked as if it had roots that went deep into the Earth. Carved creatures raced across its sides, while crystals glimmered here and there within the deeper carvings.

Every stroke of her hand brought her close to the great tree the counter had once been a part of. From its highest branches, eagles had watched the sea, and among its roots, humans had sheltered, so long ago that they didn't quite look like people. Her eyes closed, Keelie wished she could get closer to them. Maybe they weren't human after all.

"Are you ready?"

She jumped and her eyes shot open. Master Oswald stood before her, floppy Elizabethan hat cocked jauntily over one eye. He smiled. "I'm sorry, I didn't mean to startle you." He looked around appreciatively. "Zeke has outdone himself. I've wanted him to participate for years, and I'm so happy that Heartwood is finally here. Very fine work." He tapped a nearby chair with his pen. "Very fine indeed. Call if you need anything," he said, trotting off. His tone said, "You'd better not need me." He was a little cold, but still so much better than Finch, the flame-haired administrator who had screamed and cursed her way through each day at the Wildewood Faire.

The bagpipes skirled again and Keelie flinched. She liked a bagpipe tune, but not nonstop. She added aspirin to the list of things to buy when she had a chance to escape. Maybe if the day was slow she could leave Grandmother in charge and drive into Juliet alone. Who would notice? Certainly not the big sleepy trees. At home in the Dread Forest (it still tickled her to think "home" and "Dread Forest" together), the gossipy trees would have alerted Dad before she'd even turned the key. They were awful, now that he was head of the forest.

A creak of wheels and shouted instructions caused Keelie to look up. Risa had set up her Green Goddess cart outside.

Was she cursed? Keelie ran out to confront the elf girl. "What are you doing here?"

Risa adjusted her snug bodice, pulling it lower as she smiled coyly at Keelie. "Master Oswald told me to set up here. Take it up with him."

A group of visitors had already come down the road. The men veered off to talk to Risa. The women stood by, disconcerted, but then one noticed Heartwood.

"Look at the beautiful furniture, Sylvia. Let's go inside."

The other woman glanced back at the man who was probably her husband. His face was inches from Risa's chest. She shrugged. "I've got the credit cards."

"I take Master Card and Lady Visa," Keelie said, following them inside. She grinned. Maybe this would work out after all. She could stay inside the shop and Risa could lure the customers. If Peascod came back, Risa could deal with him.

Knot sat on the counter, eyes closed and tail tucked underneath his paws. The shoppers admired him, then walked on to look at furniture. A few minutes later, Risa sneaked in to coo at him.

"Out!" Keelie pointed.

"You can't make me." Risa glowered.

Knot purred.

"Listen to him. What an enchanting sound." Risa reached out to scratch Knot's ears. He tilted his head and let her have her way with him.

"I wouldn't do that if I were you," Keelie said. "You'll need to get a round of rabies shots if he scratches you."

Keelie knew that wasn't true, but Risa didn't.

Knot growled and opened his eyes.

Risa pulled her hand back. She tossed her hair over her shoulders, and Keelie wondered if there might be a flea charm in the pest section in the Compendium. To draw fleas, that is, not chase them away.

Grandmother finally appeared, on the path opposite the shop. She'd changed into an outfit with a wide dark green skirt, a pointy-waisted, tightly cinched matching bodice with a black velvet collar, and a brimmed hat that covered her silver hair. A long gold chain hung from her waist, a little golden acorn hanging from its end.

Keelie realized that her mouth was hanging open. She shut it and hurried forward, dodging the mundanes (the street-clothed members of the public) who filled the path.

"Good morrow, Keliel," Grandmother said, bowing her head regally. Okay, that part was still normal.

"Good morrow to you, too, Grandmother." Keelie bowed. Grandmother looked sharp. Keelie leaned forward and whispered, "What gives with the new garb? Did you buy it this morning?"

Grandmother beamed at her. "I did, indeed. I was speaking with Master Oswald at the Player's Pub this morning and he suggested I wear something a little more in keeping with the Shakespearian theme. He has a little part he wishes me to play onstage, too." She twirled, her skirt belling out around her. "What do you think?"

"Beautiful." Great. Keelie was stuck running the shop while Grandmother was doing the Elizabethan version of the Shopping Channel and playing with the actors.

Grandmother eyed Keelie's costume. "That boy's garb isn't becoming. Why don't you buy something more in keeping with the festival?"

Keelie stared at her grandmother, torn between outrage because she'd been working nonstop to make money for the family while Grandmother fooled around instead of looking for the missing tree shepherd, and excitement at the thought of going shopping.

"I don't have any money," she said quickly.

Grandmother waved a hand airily and watched a family

approach their shop. "Tell them to bill me. Now, what do we do when people come?"

Keelie hurried forward. "Good gentles, allow me to show you our wares." She spent the next ten minutes answering questions about her father's furniture, and the mother finally plopped her purse on the counter and wrote a check for a set of porch chairs. While Keelie made arrangements to ship them to their home, she noticed Grandmother speaking to a woman who was admiring a hall tree.

Moments later, Grandmother came running over. "Who is Lady Visa?"

"Ah, Lady Visa and Master Card. Our excellent friends," Keelie said. "I'll show you how to ring up purchases."

It was three more hours before there was a lull in the festival traffic. Lunchtime was approaching, and the big crowds were now headed toward Pieman's Green, where all the food vendors sold their wares. Keelie sat down behind the counter while Grandmother leaned against the back wall and fanned herself.

"If I sit, I may not be able to walk."

"We just need a little rest." Keelie nodded at a passing woman pushing a stroller. The baby wore a jester's hat and was chewing thoughtfully on one of the four dangling points. The cute scene chilled Keelie, reminding her of creepy Peascod. Then her stomach rumbled, reminding her that she'd had no breakfast.

"Can you mind the shop while I go get lunch? I can bring you back a meat pie and a lemonade."

Grandmother shuddered. "What manner of food is that?"

Keelie sighed. "Faire food. How about a turkey leg, then? Steak on a stake?" That last was not Keelie's favorite—she'd had a bad experience working at Steak-on-a-Stake at the Wildewood Faire.

"Ah, sweet Lady Keliatiel. Madam, I have sought you long this morn." A tall man with a beautiful silver beard bowed elaborately before them, showing off his slashed leather sleeves, which had bits of purple satin poking through each cut. He extended a pink carnation. "A bloom that withers when compared to thy beauty."

Grandmother blushed. Keelie stared from one oldster to the other. What had gotten into her grandmother? Were people allowed to flirt when they were ancient? She wondered what the old dude would do it if she revealed that his "bloom" was hundreds of years old?

Grandmother stood. "Keelie, I believe Lord Mortimer and I will take a stroll. Mind the shop."

The two drifted down the path, drawing admiring glances from the mundanes. Keelie sat there, thunderstruck. She'd just been ditched by her grandmother, she was starving, and she had no backup.

Scott came out of his shop and leaned against the doorway. Keelie gestured frantically. He trotted over. "Something wrong?"

"Yes. My grandmother's gone bats. She just took off with some guy called Lord Mortimer." She pointed down the road. "She's abandoned me here with no lunch, no backup, and who knows when she'll be back?" Keelie aimed a kick at the post, but stopped before she hurt her toe and made her day even worse than it was. "I'm starving, too."

"I'll get us something." Scott looked really good in the afternoon sun. "The meat pies are tasty. Want me to get you one?"

She smiled at him. "And lemonade?"

"You got it." Scott raced off, abandoning his shop.

Keelie stretched and grinned at the passersby. Life was suddenly looking good. She would never have guessed that Scott would turn out to be hot and nice. Maybe she had a little elven charm and didn't know it. On the other hand, it could just be the power of womanhood.

"Do you have a human stashed at every festival?" came Risa's sarcastic voice from behind her. Keelie swore to herself. She'd totally forgotten the elf girl.

"Gosh, Risa. Some folks got it, and others have to flaunt it to get attention." The power of womanhood was still roaring through her when Sean walked by, Peascod trailing behind him. Keelie decided to try it out on him and sauntered out, swinging her hips. "Hello, Lord Sean. How goes your day?"

Sean stared at her. She ran a hand over her shirt front. She noticed that Risa was watching from behind her cart, which gave her a taste of déjà vu. It was like her daydream, Keelie thought. Risa watching as she flirted with Sean. She shivered.

"Keelie, they only had diet lemonade, so I got you an

iced tea." Scott's arms were laden with bundles from the food court. His eyes grew tight as he saw Sean close to Keelie.

Peascod, who had also stopped walking, pointed toward Scott. "See?" he said to Sean. "I told you he's always around her."

Keelie's face burned. Sean looked Scott up and down. "Gone for the groceries, lackey?"

Scott dropped the wrapped packages as his fists came up and he assumed a martial arts stance. Knot dashed in, grabbed a mouthful of greasy paper, and started to haul a meat pie backwards to safety.

"You two stop it," Keelie said. "Scott, you dropped your stuff."

"That is not 'stuff,' Keelie," he said, eyes on his rival. "That is the lunch that we were going to eat together."

"Oh, together." Sean looked him up and down. "Like a lady and her dog."

They were acting like toddlers, but Keelie didn't know what to say that wouldn't make them madder. Peascod was grinning broadly from the sidelines.

"Mind your shops, m'lords and m'ladies." Master Oswald's booming voice filled the clearing. He strode and stood, fists on his hips. He glared at Peascod. "You, jester. The fairies need you at the Globe." Peascod slunk away without answering.

Master Oswald glared at Scott. "I expected better from you, sirrah." His head swiveled to include Keelie. He shook his head, as if he'd heard she was a troublemaker and expected no better. "Lady Keliel, a word with you in private, please."

Risa grinned and followed, clearly enjoying the moment, as Oswald escorted Keelie into her shop.

Keelie cocked her thumb toward the road. "Hit it. Go on, Risa. You're not a part of this."

Master Oswald frowned at Risa. "Tend your cart, lass. Curiosity killed the cat."

At the word cat, Risa's eyes widened and she looked around frantically. "Where's Knot? Oh my beloved kitty, where are you?"

She ran outside, looking for him. Scott had picked up the remaining sandwiches and was now eating alone and looking miserable on a chair in front of his shop. Sean was nowhere to be seen.

Master Oswald cleared his throat. "You know your lady Grandmother is helping us by playing Queen Elizabeth at the theater?"

Keelie's mouth dropped open. "Is that why she has a new costume?" Little part, indeed.

"We've invited her to play the Queen throughout the run of the festival. She's a natural."

Keelie stared at the big man, dismayed. "The whole festival? I can't run this shop alone." And she couldn't search for Viran as often, either.

"Nor will you. Peascod has volunteered to help you."

"Oh, no. No need. I think I can manage."

"Are you sure?"

Keelie nodded emphatically, and Master Oswald bowed and backed out of the shop. The shop that she now had to run by herself.

Under the counter, Knot lifted his face from the remains of the meat pie that he'd snagged. Keelie didn't mind. She'd lost her appetite.

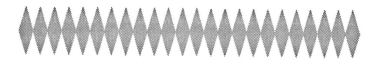

# nine

"Here ye, here ye. The play begins at the stroke of six bells."
A town crier yelled. He wore a big green poofy hat that
matched his doublet and hose. "Hie thee to the Globe, good
gentles."

People began to stream out of the shops near Heartwood.
Several patrons stumbled out of the Queen's Alehouse. The
din of loud conversation filled the air as the costumed crowd
followed the crier. Each day was to begin and end with a
Shakespearean play at the Globe. Today's evening performance of *A Midsummer Night's Dream* would be performed
by the professional actors, with the vendors helping out.

Keelie glanced around Heartwood, glad that the shop was empty and that it was time to close. She was tired, but she wanted to watch the performance. She started to put away the cash box and receipt book.

Scott waved to her from Tudor Turnings. He had one last customer in his shop, a woman hemming and hawing over a chair. Keelie wasn't going to say anything to Scott, but she thought the quality of his pieces wasn't up to Heartwood standards. She hoped he wouldn't mention the confrontation with Sean next time they talked. She'd flirted a little, yes, but this was the real world, not some Shakespearian tragedy. Men didn't start fights over meat pies and sandwiches.

Keelie ran her hand along the counter. The heavy Compendium she was supposed to be studying rested on a shelf beneath it. The board was barely strong enough to hold it. She ignored the ominous bend in the middle of the board and would continue to ignore it, at least until her guilt at not getting her charms memorized grew as heavy as the book. She was always good at cramming, though. How hard could it be to study a few little spells? Make that a few hundred spells.

Risa had packed up her cart and left for the Globe earlier in the afternoon, since she had a costume fitting. She was to be one of Queen Titania's backup handmaidens. This would give her something to feel superior about without actually adding to her workload. Typical.

The laughter from the Queen's Alehouse proved to be two women, one dressed in a cerulean blue overdress who lifted her skirts delicately as she stepped down from the deck and onto the road. Her friend, wearing a maroon velvet Francesca costume, laughed as she held up a pewter tankard. Beads of condensation dripped down its sides and onto her skirt. Knot walked beside the woman, tail held high as if he were her escort. He leaned a little to the left and teetered. The cat had been hitting the mead again, Keelie knew. Maybe the stress of dealing with Risa had driven him to drink. Keelie so understood.

She narrowed her eyes. Wait a minute. Knot was supposed to be her guardian. Ever since the ale house had opened he'd forgotten all about his guardian job. Keelie leaned out and saw that a tree spirit disguised as a cloud was hanging over the shop. People were glancing up, noticing the cloud in the otherwise blue sky.

By the time the crowd thinned, Keelie had closed Heartwood. She stretched her arms back as she stepped out on the path, then reached overhead, moving her muscles. Furniture selling was hard work, and it felt good to be finished. Dad would be pleased at her sales today. She glanced over at Tudor Turnings. Scott was still dealing with the customer who couldn't make up her mind, and she could tell he was losing his patience.

Keelie was glad that he was the one stuck with a customer, not her. She was anxious to catch up with the crowd headed to the Globe. She didn't want to miss the opening act, and she wanted to get a good seat.

"Keelie, wait up."

Turning, Keelie was astonished to see her Earth magic

teacher, Sir Davey. His elegantly garbed and very short figure was hurrying to catch up with her.

"I didn't know you were here already!" Keelie rushed back to where he stood, huffing and regaining his breath.

"Your father got me here." It was unusual for an elf to be close friends with a dwarf, but Dad and Sir Davey were best buds. Keelie was torn between feeling relief that she had Sir Davey to rely on, and irritation at Dad for thinking that she'd need help. "Did you set up your rock shop here?"

He looked at her sideways. "The Dragon Hoard, milady. Didn't you hear that we must call each other lord this and lady that and mention our shops by their full names? Admin says it's good for business."

"Don't want the mundanes catching on to the fact that everyone leaves here and returns to being schoolteachers, actors, and carpenters, right?"

Sir Davey put a finger along his nose. "They might even believe in elves and fairies," he said.

"Or dwarves who can pull magic from the Earth." Keelie smiled, enjoying herself. Sir Davey was like a favorite uncle. Even when he was teaching he had a way of making everything fun.

"Exactly so."

They hiked up the hill to the Globe. Keelie's leg muscles ached from her midnight stroll the other night. But she sensed no tree wraiths hanging around. From up here she could see glimpses of the Pacific ocean through the trees. Today was a cool day—sweater weather, and just right for the garb she wore. No clouds of mist hung over the ocean. This could change, but right now, Keelie enjoyed a delicious sense of freedom.

At the Globe she set aside her anger at her grandmother and was thrilled to see her sitting in the middle of the theater on a carved throne, dressed as Queen Elizabeth the first, waving to the crowd. Several of the costumed actors had gathered around and from the expressions on their faces, they were enthralled. They'd tone down the admiration if they knew the person under the clown-like white makeup.

She noted that the actors weren't under any sort of enchantment now. They were livelier, and definitely into their parts. Keelie wondered if they remembered anything from the other night. She thought about Bloodroot's power over humans, and Peascod, who seemed to be immune to it.

Just as Keelie was about to walk inside the Globe, one of the Admin people stopped her and handed her a sheet of paper with instructions for the "townspeople."

"You don't get a speaking part in this festival, but you'll need to know how to act when street theater happens around you for next week's performance."

Keelie was peeved for a moment that she didn't have a speaking part, but then she laughed. She sure didn't want one. She had enough to do.

"I wouldn't be so upset if I were you," Sir Davey said as he glared at the departing Admin person. "Last vendor in gets the only part available," he groused.

"I don't understand," Keelie said.

"I'm going to be the Mustard Seed Fairy."

Laughter overcame Keelie. She envisioned Sir Davey

dressed in a glittering costume with gauzy wings, flitting around like a bearded cherub.

"I can't wait to see you in cute little wings." Keelie wiped her eyes and leaned against a tree (hemlock).

"If you're through having your hissy fit, then I'd like to show you something. Laurie contacted me."

Sir Davey held up an iPhone. Keelie felt saliva gathering in the back of her throat. "Oh, my precious!" She swallowed hard, afraid of drooling like a bulldog anticipating a steak.

He held it out, and Keelie took it reverently. She missed technology. It wasn't like she didn't have a cell phone, but hers was hooked up to trees, and regular cell phones often didn't work either in the town of Edgewood or in the Dread Forest. Zabrina said sometimes magic and technology canceled each other out.

Keelie read the message:

> Leaving L.A. On way 2 Redwd.
> Stopping to shop
> Arriving Monday
> Can't w8t 2 C U
>
> XOXO
> Laurie

"She'll be here Monday." Reluctantly, Keelie gave the phone back to Sir Davey, who slipped it into a leather pouch.

Sir Davey nodded. "It'll be good for you to have your friend with you. Your father called her mother, and the woman said Laurie had her permission. She's driving a BMW, and that's a perfectly safe automobile."

"Laurie's mom has always had a different view of the world." Keelie was quoting something Mom always said about Laurie's mom.

Loud feminine laughter, mingled with a horse's whinny, drifted to Keelie. For a brief moment, it was hard to distinguish the two. Sean and the other jousters were leading their horses to the nearby paddocks.

Maybe that feminine laugh had been one of the horses. Weird.

Sir Davey motioned his head toward the jousters. "Have you forgiven them for being Niriel's army?"

Keelie blushed. "Shh. Sean is coming near, and Niriel is his Dad, you know."

Nodding, Sir Davey smiled mischievously. "I get it. You're still sweet on the elf."

"Niriel is doing community service," Keelie said out of the side of her mouth.

"Prithee, tell me what that rapscallion is doing that could be recompense for his actions." Sir Davey's smile transformed to a tight line as he pressed his lips together.

"Niriel is helping Uncle Dariel, and he's working with Zabrina. Together they're mending the rules that the mayor of Edgewood broke when he let humans into the forest. Niriel has people skills," Keelie said in a soft voice. She wondered if Niriel was using his elven charm to help convince the Edgewood city council.

As Sir Davey and Keelie neared the jousters, she saw Risa was with them, standing close to Sean.

Keelie's eyebrows rose when she realized it hadn't been a

horse that had laughed. Risa tossed her red hair across her shoulder. She was dressed in a green satin gown with fake fairy wings that glittered cheaply in the early evening light. Keelie could almost imagine Risa being one of the Shining Ones, even with the tacky wings.

Sean turned to look at Keelie, and flashed a smile at her. He waved to her, secretly pointed at Risa, and crossed his eyes.

Warmth flowed through Keelie as she waved back. Sean wasn't falling for Risa's flirtation. Instead, he was making a jest about her, and Risa was oblivious to it.

Keelie watched as Sean said something to Risa and the other jousters. He motioned toward Keelie. Risa smirked and finger-waved at Keelie as if saying "Look at me, I'm with Sean, and you're not." Then she grinned wickedly as she placed her hand on Sean's shoulder and leaned intimately against him.

A growl formed in the back of Keelie's throat. If she had a wand, she'd make Risa's wings become real and take to the air, and then elf girl would crash into the ocean. The image eased Keelie's jealousy. She shouldn't think things like that, but sometimes a girl couldn't help herself.

Sean shrugged Risa's hand off and moved away from her. Risa glared malevolently at his retreating figure.

"Holy Granite. That girl never gives up," Sir Davey said in a loud voice, loud enough that Risa must have heard him because she turned around and scowled at them.

As if on cue, Knot threaded his way through the jousters and sat down near Risa. He started washing his tail. Risa's expression transformed from evil-vulture glower to besotted love ogle. She dropped to her knees and her wings bounced up and down as if preparing to take flight. "Knot, my love, come to me."

The cat stood and backed away from Risa. His tail swished back and forth as the jousters gawked at the spectacle. Sean laughed. He left the group.

"Earthworms from Mars, what has happened to that girl?" Sir Davey said, his eyes popping out of their sockets.

Risa advanced on Knot. He leaped, and then bounded away and was lost in the gathering crowd of people waiting to attend the play.

"What is that about?" Sir Davey looked up at Keelie.

Keelie explained about the mixed-up potions and the result: Risa being hopelessly in love with Knot.

Tears formed in Sir Davey's eyes as he laughed. "'Tis certainly hilarious, but that cat needs to careful. He is your guardian, and Risa is a distraction that he doesn't need at this time. There is danger here, and I can't put my finger on what it is."

Keelie rubbed her hands over her arms as a chill spread through her body. Several tree spirits now hung over the Globe. Sean was weaving his way through the crowd to her.

"You're right, and I can't rely on the trees, either." She started to tell him about the trees, but there were too many of them about. Maybe in town it would be better.

"Milady Keliel," someone called out.

Keelie turned and saw Tavyn step out from behind a hemlock tree. He was dressed in his dark brown gambeson, green hose, and tall boots. His dark brown hair was loose and free. A pointed ear tip poked through the strands. Keelie assumed it would go unnoticed—there were mundanes here with fake elf ears.

He bowed his head. "I'm sorry to disturb you, but I was wondering if you will allow me to sit with you."

Surprised at the request, Keelie looked at Sir Davey, who winked at her. Then Sean came over to join them. He nodded politely to Tavyn.

The Redwood elf clasped his hands behind his back and returned Sean's nod with a distinct not-glad-to-see-you gaze. There was definitely an undercurrent of tension between the two elves.

Sean stepped close to Keelie. "I was going to ask Lady Keliel to dine with me, and you, too, Sir Davey."

"I'd like to, but I have to go for my fitting." Sir Davey pulled out a slip of paper from the leather pouch holding the iPhone. "'Costume fitting: 6:30.' I'll see you later." Sir Davey wandered away—mumbling about how vendors shouldn't be forced against their will to be in a stage production.

Keelie gritted her teeth together, trying to repress a laugh as the image of Sir Davey in wings returned to her. She wondered if his wings would be like Risa's, cheap and glittery. Nah, Sir Davey would carry the whole fairy handmaiden look much better than Risa could ever do.

"Lady Keelie, if you're ready, I'll escort you into the theater." Tavyn held out his elbow in an invitation.

Sean stepped forward. "May I interrupt? I need to speak to you, Keelie, about your father."

"Is something wrong?" Keelie's heart had started thumping, either from Sean's nearness or his mention of her father.

"Not at all," Sean replied quickly. "But it's a personal matter." He stared coolly at Tavyn.

Tavyn stepped back. "Of course." A flash of irritation crossed his face. "Until later, Lady Keliel." Tavyn took two steps back, turned, and walked away, blending into the crowd.

What was up with Sean? He'd acted all macho elf when Scott had been paying attention to her, and now he was doing the same thing with Tavyn. Part of Keelie was secretly thrilled that he was acting like a boyfriend, but there was another part of her that wasn't too happy. Relationships were so confusing.

Knot had returned. He sat down next to Keelie and proceeded to wash his butt. Risa was nowhere in sight. That was a small favor, and one less thing to deal with.

Sean held out his hand toward Keelie and motioned with his head to the path leading back down to Juliet City. She accepted Sean's hand, and a tingle skipped up and down her spine.

As they walked, a cloud was following them from above. It had to be the same tree spirit Keelie had noticed hanging around the shop. It was so obvious. Sean turned, and the cloud floated up. He looked puzzled, shook his head, and continued walking.

"You said you needed to talk to me about Dad. Why?"

"Your father wants me to go with you and Laurie to L.A. next week. I know he didn't tell you that. Typical Zeke."

Sean in L.A.? Keelie was thrilled, but her head spun at the concept of her lordly elven boyfriend in worldly Los Angeles. Of course, with his surfer good looks, he could fit in. She'd have to come up with a good costume for him.

The cloud was back, floating along. It was trailing them again like a bad detective. Keelie saw, from the corner of her eye, that Knot was watching it too, his eyes dilated.

All of a sudden, Sean stopped. He glanced up. The cloud scooted into some bushes. It could at least try to act like a cloud. Knot darted off into the rhododendrons.

"What is going on?" Sean pointed in the direction of the cloud and cat.

Keelie looked to the left and the right of the path to make sure no one was around. She leaned close to Sean and whispered, "It's a tree."

"It's a tree?" Sean blinked as if he couldn't quite believe what he was hearing.

Keelie nodded. "It's a tree spirit. The redwoods can spirit walk, and allow anyone to see them. Even humans."

Sean's eyes widened in surprise. He turned to look for the cloudlike form and found it hiding behind a large rhododendron. Sean gestured in the direction of the ocean. "What about the mist. Is that a tree, too?"

"No, just mist. But they use it for camouflage. They blend in with it."

A small breeze began to blow. The tree spirit flew out of the bush, carried by the wind, then dissolved. Knot walked out from underneath the bushes. The end of his tail was crooked.

Sean made a grim face. "There were always stories about the power of the redwoods, but this goes beyond what anyone imagined."

"I think it's just the tip of the branch," Keelie said. Now that the cloud was no longer following them, she felt free to talk to Sean, although the tree spirits were probably all around, listening. "Tonight, Grandmother, Norzan, and I are going to hunt for the missing tree shepherd. Want to come?"

"Why not do it during the day? It seems dangerous to go out into the forest at night. You could twist your ankle."

"You are so sweet to worry. But Grandmother has this Queen gig, so we have to work around that. You can come and protect me."

"What time? I will defend you against any evil ferns and fog." He smiled down at her.

"Don't worry, you're excused. I know that jousting is hard work, and I'll have plenty of company in the woods. If too many of us go hiking at night, it'll look weird."

"Then it will just have to look weird. I'll be there to protect you."

Keelie smiled and squeezed his hand, but she had the disturbing feeling that the woods were more dangerous than either of them knew.

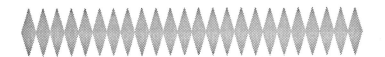

# ten

"Grandmother, don't you think it's weird that the smaller trees don't talk to us at all?" Keelie sipped from her water bottle and looked down the path at her grandmother, dressed in twenty-first-century hiking togs. They'd been searching for Viran for an hour, senses open, looking for signs of the missing tree shepherd, but feeling none of his essence.

"I think they're frightened." Grandmother put her own bottle back into the special holster at her belt and glanced at Norzan, who was frowning up into the canopy far above them.

"There could be another reason, but we don't know yet.

It will take a while to understand," he said. "The rules of this forest are different."

"I'll say." Keelie replied. The strange quiet extended all the way to the forest floor. Except for the small animals, there was no motion in this forest. No fairies at all, no clicking of the sticklike *bhata* or humming wings of the *feithid daoine*. "What's next, then? It's pointless to just wander around looking for him, especially if the trees can't find him either." Keelie placed a hand against the young tree's bark and didn't feel its presence. Tree silence, just as it had been before her gift had grown.

Grandmother frowned. "I believe I may know where he might be," she said slowly. "But we can't move too fast, if he's in danger."

"So you don't think he's just lost or hurt—you think someone has him? If he's in danger, shouldn't we move faster?" Keelie looked from Grandmother to Norzan.

"We can't rule anything out." Norzan gestured toward the coast. "Don't you feel it? Something is definitely wrong here."

Keelie remembered the blinding headache that had hit her when she'd first entered the forest, and the black spots she'd noticed along the edge of the tree magic. Norzan was right. These woods were unlike any she'd ever seen.

"Trees, Keelie," Grandmother intoned. "These aren't teenage girls. They are ancient trees. And their ancient tree shepherd moves slowly as well." The ancient sequoias were like great buildings that rose straight up, the open spaces around them filled with great ferns and smaller trees and bushes. Keelie couldn't relate to a tree of this size and age.

A dark shape suddenly plummeted down toward them and Keelie ducked, arms over her head, until she realized that it was an owl. It soared through the dark forest, a blacker shadow against the darkness.

They marched on, heading deeper into the forest, with Norzan leading the way. Keelie walked behind Grandmother, listening for signs of tree speak or Viran's presence. She heard nothing... except, once, the faint, far jangle of bells.

Laurie arrived on Monday as promised, black D&G wraparound sunglasses hugging her spray-tanned face, freshly highlighted blonde hair whipping around her head as she drove her BMW into the parking lot, honking the horn and leaning out the window yelling, "Woohoo, faire people!" She swung expertly into a parking space and hopped out of her car.

Keelie envied her friend, who looked fresh and just out of the salon. As opposed to Keelie, who'd spent the weekend manning the store and trudging through the woods looking for Viran—with no luck. At least sales at Heartwood were good.

Tavyn was standing at the edge of the parking lot near Keelie and Sir Davey. He stared, frozen, at Laurie's bright hair and tight jeans. "Who is that?" he asked.

"That's my friend, Laurie," Keelie replied. "She's from Orange County."

Tavyn nodded as if he understood. "We have people who come up from Orange County. They always seem so unbalanced, removed from nature." But his admiring looks didn't agree with his words.

Laurie hurried over to hug Keelie and Sir Davey. "You've got to give me the two-dollar tour!" she demanded, looking around. She beamed at Tavyn. "You are all so cute!" Laurie kept talking as she pulled Keelie aside. "When I told Mom you're staying where they put on a Shakespeare Festival and you wanted me to visit, she was all for it. She said it would be educational for me, so she let me skip school. She booked a week at a Catalina spa. She said you were a good influence on me, and Mom thinks your dad is hot. She calls him Sexy Zeke."

Eww! Keelie just couldn't imagine Laurie's mom and Dad together. She needed to change the subject. "Let's go watch the actors get ready for the show."

The morning performance of *A Midsummer Night's Dream* was packed. Tavyn had been right. The parking lot was crammed with cars from up and down the coast, here just for the show. When Peascod strode onstage, playing Puck, he was wearing his red and green harlequin's costume. Didn't the man ever change his clothes?

Knot hissed as the actor took his place onstage.

"That is one strange guy," Laurie noted.

"I'm glad you picked up on that, because we all agree that he's very creepy."

The bearded actor playing the part of Bottom said his line, "Enough; hold, or cut bow-strings," and left the stage. One of the pie sellers came in with fairy wings strapped to her back. Peascod strode in from the other side of the stage. "How now, spirit! Whither wander you?"

Or rather, his lips moved to the lines, but all anyone heard was Knot's loud yowling.

Peascod glared in their direction, and so did everyone sitting around them.

The fairy said her next lines undisturbed, and then Peascod opened his mouth and Knot started to howl again.

Master Oswald leaped up. The actors stopped, and everyone in the Globe looked at Keelie and Laurie. Master Oswald pointed toward them. "No cats allowed in the Globe."

Knot looked very satisfied with himself as they slunk out of the theater.

"I can't take you anywhere," Keelie groused.

"Personally, I think it's kind of cool. First time I've ever been evicted from a Shakespeare play," Laurie said.

They headed to Sir Davey's RV, ready for lunch. The RV was uber-luxurious and retrofitted for everything the dwarf wanted.

"So, when we get to L.A., want to go shopping?" Laurie asked as she picked the tomatoes out of her salad.

"I'd love to go shopping."

Sir Davey plunked a tuna fish sandwich in front of Knot. Knot meowed piteously.

"What?" Sir Davey looked hurt. "I made you a sandwich."

Keelie wiped her hands on her napkin. "He wants you to cut the crusts off." She sawed off the crusts and set the sandwich back in front of Knot. He swatted at her hand.

She nudged him with her foot. He purred as he ate.

Laurie shook her head. "He's so weird."

Sir Davey snorted. "You don't know the half of it."

Laurie nibbled at her salad.

"Knot should act more like a guardian," Sir Davey added, pointing with his fork at the cat. Knot's eyes turned to slits. His tail twitched.

There was a knock at the door.

Sir Davey looked alarmed. "I hope it's not the costumer."

He opened the door, and in walked Risa. Keelie wanted to hiss. She'd been hanging around Knot too long.

"There you are." Risa glided into the camper. "Your grandmother suggested I'd find you here." Her eyes drifted to Knot. "I've been searching for you all morning," she continued, her voice rising in pitch as she dropped down to her knees and gazed at Knot. His eyes dilated and his tail trembled with agitation.

"Who is that?" Laurie asked, as she and Keelie exchanged looks.

"Risa."

"Oh," Laurie's eyebrows rose. She shifted in her seat. "That Risa."

"That Risa." Keelie glared. She wondered if the Elven

Compendium of Household Charms contained a "charm" to get rid of pests. She needed to study more.

The elf girl turned her head and glowered at Laurie and Keelie. "Yes, I'm that girl." She pushed herself up to her knees. "I'm that girl who was betrothed to Sean, but now my heart belongs to Knot." She stood. Even while proclaiming that her heart belonged to a cat, Risa held herself with dignity and grace. Keelie always felt those certain qualities were lacking in herself.

Sir Davey walked over to Risa. "I think this upcoming trip will be good for you, too."

"What upcoming trip?" Risa asked, turning to Keelie for answers.

"The one Keelie and Knot are going to take to L.A. It'll do you some good to be away from Knot. See if you can break that spell. Shouldn't have cast it in the first place, but I think you've suffered enough." Sir Davey stroked his Van Dyke beard as he studied Knot.

Keelie's mouth dropped opened and she stared at Sir Davey. Whose side was he on, anyway?

Risa shook her head. "No, that's impossible. I can't be separated from Knot. I have to go to L.A., too."

"She can't go to L.A." Keelie said. Laurie kept eating. Knot hopped up beside her and looked at her as she ate. She ignored him.

"Besides, where I'm going there aren't a lot of trees. Canyon lands, scrub brush, freeways, malls, you know. Urban nature."

"All the more reason I need to go. How dare you take

Knot into such a dangerous and polluted environment? He'll need my healing powers to help cleanse his system of the toxins."

Waving her hand, Laurie pointed to Knot, who now sat in her lap. "He's already polluted. He needs a breath mint." She pushed her salad away. "And that's just his sweet side."

Risa's eyes narrowed to dangerous slits. "What charm have you used, sorceress, to make Knot sit in your lap?"

"I'm not a sorceress. I'm a junior at Baywood Academy," Laurie said defensively.

Sir Davey looked from Laurie and Knot to Risa, then back to Keelie and shook his head. "It's a good thing Sean is going with you to L.A. You're going to need all the help you can get on this trip."

"Sean is going?" Risa stomped her foot. "And Knot? That does it. I'm coming, too."

Keelie felt nauseous as she imagined the clown-car effect of having two elves, a fairy, and a mall brat in the same car with her.

In the afternoon, Keelie gave Laurie a tour of the festival. Even though the shops were closed to mundanes during the week, the streets were lively with vendors cleaning their booths and calling out to one another. Knot accompanied them everywhere they went, apparently trying to overcome the accusation of being a slacker guardian. Then, leaving Laurie with Sir Davey to happily discuss precious and semi-precious stones and their metaphysical properties, Keelie went to find Grandmother.

Lady Keliatiel was at the Globe. She was dressed in her

elven robes that had embroidered trees on the bell sleeves. Her hair was pinned up in an intricate bun, held in place by two gem-studded sticks. She looked very fashionable, not as dusty and uptight as she once did. Acting was good for her.

Grandmother walked with Keelie around the stage.

"I'm going to L.A. tomorrow," Keelie told her. "Remember? I have to handle some things for Mom's estate. They're selling the house."

"I'm not senile, Keliel. I know all about your trip. Why have you not introduced me to your friend? She must be a charming girl, for Alora to think so highly of her."

Keelie grinned. "You'll meet her tonight."

"While you're away, I will be meeting with Bella Matera," Grandmother said. "The redwoods are growing more and more worried with each passing day about Viran, and I am, too."

Keelie didn't know if she should bring it up, but she decided to go ahead. "I'm not exactly sure about the redwoods' motives, especially after Bloodroot and his demonstration last week."

"I'm going to ask Bella Matera about him," Grandmother said. She looked up at the stands, as if practicing hearing the applause.

"Don't say too much to Bella Matera until we know more about the redwoods," Keelie replied.

Grandmother's face became pinched and drawn, and she was once again the more serious, uptight woman Keelie knew. "Child, I am centuries older than you, as old as many of these trees. Give me credit for a little sense."

"I'm sorry." Grandmother did know a lot, but she didn't have any modern street sense.

A mist rose suddenly from a corner of the stage and Bella Matera drifted forward.

Keelie backed away, seeing anger in the tree spirit's ethereal features.

Grandmother started forward, but Bella Matera blocked her path and confronted Keelie. The tree spirit ran her sticklike fingers down the side of Keelie's face. "Calm your fears, child. There are no secrets in this forest."

And that was what Keelie feared most.

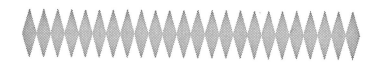

# eleven

Laurie's mouth gaped at the elven village high up in the trees. She clutched the rose quartz that Keelie had given her to fend off the sickening nausea and fear of the Dread, which was strong enough by the village to deter even the most determined hiker.

"Where are the Ewoks?" she asked.

"No Ewoks. Elves," Keelie corrected.

"How do you get up there?" Laurie pointed up, her face pale. "You're not expecting me to climb, are you? I don't climb. If you need to read the Laurie book of instructions—it says no climbing. Born with a fear of heights."

"Maybe I can find a charm for your fear of heights." Keelie had lugged the Compendium home from the shop after she'd caught Knot reading it. He had opened it to the charm for fresh breath. It had worked, too. His breath was minty with a hint of catnip. Maybe the book was going to prove more useful than a doorstop after all.

Knot sat next to her. He blinked and yawned as if saying, "Chicken."

Keelie focused on the tree. Could she do this on her own? She almost felt like she had, already, even though she'd always had an escort. "You'll have to hold my hand," she told Laurie.

"Do you need help?" Risa said, in a superior, snarky tone that grated on Keelie's nerves.

"We can do it." Keelie juggled the Compendium in the crook of her left arm.

"Fine." Risa closed her eyes. Whoosh! Away she went.

"Whoa," Laurie said. "Where did she go?"

"She's up there." Keelie pointed upwards.

Way, way up high, a small figure waved down to them.

"Close your eyes," Keelie said. She grabbed Laurie's clammy hand.

"You mean you can do this, too? How often do you whiz up and down trees?"

"First time for everything." Keelie visualized traveling up the tree, green sap pulsing in her mind. *Take us up*, she told Wena.

The glow of the tree's magic enfolded them. Beside her, Laurie's eyes bugged out.

*Whoosh!*

She'd done it! They were on the wooden rope bridge outside the tree house. Keelie tried to keep the silly grin off her face, in case Risa was looking. Laurie dropped to her knees. She stuttered as she clung to Keelie's legs.

Holding out her hand, Keelie reached for Laurie's. "You're fine. Just don't look down."

"I don't know if I can breathe."

"Easy," Keelie encouraged her. "It gets better."

Laurie accepted Keelie's hand and got shakily to her feet.

Keelie slowly scooted, with Laurie clutching her shirt, to the tree house door. Once inside, Laurie collapsed onto a chair. Her face drawn and pinched, she closed her eyes. Keelie noticed her friend's hands trembling.

Opening the Compendium, Keelie searched for a charm for fear. Under "Calming Charm," she read about the magical words and the energy she needed. It required her to tap into "nature" and pull a string of magic. Nature?

Keelie scratched her head. She wasn't quite sure what the book meant by "nature." Maybe it was tree magic. Earth magic? But elves didn't tap into the deep Earth for energy. She peered more closely at the text. She didn't want to use tree magic, not here in the redwoods.

Keelie turned to the index: "Nature: pages 1000-1003."

"You're reading while I'm dying over here." Laurie opened one eye and glared. "I've seen some weird things with you, but this ranks right up there."

"I'm looking for a cure for you."

"Nature: The energy of the living earth, the sun, the wind, and the energy of living things. When creating charms, it is important to have a base of nature to energize the magic."

Keelie closed her eyes and imagined sunlight reaching out to Laurie, wrapping her in a blanket of calm. Keelie felt warm as she recited the words of the charm. Then there was a tug from within her as she felt power flow from her. Her hands became hot, and when she opened her eyes, her hands glowed with yellow light. She lifted them up, and the golden light formed a sphere.

The light floated over to Laurie and bounced over her head like a beach ball. Then, like an egg cracking over a bowl, the light spilled out and poured into her body.

Keelie sniffed. The aroma of lemon oil and cedar shavings filled the air. It smelled like the Heartwood shop after she had polished the furniture.

Laurie bolted upright and blinked several times. "Wow! I feel like I've been to the spa and had a detox avocado body wrap with a lemon juice tonic." She stretched her arms. "What did you do?"

"I used a calm charm to help you recover from your fears," Keelie answered.

"A charm? Isn't that the magic thing your Dad did to whammy that town council woman at the Wildewood Faire?"

"It's one of the charms the elves use most," Keelie said. "I'm learning." She gazed down at the Compendium.

Laurie's expression darkened. "I'm not going to have any side effects, like growing cat ears or a tail?" She pressed her hands to her face. She touched her nose as if seeking reassurance it hadn't returned to its pre-surgery shape.

"I don't think so." Keelie hadn't thought of side effects. She'd have to ask Elianard about them. She wanted to be confident in front of Laurie, but she'd have to keep an eye on her friend.

"Is this appropriate for L.A. and the mall?" Risa walked into the room, holding out a beautiful green gown with flowing sleeves, the elven fashion norm. She held up another one, a blue empire gown (Jane Austen inspired) with puffed sleeves at the shoulder.

Laurie and Keelie exchanged looks.

Keelie hauled out the street clothes she'd packed. She had jeans, T-shirts, and tennis shoes. Her wardrobe had become sort of rustic since living with Dad. Back to basics. When you lived in the Dread Forest, you didn't wear Dolce or Stella to the Edgewood Diner.

"You want me to wear this?" Risa sneered, inspecting the clothes.

"You've been shopping online from Enviro Girl, haven't you?" Laurie said with disbelief in her voice. "I told you to stay away from that website."

"I'm a tree shepherd—I can't go around wearing Prada in the forest. I have to at least attempt to blend in." Keelie was about to pack her clothes away. Let Risa wear her elf clothes and face the ridicule.

Risa lifted a shirt with the tip of her index finger. The shirt hung limply, like the droopy flag of some forsaken country that had lost its independence.

Laurie frowned. "Your clothes aren't cute. There isn't any style to them. It says Nature Geek."

"What do you mean they aren't cute?" Keelie couldn't believe what she was hearing. She picked up a green T-shirt with a crackled and fading image of the planet and the words "arth, a Great Place to Live." The "*E*" had disappeared several washings ago.

Risa nodded. "They're ugly, too." She wrinkled her nose as she held up a pair of camo cargo pants with several pockets down the leg.

Shocked, Keelie looked at her wardrobe. Risa and Laurie were right. A lot of her clothes were various shades of green and brown—like a tree. She was dressing in forest colors. She'd buy some bright new happy colors at the mall in L.A.

"Maybe we need to stop at La Jolie Rouge," Laurie suggested.

Risa turned to Laurie. "What is this La Jolie Rouge?"

Laurie beamed. "It's this awesome store with cool clothes."

"I would like to go shopping at this La Jolie Rouge," Risa pointed to Laurie's shirt, a pink and white top with an embroidered sunflower. "I like your clothes. Maybe you can guide me in my selections?"

Laurie's face lit up with radiant happiness. "I'd love to be your stylist."

Keelie listened as Laurie and Risa talked about clothes. The two had similar styles. Laurie and Keelie used to talk about clothes at Baywood Academy, when her life had been focused on the mall, fashion, and their friends. Now it was the trees and Dad. Keelie lifted her battered "arth" shirt. She had changed a lot.

"I need to get ready for tonight's show," Risa said, looking out the window and noting the position of the sun in the sky. She turned to Laurie. "Why don't you come with me, and we can continue our discussion about fashion."

Laurie was about to agree, but she stopped and her eyes held Keelie's with a searching gaze. "I think we're going to go to that French restaurant in Juliet."

Keelie nodded.

"Perfect. We can all meet after the show." Risa smiled like she'd just negotiated a treaty for world peace.

"Works for me…" Laurie said tentatively. "Keelie?"

Keelie glared at Risa. She hated how the elf was worming her way into every aspect of her life. A sharp pain lanced through her temple, and just as quickly as it had appeared, it was gone.

Suddenly, fatigue drained the energy from her muscles. Keelie sat down. Maybe she was tired from using the charm. She didn't have the energy or the inclination to argue with Risa right now. "Sure, why not?"

Two hours later, Keelie, Laurie, Risa, Sean, and two other jousters met up under the Globe's arched doorways. Streams of theater-goers pushed past them, leaving the building.

"Your friend Scott is coming too, along with three of his friends," Risa told Keelie.

Sean scowled. "Who invited him?"

Risa batted her eyelashes. "I did. Are you jealous that Scott talked to me?"

"No, but I saw Knot sitting with one of Queen Titania's handmaidens at the Queen's Alehouse. He was purring as she scratched underneath his chin," Sean said.

Risa shot him a venomous look. "How long ago?"

Sean shrugged. "Possibly fifteen minutes ago."

"I have to hurry. I'll meet you in the parking lot."

As Risa rushed away, Grandmother appeared, still in makeup. She allowed herself to be photographed, and signed autographs while making her way toward Keelie. She motioned for Keelie to join her in a corner. "Kalix has summoned us back to the forest. It's an emergency."

"What's going on?"

"Norzan is missing."

Stunned, Keelie stared in disbelief at her grandmother. "We have to find him."

She thought about Sean and Risa being together at the French restaurant. Everyone would be having fun and hanging out while she, once again, would be trudging through the forest. A pang of envy zapped her. At least Laurie would be there to keep an eye on Risa, in case she forgot Knot and made a move on Sean.

"Okay, Grandmother. Give me a moment."

Grandmother patted her arm, adjusted her jewelled red wig, and returned to the crowd awaiting their queen.

Keelie sighed heavily and looked toward the stage. Sean now sat on the boards, one leg raised and the other dangling, looking like any other gloriously hunky teen guy. She knew that, being an elf, he was way past eighty years old. So why did she still think he was so hot?

He was laughing at something his friend Bromliel said.

Oh yeah, because he WAS so hot.

"Sean, I can't go to dinner."

He jumped off the stage and took a good look at her face. "What's wrong?"

"Norzan is missing. I have to help Grandmother find him."

"We'll all help." Sean looked over at his elven jousters.

Keelie grabbed his sleeve. "No. You'll start some kind of war here. It's tree shepherd business until declared otherwise. Go to town. I'll try to catch up with you guys."

Sean cupped her face with his hands, then kissed her. Keelie closed her eyes and enjoyed the moment, which was made even more delicious by Risa's hiss and Laurie's gasp of delight. Some moments were just perfect. It almost made up for not being able to go into Juliet City.

Back at the tree house, Keelie put on her camo pants and her "arth" shirt—tree shepherd attire. Normally, she would've opened herself to the trees and asked for their help, but that was no use in the redwoods.

Grandmother noticed Keelie's uneasiness. "I wouldn't suggest this, but given the situation, I recommend we join our magic and shore up our defenses."

Keelie and Dad had a telepathic bond. Did she share one with Grandmother? "Can you read my thoughts?"

"No, I cannot," Grandmother said. "Nor would I want to be privy to your half-human musings."

Relief flowed through Keelie, even considering the insult.

"But if we both want a door, one will open between our minds," Grandmother suggested, her gaze level with Keelie's.

Keelie recalled the first time she and Dad had a mental "talk." She wondered what they had done to make it happen.

A tickle touched her mind. It was very different from the green thoughts from the trees. The tickle became stronger and moved her thoughts to a vision of a door opening, golden light pouring forth.

*Can you hear me now?*

Grandmother smiled. *I can.*

Wow! The power of Grandmother's mind was strong, Supergranny strong. She was way more powerful than Dad.

Grandmother smiled wickedly, like "yeah!"

If she was this strong, Keelie was going to have to figure out how to keep Grandmother out of her mind. With Dad, she did it by imagining defensive walls around her mind, but she didn't know if that would work with Grandmother.

Lady Keliatiel extended her hands, and Keelie took them. She dropped her mental defenses, and once more that golden light connected them. It felt like being wrapped in strong arms—utmost safety. Keelie had never felt anything like it. She sadly realized that this was as close as she and Grandmother would ever get.

She felt a pang of echoing sadness. Startled, she looked at Grandmother and saw sadness flash in her eyes, revealing vulnerability within the power. Insight filled Keelie— Grandmother's magic was so powerful that if she unleashed it on an unsuspecting person, they would fall immediately in love with her. It was sort of like a charm. Then the aloofness Grandmother wore like armor was back.

"Norzan needs us."

Keelie nodded. They headed out.

In the Redwood Forest, with their minds bonded, Grandmother and Keelie cast their thoughts to the trees. *Ancients, we seek your help in finding the Northwoods Tree Shepherd.*

"Should we ask about the Redwood Tree Shepherd?" Keelie whispered.

"I already asked them earlier," Grandmother replied.

An unfathomable, soaring voice answered. *We cannot find either of the tree shepherds.*

This was the true voice of a redwood. But the green that Keelie associated with tree speak was tempered with dark flashes. She wanted to return by day to see what she could find there. She'd bring Knot with her—the fairy would be able to see things that she could not. She felt Grandmother's approval.

A misty cloud spiralled down from above. It was Bella Matera, her eyes pinpoints of silver light.

Terror surged from a nearby stand of hemlocks. Keelie and Grandmother turned their attention to the trees, but a wall of magic blocked them. Sharp pain pierced Keelie's mind. She couldn't break through. But then the pain disappeared just as quickly as it came.

Bella's essence swathed Keelie's mind. *You are frightening the trees. I am only protecting them from their fear. I am deeply worried that we cannot find the two shepherds. I vow to continue to search for them.*

*Thank you*, Grandmother replied. *Your trees need not fear us. We are tree shepherds.*

The tree spirit drifted into the sky, and as she vanished, the wall of magic dissolved.

Keelie turned to the hemlocks. *You can trust me.*

*We trust no one.*

Grandmother looked at Keelie, frustrated. "We must continue to search."

Although Keelie wanted to go to bed, she knew that her grandmother was right, and wondered what had happened to the little trees to frighten them. "Let's go."

Risa and Laurie were already in the bed by the time Keelie collapsed on the skinny strip of space the bed hogs had left for her. Thank goodness she was able to travel the sap by herself. She was so exhausted that she didn't think she could have waited for someone to come down and help her. She would have drifted off right there between Wena's roots. She was not going to have any problem going to sleep tonight.

She moved her feet and her toes curled up against something large, lumpy, and furry. Knot swatted at her foot, snagging a claw in her skin.

Keelie jerked her foot away, kicking Laurie in the back. Laurie, in turn, rolled over and her arms landed on Risa. Risa fell out of the bed with a large thunk.

"Ow!" Risa rose up on her knees and slammed her fists on the bed. "Somebody isn't going to live until morning."

Knot dug himself out of the covers, growling as he jumped down onto the floor.

Risa turned, watching him leave. "Don't go," she pleaded. "I'll go and you can sleep on the bed."

He stopped in the doorway, the light from the bathroom casting a golden glow on his orange fur. He meowed and walked away.

Minutes later, Grandmother bellowed, "Damn fairy!"

Soon all was quiet.

"Why can't I sit up front?" Risa's whine was like a dentist's drill. She was dressed in a Juliet City Shakespeare Festival T-shirt and a pair of Laurie's jeans.

It had taken forever to get organized, so it was evening before they were finally ready to drive to Los Angeles. Keelie proposed they drive all night, taking turns behind the wheel of Laurie's car. That left the whole next day free for L.A., then they would turn around and drive straight back.

Obviously, Risa would do no driving, and Keelie wished she would shut up.

She glanced into the back seat and saw that Laurie was rolling her window down, probably preparing to throw the elf girl out. Keelie was in the front passenger seat, and Sean was driving. It had been like a desperate game of musical chairs as they'd jockeyed for spots. After Laurie had decided to let Sean drive, Keelie knocked Risa aside as she quickly jumped into the front seat next to him. Knot hopped in next to her, further infuriating the elf girl, who ended up stuck in the back with Laurie. At one point, Knot was in the driver's seat. That was so not going to happen.

"I'm totally happy back here," Laurie called out as they bumped down the road. "I'm going to get some sleep. If I had a hammer, I'd make sure Risa did, too."

Knot was now sitting in the front seat between Keelie and Sean, the air from the vent blowing his fur. He rode sitting up, eyes closed as if meditating.

"Risa, put your seat belt back on," Sean said, eyes on the rearview mirror. He was a good driver, and Keelie relaxed after she realized that they were not going to all die before they got to the highway. He wore a Silver Bough shirt, jeans, and leather jacket. He looked good. Real good.

"I'm going to die back here."

If Risa kept up the annoying whine, she might vanish on the road to L.A., Keelie decided.

They stopped for a snack at a burrito stand on the side of the road. Despite Keelie's efforts, Knot snagged a burrito from their picnic table and wolfed it down. They'd all pay for that, Keelie knew. The gasbag kitty would be at poisonous levels.

The road down to L.A. was mostly arid, with ocean and sand and palisades on one side, and rock and gorse and hills on the other. Risa didn't like it, and even Sean looked uneasy at the lack of trees and greenery. No elves here, Keelie thought. And that's probably exactly why Mom had chosen to live here.

They neared Los Angeles as the sun was rising, and Sean pulled over at a restaurant. Everyone piled out to wash their faces, eat breakfast, and brush their teeth. Laurie decided to drive the rest of the way, and Sean gave Keelie the evil eye (or was it the "save me!" eye) as he climbed into the back with Risa. Keelie gritted her teeth as Risa cooed, but she wanted to have a front-seat view of her old hometown.

Laurie drove confidently, making Keelie jealous as she smoothly negotiated the crowded freeway and streets like a pro.

"Want to see our old school?"

"Why?" Risa sounded bored. "Let's just get this errand done, okay?"

Keelie glared at her, then smiled at Laurie, who was grinning as she drove. "You know I want to go by there."

"We can't let anyone see me because I'm skipping, but we can look."

"What's 'skipping'?" Sean asked from the back seat.

"That means not going to school when you're supposed to," Keelie explained.

"Lord Elianard would come to my house to find me if I did that. And my father would never allow it," Risa said.

Sean nodded. "We studied when it was time to study."

"Understood. There are no elf slackers. But here, a bus comes to pick you up at your home and take you to the school building, and there you spend the day working, and in the afternoon the bus takes you back home."

Sean and Risa looked interested at this insight into human life. As Laurie turned into the street that went by the back of Baywood Academy, they leaned forward to look. Laurie pulled over and they got out.

The soccer fields were in back, separated from the street by a row of slender Bradford Pear trees, now in full stinky bloom. Dozens of girls in burgundy shorts and dark blue T-shirts with the gold Baywood logo were playing soccer. They laughed and talked, and occasional blasts of the referee's whistle split the air.

Keelie's surge of nostalgia at the familiar sounds and smells was marred because she also heard the thoughts of the trees. She knew now that the Bradford Pears were watered too little and their roots were shallow, planted by landscapers looking for an inexpensive solution.

*We need water.*

*I'll try and find you water*, she promised.

Although sad for the trees, Keelie was also annoyed. She couldn't enjoy her moment of remembrance of her life that once was without it being invaded by the needs of the now.

"Why did we stop? There's nothing interesting here, just a bunch of girls playing a game. We could have stopped in the garlic fields. That was interesting, but no, you all said it was stinky and just farms." Risa crossed her arms and stalked back to the car.

Sean didn't say anything, but Keelie could tell he didn't see the point of stopping here, either.

"I'm sorry if it's boring," Keelie said. "I had some really good times here."

"It's good to remember," Sean said. "Did you wear one of those outfits to play?"

"No, I ran track. My shorts were shorter."

His eyebrows rose. She left him to think about that.

Laurie was back behind the wheel. "I don't want to be seen. Hurry up."

A moment later they were back on the road, this time passing through neighborhoods and shopping areas that were familiar to Keelie. Here was where Mom's chiropractor's office was, and there her dentist. They passed the organic supermarket, and the nail salon Mom visited every week. Now they were in Hancock Park.

Laurie turned onto Citrus Avenue, then slowed the car down and pulled up in front of the house. A "sold" sign was slapped across the red and white real estate sign.

"We're here." Laurie said in a soft voice.

Knot hopped up on the seat back and climbed onto Keelie's shoulders, then walked down into her lap and sat with his paw on the door handle.

Laurie stared at him. "Look, he's giving you kitty love."

"He's being a pain in the hiney."

Keelie looked out the car window at the house, which seemed like a vision from another lifetime. She didn't know if she could go inside. It might hurt to make the memories more real. It was like her heart breaking into shards of glass, again.

She breathed in, trying to still the grief washing over her in waves. "I can do this," she said, as if the words would be a life preserver in the crush of emotions.

Laurie reached over and placed her hand on Keelie's shoulder. "That's why I'm here. We don't have to go in until you're ready. Want to get a coffee at the mall?"

Keelie exhaled. "I need to do this. The sooner the better."

Looking at the "sold" sign, Keelie realized that soon a new family would grow up here. The story of Mom and Keelie as a family was over. Now, it was Keelie and Dad. It was a new chapter, but she wanted one more chance to see the backstory of her life.

Risa was fascinated. "So few trees, but the gardens are beautiful."

"People pay a lot of money for their landscaping," Keelie agreed. Her mother had probably chosen this neighborhood because there were so few trees here. There were trees on the other side of Citrus Avenue, but here there were none. Her house was a sparkling white Mediterranean with a bay window in the front. Colorful landscaping decorated the sides of the house, and over the roof she saw the tops of three palms that were actually a block away.

Sean and Risa jumped out. Keelie sat still for a moment, savoring the view of the small neat yard, with its river-rock borders and the flagstone path that led to the back, and the round-topped front door with the little window.

She opened the car door and Knot stretched. He dug his back claws deep into Keelie's thigh as he propelled himself out the door like an acrobat. He landed on the ground with a thud.

Stupid cat!

Somewhere nearby someone was mowing their lawn, probably Mr. Heidelman, who cut his lawn at odd hours, even at midnight. It had driven Mom crazy. "Who does yard work at midnight? You'd think we had vampires in our neighborhood."

Keelie wondered if Mom had known about Uncle Dariel. There were so many things Mom had never told her, and now she would never know Mom's side of the story.

Knot sat on the front walkway and meowed. He looked directly at her as if saying, "Come on."

Years of memories rolled through Keelie's mind. They were running into one another, a cluttered collage of film clips from her life: trick-or-treating on Halloween, Chrismases with artificial trees, Thanksgivings, even just bringing in the groceries—the years were heaped on one another.

Keelie wanted to relive them all, capture them in a locket and keep them with her. When she walked out of this house today for the last time, would she lose them?

The others were already trying the locked door and looking through the windows when she got slowly out of the car. Would she feel her mother here?

The solitary orange tree next door sang a song of welcome, and her nose burned with tears. When had she heard this familiar song? Had the trees always sung for her and she just hadn't heard them? Aching with memory, Keelie went to join her friends.

*Yes, I'm back*, she told the tree.

She would say goodbye, then leave forever.

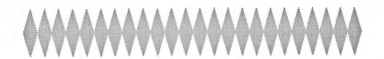

# twelve

The key was in the lock, but Keelie couldn't make herself turn it. Laurie stood beside her, hands on her hips. She studied Keelie with concern in her eyes. "You ready to do this?"

Risa stared at them from behind Laurie, frowning.

Warm fur rubbed up against her leg. Knot meowed, then reached up and impatiently tapped the doorknob.

She felt Sean's strong hand at her waist. "You don't have to if you don't want to," he whispered, "but we're here for you."

Keelie nodded. She turned the key in the lock.

Knot rose up on his paws and pushed the door open a

crack, then squeezed in, marching past Keelie. He stopped and sat down in the middle of the living room. Sunlight streamed onto the hardwood floors. Knot sat in the center of a warm patch of light, his fur shining with an orange glow. He turned his green eyes toward her and blinked, as if saying, "Well, what now?"

Keelie's feet were frozen to the welcome mat. She couldn't move. If Mom were here, she would've been insulted that the cat had forged his way ahead of her. Mom liked to be first, and she wanted Keelie to be just like her. She would've told Keelie to walk inside and do what she had to do. She could almost hear her using that lawyer voice. The one she used when they'd argue and she was tired of debating the subject. Keelie squared her shoulders.

Knot meowed. The front door creaked open wider and Keelie looked around her home for the first time in almost a year. It was empty. The polished tile floors of the sun room on the other side of the hall gleamed, and the walls smelled slightly of fresh paint. She didn't know what she'd expected to see. Certainly not Grandmother Jo's dark red velvet settee, or the pegged shelf where they'd hung sun hats, umbrellas, and tote bags. Those were all in storage. She glanced at Sean, hoping he hadn't noticed her disappointment. They'd come all this way for a mere real estate tour.

Sean's mouth turned up a little in the corners and he pretended to be very interested in the landscaping out front.

Laurie grabbed Risa's elbow and dragged her away.

"What are you doing? I want to see what all the fuss is about. Is there a treasure inside?"

"Shut up and help me identify these plants."

It was apparently the right thing to say to Risa, because the girl fell silent.

Grateful, Keelie stepped into the house alone. The Talbot and Talbot letter crackled in her pocket, where she'd tucked it in case anyone asked who they were and why they were here. She could hear Risa and Laurie's voices moving toward the back yard.

The house was very still, as if it had been waiting for her. She tiptoed into the living room, which seemed huge without the furniture that had filled it. The floor was a little dented where the piano had pounded flat its rectangular shape.

This was where they'd argued about the belly button ring. Mom had been sorting through files on the table, her lips thin from keeping in her anger. Keelie had felt triumphant when she'd seen how mad Mom was. She'd keep it up until she got her way.

Keelie closed her eyes, feeling like Knot, who closed his eyes as if he wanted to be someplace else. Suddenly, everything came back to her clearly, so real she could hear Mom's voice as if she was standing right next to her, as if Keelie could reach out and touch her. The smell of paint faded, overlaid with the scent of Mom's bath gel and the morning's toast and strong coffee.

"Keelie, we'll talk about this tonight." Mom's dark hair was brushed up and held with an elegant clip. She wore her favorite black business suit, with a white silk blouse and a

Chinese scarf. She pushed papers into her leather briefcase haphazardly.

"Mom, everyone is getting pierced. I'm not a baby."

"Keelie, you're not getting your navel pierced, and that's final." She hurried to the door and held it open, waving at the Lexus idling in their driveway. "Your carpool is here. Get your bookbag, don't make them wait."

Keelie snatched up her backpack, narrowly missing a Waterford vase as she swung it onto her shoulder. She was going to be the only girl at the pool party without body jewelry. Everyone would stare and look at her pityingly for having such a bitchy mom. She sighed, hating the quavery feeling in her lungs. She was not going to cry.

"I love you, darling."

"Well, I hate you."

Mom sighed. "No you don't. You're just mad. Come on. I'm going to be late for my plane. Maybe we can eat at Luna tonight when I get home."

She'd never come home.

A sick feeling burned through Keelie. *I didn't mean it, Mom. I didn't hate you. I love you!*

Dad said that Mom hadn't taken her seriously, but it was the last thing she'd ever said to her mother.

Knot scooted past her, tail held high. Sean turned to look at the kitchen as Knot ducked into her old bedroom.

Ugh. Keelie followed Knot, anxious to prevent a cat accident. Knot was not above using a nice new carpet as his personal toilet, and the house belonged to someone else now.

"Come back here, Knot. Use the garden."

Her bedroom was empty. For a moment Keelie just stood, staring at the neutral paint on the walls. She blinked back tears. She would not let this get to her. She had a new life now. She thought of her room in Oregon, of the four-poster bed with its twisty carved posts, and the window with a view of the forest. She thought of the fish kite that dangled in the hallway, twirling slowly. That was home now. This—she pictured a home office. Or a nursery. That was it. She felt better thinking that her old room would belong to a baby. The crib could go there, against the wall, and a rocking chair by the window...

She opened the closet door. A rod, a shelf. No cat. Keelie walked quickly from room to room, looking for Knot, but he'd vanished. Sean was in the front room, but the rest of the house was empty.

Just as well. She walked toward Mom's room. As long as the house was here, Keelie had held out hope that Mom would come back, even though the logical part of her brain said it was impossible. She had seen a lot of magic, but none that brought back the dead. She'd come here partly to prove to herself that Mom wasn't coming back.

Knot came trotting toward her, tail swishing. "Where were you, bad kitty? You stick close, okay?"

She went into Mom's bedroom with Knot at her side. Also empty, of course. Empty, yet full of Mom. The walls were painted a soft peach, Mom's favorite color. They hadn't been repainted, and her almond and rose smell filled the room as if she'd just left. If only she could come back for a goodbye, for one last hug and kiss.

Tears sprang to Keelie's eyes, and then trailed wet and warm down her cheek.

Knot leaned against her leg, stuck to her like crazy glue. He purred, but it was a different kind of purr, a warm soothing rhythm like a furry blanket of sound that wrapped her in comfort. She felt the tension in her body slowly release. The empty room didn't contain her mother. Mom was in her memories...mornings in bed reading stories, playing games on weekends. Mom teaching her about makeup. She smiled, remembering the happy discoveries they'd made shopping. Those thoughts were locked away in her heart and mind. She never thought she could remember that happiness without hurting, but she could.

She looked down at Knot, and he blinked up at her, showing fang in a kitty grin. Keelie didn't know if he'd used magic on her, but she gave him a slight nod of appreciation.

She had another reason for coming in here, too. She opened the door to the walk-in closet. It was almost as big as Dad's Swiss Miss Chalet (she'd gained an appreciation for small spaces since sleeping in that tiny camper). Kneeling in front of the metal furnace grate on the wall, Keelie pressed the upper right-hand screw that seemed to hold it in place. The grate clicked open, revealing that it was a door. Inside was a safe. Talbot and Talbot knew nothing about this, and Keelie's hand trembled as she reached for the knob.

She knew the combination. It was the same one that Mom had used for everything from bike locks to her ATM card. Her photos and journals were inside, and just maybe, an explanation of why she kept Keelie away from Dad, why she'd lied about Keelie's "tree allergy."

The combination lock sprang open. Keelie felt a tickling wind pass her, coming from the safe. She'd broken a magical ward. Bits of it still fluttered around like a spider web that had been torn. Keelie detected a strange coldness, too. Dark magic had been used here.

She stared disbelievingly at the inside of the open safe. It was empty. She reached into its depths and felt around. Nothing. As she pulled her arm out, a torn piece of paper fluttered to the ground. She picked it up and turned it over.

It was thick and stiff like a piece of parchment from the charm book. Keelie could see images of a fairy spell forming on the page. What had been in the safe, that this charm had been tucked in there to keep it secure?

Suddenly, Keelie sensed eyes watching her from the window. She turned her head slowly. Something had moved, but she saw only the black shadows under the green branches of the shrub outside. Then the darkness shifted, and the sun glinted briefly on a pattern of red and green diamonds. Her blood chilled.

Knot leaped up and ran to the window, hissing. Keelie watched, astonished, as he pulled himself up to the window to look out and grew larger, until he was the size of a bobcat. This was new.

Whatever Knot saw outside made his green eyes glow. He pushed away from the window and ran from the room, still growing.

Keelie ran after him, down the hall, through the kitchen, then to the French doors leading to the back yard, which were opened wide.

Knot was now the size of a small cheetah. He bolted outside, Keelie close behind him.

Laurie and Risa were sitting on a stone bench, Laurie's eyes were glazed as Risa explained about the plant she held. She screamed as newly huge Knot ran through the bushes that grew at the property line. Keelie pushed her way through the bushes too, following Knot as he ran across the street and down the sidewalk to the corner, then right into the park. Darn cat was going to get shot, or lost, or captured, and it was his fault for using magic in the middle of a city.

He disappeared behind a concrete building that housed the restrooms, still intent on what he was chasing. A single frantic jingle sounded through the bushes on the other side.

*I wouldn't follow him, if I were you.*

Keelie stopped. The big tree in the middle of the park had spoken to her. She spun around and stood before the great California live oak.

The tree pushed its face outward through its trunk. It was lined with wrinkles.

"Who are you?"

*The name is Morgan Freeman.*

"Like the film star?" Something was familiar about this tree's voice. "You used to talk to me when I was a little girl and tell me stories when I played in this park." She'd forgotten until now. Her mother had told her that she was imagining things.

*I'm glad to see you broke through your Mother's spells to remember me.*

Keelie reeled back in shock, her runaway cat forgotten. "Mom used magic on me?"

*Yes, she did.* The tree leaned to one side, bark cracking like whips as it stretched.

Keelie didn't want to believe what the tree had said. She looked down at the page in her hand, but she knew deep down that the tree was telling the truth. "She used fairy magic."

*She wanted to protect you from those who would claim you and your magic, Keelie.*

"She kept me from Dad."

*She was afraid. She loved you. Sometimes fear clouds judgment.*

Keelie pointed back to the house. "Did you see someone break into my house and take something from there?"

The tree looked over at Keelie's house. *There was a storm the other night. I didn't see what had entered your house, but I sensed an Under-the-Hill creature.*

"Under-the-Hill?" Keelie shivered.

*Be careful, Keelie, for even in the Redwood Forest, evil spreads its shadow.*

"What do you know about that?" Keelie asked.

*I can say no more. I've said too much already. May you grow many rings*, the tree said. His face dissolved back into the bark.

Keelie felt a block of magic surround the tree like a shield. This conversation was definitely over.

"You know you'd better listen to him," said a voice low to the ground.

She glanced down, startled, into the sharp-eared face of a grinning coyote.

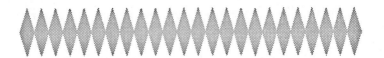

# thirteen

"What are you, the L.A. version of the White Rabbit?" Keelie had spent her fifteen years living here with no wildlife interaction, and all of a sudden she was talking to coyotes and trees.

Someone shouted out her name. Keelie looked up the street in the direction of her house. Laurie was running toward her. Keelie turned back to the talking coyote, but he had disappeared. Just like Knot. She rubbed her temple with her left hand as she examined the parchment still clutched in her right.

She was still stunned at the revelation that Mom had

used magic to block her memory. This thought was disturbing on so many levels. It would take Keelie a long, long time to sort through it. Had Mom used magic books? Since Mom was half fae, she could have—but then why keep her father out of her life, if magic wasn't objectionable?

Keelie lifted the parchment up to the sunlight, trying to figure out what it was.

Laurie finally reached her. "I checked through the house for you. It's so creepy and empty. It got really cold, like something was watching me, and Sean is going nuts. He's stalking the neighborhood like an escapee from the Lord of the Rings funny farm. Somebody is going to call the police."

Keelie held up her hands. "Stop talking. Where is Sean now, and where's Risa?"

"He said to pick him up at the end of the street. Risa is sitting in the car and refuses to get out. She's saying something about dark fairy magic. She looks sick, kind of green around the gills."

"Elves don't have gills, sprites do," Keelie said absently, putting the parchment into her pocket. "Let's go rescue Sean and Risa. Elves can't tolerate urban environments for long."

"What were you doing down here at the park?" Laurie asked. "Remember when we used to play here, and bring books and picnics?"

"Yeah, it was fun. That tree just talked to me." Keelie motioned with her head in the direction of the tree.

Understanding lit up Laurie's face. "Ah!" Then her forehead furrowed. "Did it talk to you when we were little?"

"Apparently, but I didn't remember until just now." Keelie didn't want to go into the whole Mom-using-magic thing.

Knot came dashing up to Keelie. He'd returned to his normal size, but his eyes were dilated, his fur mussed, and he meowed angrily.

Laurie's eyebrows rose. "What's wrong with him? He's acting weird even for Knot."

This wasn't weird. This was agitated. Keelie wondered if it was really Peascod that Knot had chased away from the house. "Kitty, you need a cup of catnip tea. The good stuff that makes you drool in the corner."

The temperature in the park had suddenly dropped several degrees, and a cold wind kicked up. Maybe Risa's claim about dark fairy magic wasn't too far off the mark.

Laurie was trying to act calm and collected like she wasn't concerned about anything, but Keelie knew her friend was worried. Truth be told, Keelie was, too. The trip to the old house had revealed more questions than answers.

"Storm must be blowing in. Let's go and get a latte at the mall. I think I could use a coffee," Keelie suggested.

"Sounds good to me." Laurie turned and walked down the street, back to the car. Knot surveyed the terrain like a tiger scrutinizing his territory for enemies.

Keelie looked in the same direction, and swore she saw a skinny, ugly dog watching her from the bushes. It seemed to be the coyote. A flash of dull gold fur disappeared into the greenery. Knot growled.

"Come on. I'll buy you a tall cream."

Knot swiveled his head up to stare at Keelie. He blinked

and his eyes dilated. All of a sudden, he reached out, wrapped his paws around her ankle, and bit her. His fangs sank deep into her skin.

"Ow! Let go, you crazy cat."

He did, and ran after Laurie like a spineless wuss not brave enough to face the consequences of his insane action, which was an angry Keelie.

"You have cat litter for brain cells." She loped after him. "Get back here, you psycho horror-movie excuse for a cat. A coyote would make a better guardian than you."

There was a tingle in the air, followed by a zingy harp sound. Keelie spun around, expecting to see an elf girl playing a harp. No one was there. Nothing. Still, there was a feeling of magic in the air, and suddenly she wanted to leave.

Two ladies in jogging suits watched with baffled expressions as she hobbled to the car. Knot was nowhere in sight. Laurie was waiting for her. She put on her sunglasses, shaking her head, and opened the car door.

Just then Sean rounded Mr. Heildelman's bushes and came to Keelie's side. He clasped her upper arm as he scanned the street. "Are you okay? Did you see anything strange?"

"Nothing's normal anymore, but I'm fine, thanks." Keelie forced a smile. "We're going to grab a coffee at the mall." She looked at her old house once more. "Did you lock everything up?"

"Yes. Are you sure you're done here?"

Keelie bit her lip, then released it. Mom had always told her not to bite her lip. "I'm done."

Sean pulled Keelie into a hug, surprising her. "I'm going to keep you safe," he whispered.

Keelie's legs became boneless. She pulled away from Sean and they grinned at each other. His eyes were bright.

Laurie gave a thumbs-up. From inside the car, Risa scowled and punched the back seat with closed fists.

Sean opened the passenger-side door. "Milady." Knot jumped in, his big orange butt taking up the entire seat.

Laurie shook her head. "You two, let's get going. I need a coffee." She climbed into the driver's seat.

"Move over." Sean leaned down and glowered at Knot.

"Knot, you can sit with me, my love," Risa said.

Knot scooted over and Keelie sat down next to him. He narrowed his green eyes as he looked her up and down, as if he was thinking that maybe she should ride on the hood.

As Sean walked around the front of the BMW, Laurie gazed down at Knot. "Is Keelie mean to you?"

Risa tipped forward, her hands on the back of the seat. "She's mean to him. She calls him Snotball."

Knot placed his paw on Laurie's leg as if confirming that what Risa said was true: *Yes, she's so mean to me. You should try living with her.*

Sean got into the back and closed the door. Keelie pulled the seat belt around her body. "He bit me."

"It was a love bite. Cats bite you as a token of their affection." Laurie cranked the car.

"You can forget the milk." Keelie glared down at the cat, who looked ahead.

Risa patted Knot on the head. "I'll buy you some cream."

Keelie snorted. "Let's go get that coffee."

In the mall parking lot, Laurie held her designer bag open. "Knot can ride inside like those little yappy dogs do."

"How are you going to keep him inside the bag?" Keelie asked. "We can't handcuff or tape him down."

Glaring at Keelie, Knot sank his claws deeper into the seat upholstery, refusing to be manhandled into the pocketbook.

Risa leaned over and scratched him under the chin. "If the kitty gets into the bag, then he gets his milk-milk."

"Milk-milk?" Keelie nearly gagged.

Sean was out of the car. "Ladies, we need to make this a short trip. Last night, I told Lady Keliatiel and Sir Davey I'd make sure you got home safe and sound."

With a nod to Sean, Knot stepped into Laurie's bag with his tail held high. He stuck his furry head out and blinked his eyes at Keelie.

Laurie lifted the pocketbook and gave it to Keelie, her face red from straining. "See, no prob, but you can carry your cat."

"Let me," Sean reached for the bag, but Knot growled in protest.

"No, he'll bite you," Keelie took the bag from Laurie.

Knot purred. Keelie wondered if he was kneading his paws like a superhappy kitten. What was he doing to Laurie's stuff? She wouldn't think about that.

At the mall, once her refuge of happiness and retail adventures, Keelie shuddered at the alien artificiality of the stores. Laurie chattered on and on about which stores had the best sales. "We need to find La Jolie Rouge."

Knot traveled contentedly in the bag like a pampered lap dog. The bag straps dug into Keelie's shoulder, and she was sure that she'd have rub on some Achy Bones Salve once she was back from this shopping trip.

Inside Starbucks, Laurie continued to prattle as they waited in line to get their coffee. Keelie was so tired that she couldn't focus on Laurie's words. Of course, Laurie was talking non-stop and Keelie had had an emotional afternoon.

She definitely needed a coffee to help her reenergize. Maybe six shots of espresso would do the trick. It had to have been going back to the house. Who wouldn't be wiped after an emotional experience like that?

A huge bump appeared on the side of the bag and then rolled around, accompanied by loud purring. It made the buckles and pockets pop and rattle. Knot must be doing somersaults inside. Two girls behind Keelie stared at the bag strangely. She grinned.

A pop hit jingled from inside the bag.

"Keelie, hand me my phone, would you?" Laurie was almost at the counter.

Keelie stared at the heaving bag. She was already limping. What would happen if she stuck her hand in there? She'd return to the redwoods in an ambulance, thanks to Knot her so-called guardian. "Why don't you let your voicemail catch that?"

The phone abruptly stopped ringing. "Meow?"

Luckily, Laurie didn't hear that, thank the tree rings. Keelie wondered who Knot was talking to.

The Starbucks barista was a bored, purple-haired girl. She acted like she didn't want to be there.

"We'd like two coffees," Laurie told her.

The top of the purse opened and Laurie's Vera Bradley wallet poked out. Keelie took it. "Do you want a shot in your cream?" she whispered into the bag.

The girls waiting for their coffees stared wide-eyed. Keelie grinned at them. "Just kidding."

Laurie took her wallet. "What do you guys want?" she asked Sean and Risa, who seemed confused by the menu.

"What do you suggest?" Sean asked.

"Coffee is good." Laurie didn't sound sarcastic.

"I'll have green tea," said Risa. "What is venti?"

"Big." The bored barista swiped Laurie's debit card down the register's side.

Keelie placed the bag on a nearby chair. "I'll have a venti latte with six shots, and an espresso con panna."

The purple-haired girl's eyes widened. "Six shots?"

Laurie's mouth dropped open, but she recovered. "That's what I heard, too."

"Okay." The purple-haired girl shook her head as she rang up the order.

They got their drinks and went to the atrium by the food court. Keelie sat down near a small, flowering pear tree and felt a smidge better. She took the lid off the espresso con panna (a shot of strong espresso poured over a mound of whipped cream) and put the little cup on the floor under the table. Knot squeezed himself out of the bag and dropped to the floor.

Risa and Laurie scooted their chairs close so that their legs hid the slurping feline.

Keelie stuck her head under the table. "Behave yourself."

He blinked, his eyes round and sweetly innocent, like an animated cartoon. Keelie didn't believe him for a second. "I'll be watching."

Knot went back to lapping his supercharged whipped cream with a loud licky-lick sound.

Keelie drank her rocket-fuel latte, hoping the caffeine would infuse her with more energy. Instead, she was beginning to feel more drained. She didn't know what was wrong with her. She had to keep her act together. Sean opened the lid of his coffee and sniffed the steam that floated out.

"This is the energy nectar you are always praising. Starbucks. It has an elvish name." He held his cup up and then took a sip.

"You can't tell me you haven't had coffee before," Keelie said, disbelieving.

"I didn't say that. It's just that I prefer tea. However, this was a trip for me to find out more about you. I was curious. And I wanted to drink coffee like you," he said.

Keelie smiled into her coffee. "You are so sweet."

Women of all ages shot admiring glances Sean's way. Sean noticed, then looked at Keelie and rolled his eyes. She laughed. She did wonder if people thought that Sean and Risa were a couple, because they looked more like a matched pair than she and Sean did. Jealousy stung her heart with short little jabs. It was still like having a nest of bees inside her whenever she thought about them together. Of course, Sean was eighty years old, a fact she tried hard to forget. He'd probably had lots of relationships, but she wasn't ready to know the truth. One day they would have that conversation, but until then, until she was ready, she could pretend he was her age.

Laurie stared at the purple-haired barista. "That girl needs an attitude adjustment. She needs to read the manual on customer service."

A branch from the pear tree beside Keelie tapped her on the shoulder.

*Hey, you. What are you?*

Keelie closed her eyes. She just wished she could get a break from trees.

*I'm a tree shepherdess.*

*I've never heard of one of those. Are you from the nursery?*

*No. I'm from the Dread Forest.*

*But you're human. You grew up in a forest? I've never met a human who grew up in a forest. I would love to see a forest. I hate being stuck in this pot all the time. The people that take care of us aren't very nice. They forget about me. Sometimes I get so thirsty that my leaves fall off.*

*I didn't grow up in a forest. I grew up in Los Angeles, but I live in the Dread Forest.*

The tree bent down closer to Keelie and sniffed.

Laurie's eyes widened in surprise. She obviously could see the tree bending and moving around. Sean arched an eyebrow.

Risa's eyes were riveted on Knot. "Is that eye shadow on your toes?"

*Will you stop it? People are going to notice.* Keelie looked around, but only a couple of children were pointing at the swaying tree.

The tree sniffed again. *I smell magic on you. Can you make my pot bigger?*

*Trees can't smell magic.*

*I can.* He seemed offended. *Sometimes I smell a different kind of magic on some humans who come in here. And I smell it on the gobblers, but your magic is different. You have fairy magic.* The tree's voice was accusing, as if having fairy magic was a bad thing. Guess it depended on what kind of fairy.

*Gobblers? What are gobblers?*

*They're the ugly fairies, and they're not friends of the trees. You're not a gobbler, are you? They like to steal sap.*

Keelie had no idea what a gobbler was. She felt sorry for this tree with his tight-fitting planter.

Suddenly a horrendous smell filled the air. Keelie recognized it, and jumped up as Knot vaulted onto the planter's edge and made an experimental dig with one paw.

*There's a fair-fair-fairy.* The tree swooned, and fell over with a loud crash. Everyone in the food court leaped up and looked toward them.

"Are you okay?" the woman behind the counter of the Chinese restaurant yelled.

"Fine," Laurie said. "We're okay. Is anybody a lawyer?"

Knot had landed on his feet and bolted toward an exit.

Keelie rounded the overturned planter and looked down at the tree, its branches splayed out on the atrium's tile floor.

*Are you okay?*

Silence.

Knot's loud meow echoed down the hall.

"The milk must not have agreed with him. You know, he may be lactose-intolerant," Laurie suggested.

A lactose-intolerant fairy. That figured.

"Knot, wait for me." Risa pushed her chair backwards and raced after him.

People in the food court were looking, pointing, and whispering.

Sean stood up. "I'd better keep an eye on her. She's not familiar with the ways of the human world, and she could get into trouble."

Keelie wanted to protest, but she had to agree with Sean. Knot and Risa on the loose in L.A.? Not a good thing.

The people in the food court resumed eating, but they kept staring at Keelie as if she'd been the one causing all the problems. Or as if she was paid entertainment.

She should be used to it, after all the numerous jobs she'd had at the Wildewood Faire. She hadn't been good at those, either, and people had stared after every disaster.

"Sit down, Keelie, people are looking." Laurie tried to look nonchalant as she sipped her drink.

"I hope they get this poor tree a new planter. He's out-grown this one," Keelie said loudly. She yanked on its slim trunk and the crumbly earth ball held by its roots popped out. His branches drooped and several leaves skittered across the floor as if it was autumn. Some of the nearby people nodded sympathetically.

Keelie stared down at the root ball. If the tree had been watered regularly, it would have been impossible to pull out. And the root ball was big, too. The tree's roots had been cramped, with no room to grow. It was like having a person's feet crammed into too-small shoes. She had to do something.

As two big security guards rushed forward, Keelie pointed to the tree. "You really need to talk to the company that takes care of your plants. That tree could've collapsed on me. I could be suffering from a concussion, and you're darn lucky I'm not."

One of the beefy security guards, whose nameplate said "Dan," looked uncomfortable. "Yes ma'am. Are you okay?"

"Who takes care of your trees?" Keelie demanded.

"We're not sure." The two guys exchanged I-dunno-do-you-know? looks.

The tree was beginning to come back to consciousness. Huh!

"I'm taking it with me as evidence," Keelie said.

The other security guard, with "Don" on his name tag, scratched his head. "I don't know if you can do that."

"Do you have a larger container and fresh clean soil?" Keelie asked, using her best lawyer voice.

Laurie crossed her arms over her chest. "Yeah, do you?"

Tweedle Dan and Tweedle Don shook their heads.

"I'm going to take this tree, and consider yourselves lucky I don't sue the mall." Keelie said.

"We need to talk to our boss," Tweedle Don replied.

"Go talk to him," Keelie said. "I need some answers."

"Okay!" They both left.

Once the guards were out of sight, Keelie motioned to Laurie. "Come on, we're getting out of here." She grabbed the tree by its slender trunk. "Help me carry this."

Laurie grabbed a leafy branch. "Is this like shoplifting, or more like a PETA rescue, only with trees?"

"We'll figure it out later. Walk faster." The two girls scooted through the mall and wrestled the tree up the escalator and out the front door. Few people gave them more than a glance.

"L.A. is so blasé about everything," Keelie observed. "We could have been leading an elephant around in here and no one would notice."

They found Sean, Risa, and Knot standing on a four-foot-square patch of grass in front of the mall. All three were avoiding a corner of the patch. Knot looked relieved to see them.

"Time to go," Laurie said. Sean grabbed the tree trunk, freeing Laurie to search for her car keys.

They ran to the car, the branches sticking up over their heads as if they were smuggling giant broccoli. Knot was leading the way.

"I can't believe we're tree-napping. What if those two guards put two and two together and come after us?" Laurie asked.

"That's why we need to get out of here," Keelie replied. She had no idea what she was going to do with the pear tree.

She needed to plant him somewhere safe, with lots of tree company.

When they reached the car, an out-of-breath Risa was holding her side. "I thought we were going shopping at La Jolie Rouge? Now you two are stealing a tree. We just left a forest filled with trees. We live in a forest. Can't you get enough?"

Sean's face was serious. "Come on. I've had enough of the mall."

"Thank you." Keelie's eyes held Sean's.

"We'll talk about this later," he said firmly.

Laurie pressed her key remote and the BMW doors clicked open. She tossed Keelie the keys. Knot hopped into the front seat, yowling loudly as if saying, "Hurry, hurry." The tree was too big to fit into the back seat of the car with Risa and Sean, so it would have to ride in the trunk.

Keelie could see Tweedle Don and Tweedle Dan surveying the parking lot. They were scratching their heads and talking into their remote control walkie-talkies like they were calling for reinforcements.

Like Sean, Keelie'd had enough of the mall. "We need to go."

The tree was fully conscious. *What are you trying to do? Kill me? Take me back. I'm going to tell the gobblers about you.*

Laurie pointed. "The security guards have found us." She hopped into the car while Keelie cranked the engine. Sean lowered one of the back seats, then angled the tree in, so that the branches were in the back seat and the root ball was in the trunk. He slammed the trunk door closed, then he and Risa opened the back doors and fought the branches to find a seat.

Keelie pulled out of the parking space. Looking in the driver's side mirror, she saw Tweedle Dan and Tweedle Don gesturing wildly at the BMW.

*Oh, Great Sylvus, my planter is gone. My roots will wither away and die without soil. I'm going to die.* The tree's voice penetrated the cab of the car, but Keelie was the only one who could hear him. Lucky her.

*You're not going to die.* Keelie tried to send soothing green thoughts to the tree, but they were rejected.

*I'm going to die. I'm going to die.*

*We're saving you.* Keelie was getting irritated with this ungrateful tree.

*The gobblers were right about fairies. They're all bad. They'll find you, and you'll be sorry.*

Keelie drove slowly through the crowded parking lot

"Hurry it up. Once we get on the expressway, they'll lose us," Laurie said. "Only you would come to L.A. and steal a tree."

"I couldn't leave him there with an overturned tiny planter. His root system didn't have any room to grow," Keelie insisted.

Risa leaned forward. "See, your friend agrees with me. You're surrounded by trees. Why rescue this one?"

Keelie ignored her. She glanced into the rearview mirror.

Sean rested his head against the back of the seat and closed his eyes as if he was wishing himself anywhere but here.

As they drove past a huge SUV with tinted windows, Keelie felt a sudden wash of dark power come over her, similar to what she'd experienced in the redwoods. The sharp pain pierced her forehead. "Ow!"

"What's wrong, Keelie?" Laurie asked. Knot hissed and scrambled into the back seat, climbing onto the car's rear deck to look out the windshield. Sean's eyes opened wide and he too turned to look back at the SUV.

Risa hugged herself. "I don't feel well."

Overcoming her pain, Keelie felt a primal urge to get out of the parking lot. "I think the quickest way out of here is to take the access road and then follow the state road to Baywood Academy."

"We're going back to that boring place?" Risa whined.

"I'm going to plant the tree there."

Laurie rolled her eyes. "You need to turn right. "

"No I don't," Keelie answered.

"When we get to the red light, stay on the access road and merge onto the expressway. That's the fastest route there."

Keelie slammed on the brakes. "The expressway! I can't drive on the expressway." She was as panicked as the tree in the trunk.

*I'm going to die. I'm going to die. I'm going to die*, the tree wailed in Keelie's mind.

"Don't slam on the brakes. Go. Go. Go." Laurie motioned with her hands. Cars were honking behind them.

"We'll just have to go a mile on the expressway, then you'll take the exit. No big deal. That'll take us to Baywood Academy. We can stop there and I can drive."

*I'm going to die. I'm going to die. I'm going to die.*

"Shut up," Keelie shouted loudly.

"What?" Laurie looked at Keelie in shock.

Keelie pushed on the accelerator. "I'm talking to the tree."

Somebody in a Jeep drove around them, giving them the finger as they passed.

"People in L.A. are so rude." Keelie drove on. "Maybe we can find some planters at the school,

"What are we going to do? Repot the bush?" Risa didn't seem concerned.

Sean didn't say anything. He had his hand across his face now. He was pale and had dark circles under his eyes. He needed to get out of the city.

Laurie turned around and glared at Risa. "I can't believe we stole a tree out of the mall. I'll never be able to show my face there again. And they're having a really great sale at American Eagle."

*I'm not a bush, I'm a tree. And I'm going to die if I have to live outside.*

*You will not. You'll survive and thrive in the earth. Lots of sunshine.*

You'd think the brat mall tree would be grateful at being saved from a lifetime of being inside the mall.

The tree started making weeping noises in her head, and Keelie felt a surge of sympathy for the little guy. *It'll be okay.*

As she merged onto the expressway, she hoped she was right.

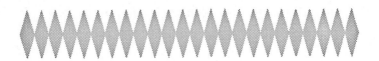

# fourteen

Keelie stroked the pear tree's smooth trunk. She'd propped him against a friendly willow so that he could soak his roots in the creek that flowed through the rear of the school property. The tree was finally calming down.

Sean sat on the bank next to it and watched the kids playing on the school's fields. "Soccer seems to be a fun game."

"Only if you're not forced to play it."

Laurie and Risa had gone to the local Orchard Supply Hardware store to buy a shovel, leaving Keelie and Sean to babysit the tree.

Knot chased a butterfly over some rocks in the creek.

"Don't get wet, kitty," Keelie warned him. "Laurie doesn't want to drive around with a soggy cat." There was a splash and an angry yowl. Knot never listened.

Philia, the willow, was crooning to the little tree in a sweet motherly tone. *He's barely older than an acorn.*

Keelie patted the pear tree's trunk. *I think he'll be happy here.*

The little tree showed Keelie his face, snub-nose and little eyes pushing through its bark. *Thank you, tree shepherdess.*

*You're welcome.* A dark blur whizzed by, followed by two others. Knot froze, intent on their movement. *Feithid daoine.* Keelie grinned at the bug fairies.

"Well, well, isn't this a lovely little scene," a voice said nearby.

Startled, Keelie looked up. It was the coyote, facing her from the opposite bank. His gold and brown fur almost blended with the woods.

Sean jumped up. "Is that a wolf?"

"No, just a coyote. They're like rats, shaped like dogs." Keelie glared at the coyote.

"I've never seen a talking rat. Or a talking wolf." Sean stared at the coyote. "But that's not a natural being. I smell fae."

"You catch on quickly." A breeze blew and the coyote turned to face it, laughing as the wind ruffled his fur.

"I saw you at the park," Keelie said. "You didn't talk then."

"Nice park. Nice old tree. He's been filling me in on you." The coyote yawned, showing sharp canine teeth.

Knot bolted up beside Keelie and shook his fur off. Water droplets sprinkled her. He glared at the coyote.

"Yeah, well, that's one reason why I'm here. I've been sent to keep an eye on you, too," the coyote told Keelie.

Knot hissed.

The coyote's ears moved forward. "He's not happy. Competition for your affections, plus he thinks he should be your only guardian."

Sean laughed.

Keelie looked from Knot to the coyote. "I don't think you're my type."

"You'll grow to like me. Chicks dig boys on the wild side." The coyote wiggled his ears like he thought he was being sexy or something.

"Who sent you?"

The coyote scratched an ear with his hind foot. "Let's just say you have friends in high places."

"You're a fairy, right?"

"You got it, Einstein."

Knot hissed. "Yeow poser."

Keelie stared down at Knot. "Wow, you must really hate him. I like him better already."

Knot ignored her and washed his butt.

"I don't know what you need to plant a tree," Laurie said, as she arrived carrying a shovel, a watering can, and a bag of plant food. Her hair was disheveled and she had a smudge of dirt on her nose. "I've never been in a hardware store before, but since I'll be banned from the mall for stealing a bush, I might as well get used to roughing it."

Risa was dragging a huge bag of potting soil, and Sean hurried to help her. Risa glared at Laurie. "I told her we needed manure, but she said not in her BMW."

Laurie stared at Keelie, at the tree, at a wet Knot, and then across the creek at the coyote. She froze.

"Hello, there," the coyote said in a deeper voice. He stood up and paced back and forth.

"A coyote! Holy cow, they carry rabies. Get behind me." Laurie dropped the watering can and the bag and held the shovel like a baseball bat. "Just let him come over here. I'll bean him all the way to Wilshire Boulevard."

Keelie couldn't help but smile as it dawned on Laurie that she'd heard the coyote talk.

"Did he just speak to me?"

Keelie nodded. "He's a fairy."

"Being your friend keeps getting weirder and weirder." Laurie lowered the shovel. Risa came to stand next to her.

"The coyote spoke?" Risa stared at him. "Do all coyotes speak here?"

Keelie ignored them and stood up. "What about me? My life keeps getting weirder and weirder."

Knot grinned up at Keelie, then began washing his tail.

"Forget the coyote. Let's plant this tree." Keelie reached for the shovel.

"What are you doing with a coyote?" Laurie couldn't seem to take here eyes off of him.

"I'm Keelie's new guardian."

Knot stopped washing his tail and hissed.

"No you're not," Keelie said. Risa took the shovel from Keelie and started to dig, laughing and ignoring all of them.

Laurie looked confused. "You have two guardians. Why do you need two guardians?"

"See, she has accepted the fact that I'm a talking coyote and that I'm your guardian," the coyote said, peering at Keelie with disapproval.

"What's your name?"

"Just call me Coyote. It'll make life easier."

"Like some cartoon character?" Keelie asked.

"I like it. It's basic." Coyote smiled, his shiny sharp teeth bright in the sun.

*I'm ready to go into the earth. You're right, I like it here.* The pear tree rustled its branches.

"Grab that sack of dirt and rip it open," Risa told Laurie.

"But he'll die. Oh, you mean the potting soil, not the coyote!" Laurie laughed.

Keelie rolled her eyes, forgetting her promise to Grandmother, and helped them pull the tree out of the creek. Risa carefully arranged its roots around the deep hole and then they poured dirt into it, patting the soil, tucking him in. Laurie filled the watering can three times to make sure he had enough water, and then they were done.

The little tree sighed with relief. He reached out to Keelie with his branches and she accepted his prickly hug. He hugged Risa and Laurie, too.

*You two take care of each other.*

*We will.* Philia sent waves of green to Keelie.

Coyote hopped over the rocks, avoiding getting his feet wet.

"You did a good thing, kid, rescuing that tree. He'll have a good life here. Before, the odds were stacked against him, being in that mall and with the..." He seemed hesitant to continue.

"And with the—what?"

"Just that the mall attracts unsavory types."

Sean sauntered across the lawn. "Finished here? I cleaned out the car."

"You made Sean clean your car?" Keelie couldn't believe it.

"Duh," Laurie said. "You should see all the dirt that your pet tree left in the trunk. It was disgusting. We could have planted crops back there."

"Actually, no," Risa said. "Crops require sunlight, although you might have planted mushrooms under certain conditions."

Laurie stared at Risa as if she'd just landed her spaceship. "I'll keep that in mind for the next time we kidnap a tree."

The minute the BMW's doors opened, Knot jumped into the back seat, followed by Coyote.

"Oh no," Laurie said. "I draw the line. He smells like a dumpster."

Coyote grinned. "The best meals are those that are tossed out. People have no appreciation for aged meat." Sean made a face and Risa looked queasy.

Keelie sighed. "I'll sit next to him."

"Hope you have your shots," Laurie said.

Risa was torn between grabbing the front seat and sitting in the back, but finally the lure of Knot's company won out. She sat next to Keelie. Sean took the front passenger seat.

"You really are, um, fragrant," Keelie told Coyote. "You're also bigger than I thought you were. Can you scooch over?"

"I don't want to muss my tail. I have it just right," he said. He looked out the window. "Are we going to the forest now?"

"I certainly hope so," Sean answered fervently.

Keelie understood. She, too, couldn't wait to return to the redwoods. She'd never thought she would want to leave Los Angeles, but this wasn't her home anymore.

Sean closed his eyes and was soon fast asleep. Knot crawled up onto the rear deck and curled up. Laurie turned onto the L.A. freeway.

"I think it's faster going up the coast road." Coyote pointed his ears forward.

"The day I take driving directions from a coyote is the day I see a unicorn," Laurie declared.

"Well, we know that ain't going to happen," Keelie muttered.

"I heard that." Laurie drove on, but then took the next exit and they made their way to the coast road.

Keelie smiled. It was funny seeing Laurie arguing with a coyote.

"How about we stop at In-N-Out Burger?" Keelie hadn't had one of their burgers in a year.

"They have great dumpsters." Coyote licked his black, doglike lips.

"Eww!" Laurie and Keelie said in unison.

The coyote turned his golden eyes to Keelie. "Listen, it's not like I can drive through and ask for a burger. A coyote has got to do what a coyote has to do to get a bite in this town."

Keelie had never thought about how hard it was for a coyote, or any animal, to exist in an urban environment. She didn't want to ask him about what else he did for survival in L.A.

"I like In-N-Out dumpsters," Coyote was saying. "It's a part of life. But if you really want to show a lady a good time, you'll take her to Beverly Hills—Wolfgang Puck's garbage cans. Delicious."

"How about we drive through and buy you a real burger?" Keelie suggested. "Let's skip the dumpster diving."

"You're kidding me? Right?"

Laurie nodded. "I think it's a great idea."

Coyote laid his paw on her shoulder. "Can we get fries?"

"Sure." Laurie glanced dubiously at the paw.

Knot snorted, as if disgusted.

At the drive-through window, Keelie got another surprise. Coyote knew how to read. And now she wondered if Knot could, too, because the two animals stared intently out the window at the menu board. Knot would meow, and Coyote would say, "Large or small?"

Risa was the only one baffled by the menu. They ended up with many white bags full of food, and stopped at a sandy-beach overlook to eat. The wind was blowing steadily from the Pacific and the waves sparkled in the sun.

The elves looked healthier here, and more alert the farther they got from the city. Keelie felt better too. There was something about the concrete and steel that had sapped her energy.

After they resumed their trip north, the elves slept deeply. Keelie didn't mind letting Sean ride with Risa in back, because they were both out of it. Coyote had curled up on the floorboard, too, and Knot was in his spot on the rear deck.

The miles went by as Keelie and Laurie talked about school and plans for the future. When Coyote woke up, Keelie listened to Laurie and Coyote talk about all the cool places to hang out in Los Angeles. Coyote and Laurie had even attended some of the same concerts.

Keelie accepted this as part of her strange new reality. She wondered what it would take to really startle her.

She glanced into the back seat at Sean, who still slept. She knew he had been wiped out, but she figured he could join the conversation. She had been thinking about how their relationship had heated up. Where were they headed? They had years ahead of them. Of course, Sean was ridiculously older than she was, even though he acted as if he were her age.

But. She turned her head and studied the long blond lashes resting against his cheeks. Asleep, and so handsome. Her heart quivered as if it had been shot by Cupid. She had no idea what her own lifespan would be. Would she be like Dad and live hundreds of years, or like Mom, who never made it to forty? That was her last thought before she fell asleep.

When she woke up, something was licking her eyelids. Before she opened them, she grabbed for the psycho feline. She was going to strangle him, but he was gone before she could wrap her hands around his neck.

"You two have a very strange relationship, even for the fairy world," Coyote commented, sounding like a nature-show narrator.

Keelie bolted upright. A big orange furry butt was climbing back into the back seat for sanctuary. She leaned back. "You'd better stay up there."

Laurie looked in the rearview mirror. "Is Keelie being mean to the sweet kitty cat?" Purring filled the car.

Sean was awake, and watching her. He reached out for her hand. He turned it around and kissed her wrist. It was such an intimate touch, even in a crowded car. In that second, Keelie's world narrowed to a sharp focus on just Sean and herself. Her stomach churned like white water in a rapidly flowing river.

He held her hand for a while, as if he had to feel her pulse and know how fast her heart was beating. She felt lonely when at last he released her and she turned back to face the road.

Knot and Coyote watched them closely.

They passed the Redwood Forest park entrance just before sunrise. Coyote lifted his head. "Let me out here."

"Why?" Keelie asked. They'd already dropped Sean off at the stables, so he could check on the jousters and the horses.

"I want to investigate." Coyote lifted his nose and sniffed. "I sense a familiar magic."

"What if people see you?" Keelie was concerned about his safety in the woods. She liked Coyote. Knot meowed darkly from the backseat.

"I'll be safe. I've been living in L.A. Nobody saw me there." Coyote lowered his eyelids, as if he didn't want to reveal too much of himself.

Keelie opened the door and Coyote slipped out. "Be careful." She watched him disappear into the deep green forest.

In the festival parking lot, a hairy fairy stood in front of Sir Davey's RV. Keelie relaxed and smiled. It was Sir Davey, except he was wearing gauzy blue fairy wings that twinkled in the sunlight. He motioned for Laurie and Keelie to come inside. Risa dragged along in their wake, Knot strolling beside her.

Sir Davey held open the door of the luxurious motorhome. "Ladies!"

Keelie pointed toward his back. "Very fashionable!"

He shrugged. "I just got back from the costume shop. If you ask me, I think they bought them at the local discount store."

Risa grimaced as she joined them and studied Sir Davey. "Your wings are prettier than mine. That's not fair. I'm going to register a complaint."

"Talk to the costume shop," Sir Davey suggested.

"I will. If I'd known that I had to go back there, I would've gotten out with Sean." Risa twirled on her heels, but then pirouetted around like she'd suddenly remembered something. She looked down at Knot, who was enjoying the fresh morning air. "Are you coming?"

He bolted inside the RV.

Shaking her head, Risa stomped off in the direction of the Globe theater.

Sir Davey arched an eyebrow and smiled mischievously. "Problems with the lovebirds?"

"I think the feelings only run one way." Keelie gazed in the direction of the RV door. "In fact, I'm worried about Knot. He seems stressed."

"How so?" Sir Davey asked.

"His fur is all mussed up. He's not being himself." How did you describe a cat not acting like a cat? It could be that Knot was stressed out about Coyote showing up, too.

"Maybe he needs a nap, and being away from Risa will do him a world of good. As long as he sticks by you and does his guardian duties, then I say he'll be fine," Sir Davey said. "Some days we handle stress better than others."

Laurie walked up the RV steps, yawning. "That nap idea sounds great." She yawned again. Sir Davey and Keelie followed her.

"Your grandmother wanted you two to stay around here, rather than go to the elf village. She wants you to help with some tree shepherd stuff while she's busy with the play. Her performance as Queen Elizabeth has impressed everyone."

Keelie rolled her eyes. Great, her grandmother would win a Ren Faire Oscar for her supposed acting ability. What everyone didn't know was that she was like that all the time. A grump. An imperious grump.

As she shoved her hands into her pockets, Keelie felt the parchment. She pulled it out and looked at it.

"What can you tell me about this, Sir Davey? It was inside my mother's safe at our old house, but everything else was missing, and there was some kind of spell on it."

Frowning, Sir Davey took it. He held it up to the light. "It's not parchment." He sniffed it and nibbled an edge. "Not vellum, either. It doesn't look like anything I've ever seen."

He waved his hand over it, closing his eyes and making a strange humming sound. Keelie hadn't seen him do this before. Maybe it was a new way of doing a magical analysis. Finally, Sir Davey opened his eyes. He shook his head. "If it's associated with magic, it's not Earth-based magic. If it's fairy magic, then stay away from it, Keelie lass. You've messed with that once, and it changed you."

Keelie took the scrap of paper from him. She rubbed it between her fingers, remembering the fairy spell that had briefly appeared when she first held it. It wouldn't take a giant mental leap to think that Mom had used fairy magic, given her fairy blood. Of course, anyone who'd known Mom would have denied it. Keelie remembered how her mom had tried to scour anything magical or fantastical from their lives. The only toy that Keelie ever really played with were her My Little Ponies. The beautiful wooden toys that Dad sent her were special treats; Mom always gave Keelie nonfiction books and toys that had educational value.

Keelie studied the paper scrap. She had to know what this was from. The more she learned about her Mom, the less she really knew her.

"Why don't you call your father?" Sir Davey suggested. "The cell phone is on my dresser. Let him know what you've been up to. I need to run to Admin," he added. "They've received a delivery from my brother in Arkansas."

Keelie went back to the bedroom to get the phone, and was not surprised to see the movie *The Two Towers* playing on the big-screen television mounted at the foot of Sir Davey's bed. Saruman was commanding the Uruk-hai to destroy the humans. Something about Saruman reminded Keelie of Bloodroot. It could possibly be that the tree was a lot like a wizard. She took the iPhone from its charging cradle and went back to the front of the RV.

Laurie had crawled onto the couch and pulled a quilt over herself. Knot sat in the window looking out into the parking lot. She knew something wasn't right about him.

"Are you waiting for your girlfriend?" she asked.

He didn't turn around. She reached out to pet him and he moved his head so she couldn't touch him.

"Are you mad about Coyote?"

Knot wouldn't look at her.

"You're my guardian. He's just a friend." She didn't like having Knot upset with her.

His tail twitched angrily.

"Maybe you could use the extra help." Keelie had to be honest with him. "I feel like you've been preoccupied ever since we came here. And I don't trust the redwoods."

Knot turned and stared at her. Keelie reached out to pet him and he snagged her arms with his claws.

Keelie disengaged them and rubbed her arms. "Good. Glad to know we have an understanding. If you're stressed, I can make you some catnip tea."

Knot gave a slight nod.

"Okay, I'll make you a cup." She put water on to boil and rooted in the cupboards until she found a baggie of catnip. She wanted to hear Dad's voice, but first, she'd call the person who knew the most about fairy magic.

# fifteen

Keelie reached for the iPhone and tapped in a number.

"Hello." Zabrina's chirpy voice warmed Keelie up like a ray of sunshine. She missed her friend and her home in the Dread Forest—and she never used to think that was possible. Keelie even sort of missed her lore lessons with Elianard. She thought of the Compendium, which she'd left at Heartwood. She'd go get it this afternoon and study. The lore lessons were proving to be very useful.

At least in the Dread Forest, she'd had her routine. She had a rhythm to her days and knew her place. Here, everything had changed. California was no longer the home she'd held precious. The memories of growing up would always be with her, but L.A. wasn't home anymore. Her childhood home was in her heart.

"Hey. It's Keelie."

"Hey, Keelie. How are the redwoods? Are they full of good energy vibes?"

"Well, they're sending vibes. Their tree shepherd is missing. They're a different sort, these trees."

"How different?" Zabrina's voice held concern. "What kind of trouble are you in? Missing tree shepherd—it sounds like you're starring in one of those detective shows where the detective goes to a different location to solve a mystery. Except in your case, it's with trees."

"I need your help."

"See, you're the detective calling the friend to check on some evidence for her," Zabrina said.

"You need to stop watching cable television." Keelie filled a tea ball with catnip leaves. Knot appeared on the counter, nostrils flared.

"Hey, I just got that satellite dish and I'm catching up. So, what do you need help with?"

"I have this piece of vellum-looking paper that was in my mom's house, and it looks like it came from a lore book. But Mom wouldn't have owned anything like that. Anyway, I thought about your glasses. Maybe if you looked at it, you could tell me more about it."

Zabrina had a pair of enchanted glasses that allowed the user to see through glamour. Useful when dealing with fairies. Keelie dipped the tea ball into a mug and poured boiling water over it while Knot flopped over onto the baggie of catnip and writhed. She yanked the bag out from under his furry bottom and put it back in the cupboard.

Zabrina hummed a bit. "Yes, I can. But there's a problem."

"What?"

"I can't see over the phone."

"Oh!" Keelie felt her cheeks get hot. She should have thought of that.

"Mail it to me, and I'll let you know. Or wait until you get back and show it to me."

"Would it work if I emailed you a picture of it?" Keelie didn't want to wait for the mail.

"No. Then I would just be looking at an image, not the real thing. Can you send it by overnight express?"

"I can. Be on the lookout for it."

"Bye, kiddo." Zabrina hung up.

Keelie really missed her. It felt like clouds had come back, and a chill permeated the air. She wondered if her watcher tree was hanging around nearby. She was going to have to corner it and get some information.

Knot licked up hot tea while surveying the parking lot. His ears twitched like little furry radar antennae.

"I'm going to Heartwood to grab the Compendium. Want to come?"

Knot looked interested. Keelie glanced at Laurie, who was still snoozing, and let herself out quietly. The Compendium was just where she had left it. She'd taken a chance leaving it like that, because it was one of the elves' treasures and she'd put it under the counter where anyone could have snatched it.

Keelie opened it up randomly on top of the counter, and glanced down at the chapter titled "Goblins." Interesting, since she'd encountered a Red Cap. She read,

> *Goblins are an Under-the-Hill species that live in urban areas, although they are also known to live in forests. Large populations live in Seattle, Washington; London, England; the Northwest Territories; and Moscow, Russia.*

Unusual locations. At least L.A. wasn't polluted with them.

> *Goblins are practitioners of dark magic, and using their blood in spells and charms guarantees a grim outcome. A strong charm must be used to deter these foes of elves.*
>
> *Suggested charms:*
>
> *Air charm—Harnessing the powers of the wind can create a thunderstorm; thus, an elf can call lightning down upon the goblin.*
>
> *Spirit Charm—Binding the goblin's spirit to a place, object, or sometimes a live container will keep him locked in this place until he is freed. One must be careful to remember where one has bound the goblin. A goblin's spirit can taint a location, an object, or its living container the longer it stays in that location. A goblin's death can taint a locale even more strongly.*
>
> *Hay-fever Charm—Goblins suffer from hay fever,*

*and recreating the conditions of newly mown grass will immobilize your enemy as they sneeze their way to defeat.*

Hay fever? So Mr. Heidelman was keeping the goblins away all that time with his midnight mowing. Who knew?

Knot placed his paw on Keelie's leg and meowed.

"Okay, buddy, let's see if that calm charm will help you."

She turned to the page and said the magic words, visualizing a calm beach with palm trees as she patted the cat on the head.

Knot eye's widened, and Keelie definitely smelled the scent of suntan oil. Knot purred and slunk away, kitty muscles relaxed, his lofty tail held high.

Keelie liked the Compendium. The goblin stuff was creepy, though. She wanted to think they didn't exist. She pushed all thoughts of goblins to the back of her mind. Anyway, she'd just avoid Seattle. No big deal.

Gobblers.

The word came back to her like a wave of cold Arctic air. It chilled her all the way to her bones. The little mall tree had said the gobblers had told him fairies were bad. Could his gobblers be goblins?

And the little tree lived in L.A., not too far from her old house. She shivered.

Keelie grabbed her charm book and the piece of parchment. She was going to have to mail this to Zabrina as soon as possible. She slammed the book shut and ran back to the RV.

"Laurie, wake up!" She shook her friend. "I need you to take me to Juliet City. I need to go the post office."

"What?" Laurie opened her eyes.

"I need for you to drive me."

Laurie reached into the pockets of her jeans and placed the BMW keys in Keelie's hand. "You drive. I was having the best dream. Orlando Bloom was fighting for me."

"That's Sir Davey's TV," Keelie laughed. The sounds of the elves and the Uruk-hai facing off in battle still came from the bedroom. Keelie went and watched for a second before turning off the TV, wondering what real goblins looked like.

There were no problems driving to and from Juliet City. Keelie enjoyed the sense of freedom driving gave her. With the parchment on its way to Zabrina, Keelie felt satisfied. Back at the festival grounds, she parked next to Sir Davey's camper.

Sean was leaning against the RV, his hands crossed over his chest. "Where did you go?"

"To Juliet City. Why? What's wrong?"

"Nothing. I was worried about you," Sean said. "Laurie said you asked for her car. With Norzan missing, I don't feel comfortable with you going out by yourself. Did you take Knot?"

"No. I put a calm charm on him."

"A calm charm?"

"Yeah. He's stressed out with Risa stalking him all hours."

Sean snorted. "He's a big boy; he can handle her. Well, how do you feel about going back to town and having an early dinner with me? I thought you might like to walk along the beach?" He raised an eyebrow. "I mean, we could be alone."

Keelie smiled. "Are you sure?"

"We might get a whole twenty minutes together. I'm hoping for an hour."

"Dare we hope we have that long?" Keelie asked with a smile. "We're always being interrupted."

Sean nodded "Yeah. Well, I'm in charge of the jousting company, and you're a tree shepherd—both jobs are twenty-four-hour gigs. We have responsibilities ..."

They exchanged understanding looks, and Keelie felt something connect between them liked they'd never experienced before.

"Do you ever get tired and want to run away?" Keelie asked. "Sometimes it's all so overwhelming, and I need to be alone."

"We can't forsake those that depend on us." Sean took her hand. "We've been chosen. Me to lead the jousters and uphold traditions, and you have the forests to help and to heal. What we do makes a difference." He really understood.

"I know, but sometimes I just want to escape and be normal."

"I understand. You want to go and hide, and let someone else take care of the problems." Sean nodded. "I know all too well what you mean. You always have to be there, and sometimes you feel lost in the role assigned to you by our people."

Keelie's stomach became light. She leaned her hand against

the RV to steady herself. She looked directly at Sean. "You said 'our people.'"

"Yes. You're part of the Dread Forest elves. Our people."

"I don't think anyone has ever said that to me." Keelie felt warm but confused. Sean was thinking of her as an elf.

"I thought you knew you were one of us." He grimaced. "Keelie, I know there have been difficulties, but know this— the jousters and I will do whatever we have to do to protect you. You are one of us."

She rubbed her round ear. "Sean, what about Risa? The other elves? They don't think of me as one of them."

Sean grabbed Keelie's upper arms and turned her around, tilting her face up with his hand. "What does it matter what other elves or people think? You have to be true to yourself, Keelie, and you are. That's one of the things I…"

He stopped. She held her breath.

He moved strands of hair behind her pointed ear, then behind her round ear. "Did you know that Etilafael sings your praises at the Council meetings?"

Keelie shook her head. "Still, Risa and some of the other elves will never accept me."

"Why is it so important to have elves like Risa accept you? You can't please every elf in the forest. Anyway, Risa has issues. She's still working out the fact that we're not going to be married. Elves don't handle rejection very well. Remember the love potion?"

"Knot sure does."

Sean arched an eyebrow. "Do you know I'm jealous of that cat?"

"You're jealous of Knot?" Keelie couldn't believe what she was hearing. "Why? He's an obnoxious fairy cat."

"Because he's with you all the time."

"He's a pain in the butt."

"Nevertheless, he's with you all the time." Sean threw his hands up. "It's hard to leave you when I have to lead my men, or you have to go and be a tree shepherd."

"What are we going to do?" Keelie leaned against him.

"We cherish the moments we do have, and we begin now. Let's go." Sean held out his elbow, and Keelie slipped her hand into the crook of his arm.

They ate in town, at the Capulet Café, and afterwards walked along the beach. At first Keelie was reluctant, seeing the large shapes of the sea lions that called this stretch of beach home. Sean assured her that it was safe. He'd cast a charm that made them invisible to the beasts. Keelie should have known, since she'd smelled the cinnamon that signaled elven magic.

She was amazed at how large the sea lions were. They reminded her of Knot when he lounged out in the sun, except the sea lions didn't have fluffy kitty fur. They had to be anywhere from six to eight feet long, and weighed hundreds of pounds. They brayed and went back to sleep on the beach as Keelie and Sean passed.

As they walked up the hill back toward the outer edge of the forest, Keelie didn't want to go home. She and Sean had never talked to one another as much as they had today. They had opened up to each other.

As if sensing her thoughts, Sean wrapped his arms

around her and lowered his lips to hers. He kissed her softly. When their lips parted, Keelie knew that she wanted it to be like this all the time.

Sean trailed soft kisses along her cheek until his lips rested against her lips again. Then he whispered, "Let's keep walking. Someone is watching us. Don't look."

Behind them, the ocean surged and crashed on the rocks that bordered the beach. She couldn't hear anyone around them, but didn't want to ask questions out loud. She sensed the magical dark spots in the forest, the same murky energy she'd felt when she'd arrived here.

They hiked up a path that led to the cliff. A small green energy filled her mind. She recognized it as the hemlock. It was suddenly overpowered by an all-encompassing wave of green magic. The redwoods. The green was streaked with darkness, and fear washed over Keelie. This wasn't the Dread; this was a cannibalistic entity that overpowered those it came in contact with.

Before the fear could overtake her mind, Keelie immediately thought about the calm charm she'd used on Laurie and Knot. She pulled on a thread of Earth magic and from deep within, her fairy magic. Creating a shield, she pushed the fear out of her mind. She would have to say thank you to Elianard for the Compendium.

Sean steadied her when she stumbled.

"Are you okay?"

"I feel the dark magic. It's very strong. We need to get out of here."

A loud, discordant jangle filled the air. Keelie had heard

the sound before. Sean pressed his finger against his lips, and they ducked behind the spreading rhododendrons.

Keelie caught a glimpse of shiny red among the tree trunks. Sticks crackled loudly on the ground. Sean motioned for Keelie to get lower in the bushes.

Images from serial killer movies featuring teenagers walking alone in the woods flashed in Keelie's mind. Suddenly, she didn't want to be here.

There was a sharp snap as something or someone stepped on a stick.

The tension in the air was thick. They could see Peascod step out into a clearing, his bells jangling horridly.

"I don't like him," she whispered to Sean.

Peascod was holding a compass and a book in his hand, searching for something. He mumbled to himself and his hat jangled as he moved east away from the beach.

Keelie was about to rise when Sean put a hand on her shoulder and shook his head. He pointed. Tavyn now stepped into view. He turned and peered about the path, then lifted his head like he was sniffing the air for his prey. He must have found Peascod's scent because he too turned east, away from the beach.

This was all so weird. Why was Tavyn following Peascod? The redwood elves must be suspicious of the jester. Keelie wondered if he had anything to do with Viran's disappearance.

Moments later, Coyote trotted into view.

Peascod, Tavyn, then Coyote. What was going on here?

Coyote's nose was low to the ground. He stopped, then

lifted his gaze to Keelie's. Their eyes locked. He gestured with his head back to the south, back toward a stand of hemlocks. Keelie detected that something wasn't right in that direction—somebody needed help.

Then Coyote darted after his quarry, Tavyn and Peascod.

"Come on, Sean. We need to go this way." She started moving in the direction Coyote had signaled.

"No, you need to get back to Sir Davey's. I'm going to follow them." Sean's eyes were glued to the coyote.

Keelie knew just where to go. It was as if there was a homing signal in her brain. "Coyote will follow them, but he signaled that we're needed over there." She pointed to the large group of hemlocks and started walking toward them.

Sean kept pace beside her. "I still think we need to call for help. You shouldn't be out here if the shepherds are in trouble."

Keelie opened herself to the hemlocks. *What is wrong?*

A small weak voice answered. *Hurry, the shepherd needs you. He tried to help us.*

The shepherd! Viran! Keelie broke into a run, leaping over fallen limbs and skidding in the wet soil, Sean at her heels. She saw the body and dropped to her knees. Their search was over.

But when she turned over the still body, she was staring into the unconscious face of Norzan, the Northwoods Shepherd. His skin was the sickly green of chlorophyll poisoning.

"He looks moldy," Sean said. "Is he sick?"

"No, it's a spell. We've got to get him back to the elven camp."

Sean lifted Norzan as if he weighed no more than a teacup. Keelie followed, fighting not to look over her shoulder as they hurried out of the forest.

Inside Kalix's tree house, the unconscious form of Norzan rested on the couch. Grandmother, in her Queen Elizabeth costume, stood in a corner of the room and spoke with Kalix in whispered tones. Keelie sat at the oaken table as Sariela brought them tea. Sean was looking around, taking in every detail.

Keelie was worried about Norzan. The Redwood Forest's elven healer hadn't been able to awaken him.

The windows blew open as a cloud rushed into the living room. Sean pushed his chair back, ready to protect Keelie. Somebody's adrenaline was pumping overtime. Keelie reached out and grabbed him by the wrist. "It's a tree spirit."

"A tree?" Then understanding filled Sean's face. He nodded and sat back down. They watched as Bella Matera materialized in her wraithlike tree form.

"What has happened?" Bella Matera floated over to Kalix and Grandmother.

"We do not know." Kalix bowed to Bella Matera.

"I will take him with me, and I will have Bloodroot see what he can do to awaken the Northwoods shepherd."

Fear for Norzan's well-being and distrust of Bloodroot filled Keelie, but Kalix nodded.

Grandmother stepped forward, her face was as hard as stone as she faced Bella Matera. "He needs to return to his home forest as soon as possible. There, among the trees that know and love him, will he be restored."

*Go Grandmother.*

Bella Matera grew until the top of her branchlike "hair" vanished through the ceiling. Her voice deepened into a loud thrum that they could feel in their bones. "Bloodroot will heal him. Norzan goes with me."

Grandmother lifted her head and glowered, fiery determination flashing in her eyes. "The Northwoods elves and healer are on their way. They will be here in two hours."

Bella Matera's eyes darkened. "Who gave you authority? We are the Ancients, and we are the ones who determine what happens and does not happen in our forest."

"Am I hearing tree speak?" Sean asked Keelie, his voice low and excited.

"No, these trees can actually talk out loud."

Sean stared at Bella Matera's ghostly form and a frown slowly settled on his features. He held Keelie's hand tightly in his.

"I am a tree shepherd, and even the Ancients mind the accords of the Great Sylvus," Grandmother was saying.

Bella Matera lowered her eyes, away from Grandmother's blistering gaze. She bowed her airy branches. "Then so be it."

Relieved that Norzan was going to the Northwoods, Keelie sat back in her chair and picked up her tea, holding it with trembling fingers. It had been so close. She was sure that if Norzan had left with Bella Matera, he would not have returned.

Bella Matera drifted toward the window, but turned suddenly to face Grandmother. "Lady Keliatiel, Norzan's death will be on your head. The Ancients will ask for blood price." She vanished in a dramatic swirl.

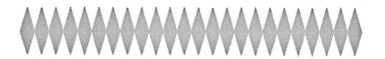

# sixteen

Kalix turned around, anger lining his face. "How dare you disrespect the wishes of Bella Matera. You must do as she says. It is our way."

"It may be your tradition to follow the trees," Grandmother retorted, "but when the trees no longer obey the rules of the Great Sylvus, then it's time a shepherd guided them back to the path. I will speak no more of it."

Kalix turned to Sariela. "We must call a Council meeting immediately."

Sariela nodded stiffly, glancing at Grandmother with fear on her face.

Grandmother slumped into a chair the minute the two elves stormed from the room. She seemed every one of her hundreds of years.

"Are you going to be okay?" Keelie kneeled at her grandmother's feet. "I'm so proud of the way you stood up to them, and to Bella Matera."

A faint smile brought life to Lady Keliatiel's face. She put a hand on Keelie's head. "I just beat you to it, and I'm more powerful than you. I could see your outrage at their suggestion to move Norzan into the forest."

"What can I do to help you now?"

Grandmother opened her eyes. "I have to go to the Globe. We're doing a special fundraiser performance tonight."

"They'll find someone else to play Queen Elizabeth."

The look Grandmother shot Keelie would have drilled holes in steel. "They will not. I'll be there."

Keelie turned to Sean. "Will you walk with us to the theater?"

Sean nodded. "I'm glad you invited me, because I would have come anyway." He looked worried, although his tone was light.

Grandmother looked at him. "Keelie cannot go. She must remain here to guard Norzan until the healer arrives." She glanced toward the doorway. "I'm not sure he'll be safe, otherwise."

"I'll stay as well, then," Sean added quickly. He winked at Keelie, but went to the doorway and casually looked outside.

"I trust you to behave with decorum." Grandmother looked toward Sean.

"Of course." Keelie smiled and put her hand on Grandmother's shoulder. "You're the Queen, right?"

Grandmother's eyebrows rose. "Perhaps Knot is the wrong guardian for you. You seem to be picking up his ways." She smiled and stood up, wincing. "Perhaps I need some of this coffee you speak of with such fondness."

"Radical." Keelie smiled. "You might never be the same. But be careful, okay?"

"I shall."

Keelie stood by the window and watched Grandmother walk through the forest below. The faint sounds of a harp wafted by. Sean came up behind her and they stood together silently.

"I'm getting used to being alone with you." Keelie leaned back against him. "Could you live way up in the trees like this?"

"I'm sure it would be fine if you grew up with it." He put his arms around her waist. Keelie loved the feel of his strong arms next to hers and his warm body behind her. He smelled spicy, but more like soap than the forest. "Of course, I'll be happy anywhere you are." He spoke into her ear, making her shiver.

Keelie turned her face toward him, hoping he'd get the hint. He did. His green eyes darkened and he touched his nose to hers, then kissed her.

Oh, god. Keelie was going to die of bliss. All thoughts of tree spirits and missing shepherds vanished. She turned in his arms and kissed him again, snaking her arms around his neck. His hands pressed the small of her back, squeezing her closer.

"Let's find a way to be alone more," he whispered. "We've managed fine so far today, despite our responsibilities."

"I'll make it a priority. You'll be number one on my agenda." She stopped talking as he nibbled her jaw.

Someone rapped on the door three times.

Sean swore, and Keelie swatted him on the shoulder. "And what's with the 'you'll be happy anywhere I am?' Sappy, but good try."

He groaned. "Was that an awful line?"

The knocking started again, louder this time. Keelie reached up to smooth Sean's mussed blond hair. "There. You look better now."

He straightened his tunic and cautiously opened the door. Three tall elves bowed to him. "We are the healers of the Northwoods, come for Norzan," one said.

Keelie sighed. Her romantic moment was over. "Welcome, healers," she said. "I'll show you where Norzan lies." How did they travel, cross-country sap?

Sean stepped aside and, as Keelie passed him, he swept a hand down her shoulders in a delicious caress, a promise of more to come.

The Northwoods elves seemed familiar. Keelie walked down the hall ahead of them and saw Kalix duck back from a doorway.

The healers surrounded Norzan, and then one turned to glare at Keelie. "You may wait on the forest floor."

"Yeah, sure."

Sean grinned. "Why the frown, Keelie? We've been ordered to wait alone, together. Doesn't sound so bad to me."

"Come to think of it, you are absolutely correct." Keelie linked her arm through his. "Let's go."

They were interrupted again an hour later, when Wena the tree gave a great groan. The wicker gurney bearing Norzan's still form appeared near them at the base of the tree, flanked by two of the healers. Wena's spirit was suddenly there too, leaning against the rough bark of her physical form. She looked exhausted.

"Too many traveling the sap," Wena gasped to them.

"Yeah, it's sort of a hotel these days, isn't it?" Keelie sympathized. "I'm sorry, Wena."

Wena waved them away with one spectral, stick-fingered hand.

The tree creaked as the third healer appeared. The female healer gave Keelie a curious look. "You are the half human, Keliel?" Her tone was snooty, as if she'd been looking for a lioness and found a possum.

Keelie inclined her head regally, as she'd seen her grandmother do. "I am Keliel, Daughter of Zekeliel of the Dread Forest." *Take that, blondie.*

The elf woman sneered, and Keelie suddenly knew why these elves seemed familiar. "Are you kin to Elia, daughter of Elianard?"

The woman's eyes darkened. "She is kin."

Oh yeah, they'd probably heard that their precious elf

princess had married a unicorn. Uncle Dariel, that is, when he took a human form.

"Dear Auntie Elia." Keelie didn't even pretend to hide the fake fondness. Even though Elia had somewhat redeemed herself, Keelie could never consider her a true friend. She was wandering around the Dread Forest right now, making everyone fetch things for her just because she was the first elf woman in a generation to get pregnant. And elf generations were three times as long as human ones.

The Northwoods elf woman sputtered, probably trying to think of something mean to say, but then one of the others called her and she hurried to catch up with them.

"Gee, she didn't even say goodbye." Keelie waved cheerily.

"Let's see how they got here." Sean's hand closed around Keelie's. Ahead, flashes of silver marked the movement of the first two healers as they made their way out of the forest, Norzan between them. The woman healer walked behind, holding a glowing light ball aloft and glancing back at them every third step.

In the clearing by the road, a helicopter waited, rotors whirring almost silently.

"Is it electric?" Keelie thought electric helicopters were just for toys. "I didn't think elves were big on motors."

"I don't know much about them myself." Sean's arm draped over her shoulder as they watched Norzan get loaded into the back. The female healer turned and walked back toward them.

"Our thanks to Lady Keliatiel for calling us. It will take Lord Norzan long to heal, but he will recover. We shall see you at the Quicksilver Faire." She bowed, all business, and Keelie and Sean returned the bow.

Keelie wasn't so sure she wanted to attend the Quicksilver Faire. The snooty factor promised to be high there.

A loud "huzzah" echoed from the direction of the Globe.

"I wonder if the play has started," Keelie said.

"No telling." Sean put his arm back on her shoulder, pulling her close to him. "Let's watch Norzan off and then we can head that way."

"Sounds like a plan."

If the healer elves thought it strange that the daughter of the Dread Forest's tree shepherd considered kissing her bodyguard's face to be an important part of their farewell, she'd hear about it later. Right now, she enjoyed it too much to care.

Sean and Keelie watched the helicopter vanish above the trees, then cut through the festival grounds to the Globe. They passed Heartwood and Tudor Turnings.

Scott appeared at his doorway. "Are you heading toward the Globe?" He fell into step with them. Sean didn't seem pleased that Scott had joined them.

"I asked Laurie to join me for a late dessert and coffee after the show," Scott said. "Want to join us?"

"We might." Sean dropped his arm over her shoulder. Keelie smiled at the possessive move. "We have to check on Keelie's grandmother first."

Laurie met up with them as they passed Sir Davey's RV in the parking area. A smile erupted on Scott's face when he saw Laurie. "Guess what? Sean and Keelie are coming, too."

Laurie grinned. "Great. It's a double date." Her eyes widened when she got a good look at Keelie. She pretended to straighten her hair.

Had she gone nuts? Then Keelie realized that Laurie was signaling that Keelie's hair was messed up. She reached up and quickly finger-combed it down. She wondered what the Northwoods elves thought of her 'do.

Keelie saw Coyote standing at the edge of the forest, camouflaged by the trees. He lifted his head, then, nose to the ground, took off in the direction of the festival. She hoped he stayed out of garbage cans and out of trouble.

The Globe was packed full of jostling, good-natured theater-goers. Luckily, the fundraiser show was running a bit late, and the ticket takers recognized them and waved them inside. Sean led the way, his height letting him see above the milling crowd in front of the stage.

As in the real Globe Theater, there were no chairs in the area directly in front of the stage. The groundlings had to stand, just as they had in London hundreds of years ago. Several of Sean's jousters were guarding the backstage entrances.

Keelie wondered how her grandmother was doing. "I'm going to check on the old lady," she told the others. She chinned herself up onto the stage and walked toward the doorways in the back.

"Please, milady, actors only back here." A wide woman opened her arms to shoo Keelie away. Keelie ducked under her arm, scooted through the doorway, and froze. The carefully aged look of the Globe was all for show. Back here, walls were made of raw lumber and a water cooler hummed in a corner. Actors and actresses, some dressed, some half-dressed, buzzed around, concentrating on the upcoming performance. A few muttered lines to themselves like crazy people.

A girl with long, flowing golden hair leaned against the doorway, watching the action. She smiled at Keelie.

"Excuse me," Keelie asked. "Have you seen a lady dressed as Queen Elizabeth? She's my grandmother."

The girl laughed. "I certainly have." Her voice was startlingly deep. She pointed a thick finger toward the left, and Keelie realized that she was a he. "Through there."

Keelie rushed in that direction, anxious to get away from the confusing place. Why did Grandmother like this so much? A discordant feeling rippled through her body.

She heard a familiar jangle and turned, searching for the source of the sound. Peascod. She expected to see him in his familiar red and green suit. She didn't see him, but she sensed him nearby. Keelie shivered, but kept moving. She didn't want to meet him in a dark hall tonight.

A low murmur of voices came from behind a door. A religious service? A poetry reading? She opened the door carefully, not wanting to make noise. Inside, a circle of folding wooden chairs, each holding a costumed courtier, surrounded a small armchair upon which sat Grandmother, sumptuously costumed as Queen Elizabeth. She wore a white and crimson gown, and her face was painted white in a style Keelie knew had been popular in Shakespeare's time.

A woman in street clothes stood behind Grandmother, gluing pearls onto her tightly curled red wig.

Grandmother lowered the jeweled hand mirror she was using to observe the woman's work. "Keliel, my dear, you should not be back here."

Keelie wanted to tell her about the Northwoods healers, and about Peascod and Tavyn in the woods, and also ask what she thought of Kalix and Sariela's strange behavior, but she couldn't do it in front of all these people. Suddenly uncertain, Keelie backed up a step. "I wanted to be sure you were okay. I'm out front with Sean and Scott and Laurie."

Grandmother made a motion as if to dismiss her. The courtiers looked at her curiously, but Grandmother did not introduce her. Embarrassed, Keelie closed the door gently behind her and pushed her way toward the stage.

The boy in the long golden wig smirked as she went by. "Granny didn't care to see you?"

Keelie ignored him. Sure, Grandmother's indifference stung a little, but she knew her better now. Grandmother was unpredictable. And she was glad for her—Grandmother was probably having more fun than she'd had in centuries.

Laurie waved to her from one of the upper balconies. Sean appeared a moment later with bottles of water, and the four of them sat packed together tightly on the bench seats.

Sean and Scott talked to a nearby group of vendors. Sean quickly introduced her to everyone, and they discussed taxes, inventory, foot traffic, and whose food shop was likeliest to induce food poisoning. Even Laurie joined in. After a while Keelie felt almost normal again.

By now the Globe was bursting with people. They hung over the balconies and swarmed in front of the stage, holding drinks dispensed from a bar by the tall, splintery doors. Keelie leaned forward in her seat, holding onto the round timber banister (yellow pine from Alabama). From here she could see the front doorway, where people were still piling in, trying to squeeze through the crowd to find a good vantage point.

"I wonder if it was like this in Shakespeare's day," Keelie mused aloud.

"Before my time," Sean said, and he was serious.

"It was much like this," the man to her left confided. He wore a University of California-Berkeley T-shirt. "I come every year and bring my students."

A fanfare played on long golden trumpets, and then Master Oswald introduced the festival court. The crowd went wild as the lords and ladies of the court sashayed to their places, dressed in colorful silks and satins and wearing bejeweled hats. Peascod, playing the royal jester, followed. He seemed to look straight at her, then pointed his jester's scepter at her.

The biggest cheers were for Grandmother, who waved solemnly to the crowd, her red, pearl-sewn wig now sporting a tiny diamond crown. She looked pretty authentic, Keelie had to admit.

Grandmother held up her gloved hands and the crowd fell silent. All faces turned to her. "Play on, good folk," she pronounced, and took her seat to wild applause. A cannon shot from the top of the wall, the boom rattling the whole theater, and then the actor playing Theseus stepped onto the stage, arms spread wide and face uplifted. Everyone settled in for a night of fun.

Back in the tree house later that night, Keelie didn't have to fight to stay awake. The coffee they'd had at the Capulet Café had taken care of that. But then she'd studied the Compendium, and now she was yawning over her cup of tea. The elves could get rich selling sample chapters of the charm book as sleep aids. But Keelie had to stay awake, in order to bring Laurie up the sap when she returned. Scott had taken her for a long walk on the road that bordered the moonlit beach.

Grandmother was missing in action as well—probably carrying on with the rowdy players. It made Keelie twitch to think about it.

Keelie glanced up at the clock. It was 1:00 in the morning. She sat up, suddenly worried. Despite their active social lives, Laurie and Grandmother shouldn't be out this late. She glanced over at Knot, who slept on his back with his paws up in the air. His tail twitched in his sleep, and he meowed angrily. Maybe he was dreaming about catching *feithid daoine*. Keelie closed the Compendium. She didn't want to read about spells and charms, although the book really had some doozies. She wanted to sneak outside and be with Sean. The memory of his kisses trailing down her neck still lingered.

On the opposite side of the room, Risa lifted her eyes and scowled. She was reading a worn, leatherbound book. It looked like one of Elianard's lore books.

Keelie glanced toward the door.

Risa closed her book. "Don't even think about it."

"What?"

"It's written all over your face. You want to go down there and snuggle up to our favorite elf guy."

"I thought you didn't want him anymore?"

"I love Knot, but Sean and I were meant to be together. It's an elf thing." Her eyes rested on the cat's sleeping form.

"Like I'm not an elf."

Risa rolled her eyes. "You're half elf. I'll give you that. But you and Sean are too different, and it won't last. When he's tired of you, or you get old and ugly real fast because you're half human, then I'll be waiting." Risa ran a hand over her chest to emphasize her point. "I'll still be firm while you'll be all saggy. Patience is an elven virtue that you obviously don't have."

Risa had given voice to one of Keelie's worries: would she age faster than Sean? She wasn't going to let Risa get the best of her.

"Who knows. Maybe I won't age at all. Then what are you going to do? Dig in your garden and talk to your plants and collect cats?"

"Collect cats? There is only one cat I want, and we both know who it is." Risa's face became all aglow with adoration as her gaze fell upon Knot. "You took Sean from me, so I'll take Knot from you."

Knot yawned and stretched his paws, sinking his claws into Keelie's thighs.

Risa sighed and her eyes misted over. "Isn't he an amazing specimen of feline elegance? Angeliello, the famous elven sculptor, couldn't have captured Knot's grace and beauty in marble. I don't think any artist would be able to do justice to Knot."

Keelie wrinkled her nose at Risa's obsession over Knot. "What did you put in that love potion?"

Risa eased back in her chair and arched an eyebrow. "Why?"

"Because you need to find an antidote, and you need to find it real fast."

Risa picked at the dress material on her knee. "There is no antidote. I've been searching for one."

"What? You were going to give Sean a potion without an antidote? That's cruel and stupid. Not to mention selfish."

Risa lifted her head, her green eyes bright with tears. She rose and walked over to the fireplace. "I didn't give it to him, so it all worked out in the end. I'm the one being punished. It is my heart that is breaking. My love for Knot will forever be unrequited and I will have to endure my days upon this earth alone, knowing he is with you."

Knot sat up, twisted, and began washing his butt. Risa looked over and placed her fist in her mouth to stop her cry.

The doorknob turned. Keelie's heart raced as Grandmother stepped in. She had bright rosy cheeks and her eyes were glowing a deep green. "Why are the jousters camped at the base of the tree?"

"Sean thought I needed extra protection. There was something following us in the woods earlier tonight." Keelie spoke impatiently, anxious to find out if Grandmother had noticed anything off about the redwood elves.

"You should not be alone in these woods. We have already seen what great danger there is here."

Keelie lowered her head and sighed. "I'm never alone in the woods." She looked toward Knot.

Grandmother shook her head. "I'm glad Sean was with you."

Keelie was glad of that, too. "You know, we saw Peascod walking with Tavyn."

"There is no law governing walks in the woods," Grandmother said. "But that is indeed a curious thing. Peascod is a player, not an elf. What was he doing in the forest?"

Risa wrinkled her nose. "Peascod never changes his costume."

"What's that got to do with anything?" Keelie parked her hands on her hips. "I'm trying to tell Grandmother something serious and you're going on about fashion. It's not like jesters have a lot of choice."

"I mean, he never changes. Have you smelled him?"

Keelie shuddered, remembering her first job at the Wildewood Faire, when she'd worn a smelly purple dragon suit. Even thinking about it brought the stench back. "I could have gone the rest of my life not knowing that."

Risa sat up. "Did you hear that? Knot needs me." She went to the door and looked out. "I'll be right back."

Grandmother sighed, but the corners of her lips were raised in a little smile. "Keelie, you'll soon have some help looking for Viran. Bloodroot has volunteered to help you."

"Bloodroot the tree? Did they pin your wig on too tight?" Even his name sounded sinister. "I can do it with Knot and Sean."

"But my dear, Bloodroot knows this forest as you do not."

Kalix and Sariela glided into the room. Kalix lifted his haughty face. "Your grandmother is right. You need to listen to her."

Sariela sat down in a chair by Keelie and stared pensively toward the doorway.

Grandmother was oblivious to Keelie's bemusement. "He seems to have many interests and talents. It's amazing what the Ancients can do."

Kalix nodded. "Your grandmother is right. You will benefit from the benevolent wisdom of Bloodroot."

Benevolent? More like malevolent. Was something wrong with Grandmother? Suddenly she seemed to trust the trees. Something wasn't right. Keelie needed to talk to Dad.

The room suddenly shook strongly, causing the dishes to rattle in the cupboards. "Earthquake. Minor one," Keelie said. There wasn't much point standing in the doorway. They were in a tree, for Pete's sake.

"I suppose they have more temblors than we do farther

north," Grandmother mused. The doorknob turned and Grandmother smiled as the door opened. "Ah, there you are. We were just talking about you."

Tavyn stood in the open doorway. Keelie bit her lip. Tavyn came closer and Keelie backed away, staring. His skin had a reddish cast, as if he were sunburned, but too much sun didn't explain why the whites of his eyes were deep green and there was a loamy scent about him, very much like the redwoods.

The answer hit her as he turned to her with a ravenous stare. Her hands clenched.

"Good evening, Keelie." His voice sounded like scraping branches. Bloodroot looked out at her through the ranger's eyes.

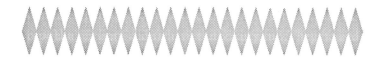

# seventeen

Keelie stared at the tree spirit–infested ranger. "This is wrong. You aren't supposed to do this. Grandmother, tell him this is wrong." She glared at Tavyn. Or was it Bloodroot? "How can you let him possess you like that?" It chilled Keelie to the core of her very soul.

Bloodroot stared at her through irises slitted like a cat's. But it was the young elf ranger's voice that now answered her. "It's okay, Keelie. The Ancients want to help us."

Keelie turned to Kalix. "You approve of this."

He looked regal and self-assured—there was no question where his loyalties lay. "We live in harmony with the trees.

If Bloodroot deems it necessary, then we are honored to do as he asks. Tavyn has been chosen to be a vessel, one who carries the spirit of the trees, so that they can walk among humans. If Norzan would see the wisdom of our ways, then he wouldn't be having problems in the Northwoods."

Turning to Grandmother for support, Keelie noticed that her face was pale with fatigue. She didn't say anything, just sat there as if overwhelmed by what was happening.

Keelie looked at Sariela, but the elven woman seemed defeated. Her shoulders sagged. "My son has chosen his path with the Ancients." Sariela bowed her head and stared down at the floor.

Keelie still couldn't understand why Tavyn would allow Bloodroot to possess him. Or why Kalix approved of it. Trees as powerful as the Ancients could override an elf's free will, even in the case of someone as strong as Grandmother. Keelie didn't stand a chance, and it scared her to think of being taken over, as Bella Matera had done to the actors at the Globe.

Tavyn-Bloodroot regarded her with a critical eye, like a scientist studying his lab rats in anticipation of what their reaction will be to the next stimulus. He seemed to be contemplating his next move. Then he spoke, deep and hypnotic, his alien eyes sparked with confidence. "Come, Keelie. You know that we need you."

Keelie's heart banged against her ribs. She wanted to go to him. His voice was working on her, eroding her self-control. Keelie took a deep breath, then pulled on a thread of Earth magic. It gave her a moment to think, and she remembered the calm charm. She said the magic words and her shields snapped into place.

"I don't trust you," she said to Tavyn-Bloodroot. "The redwood elves follow you like some cult leader, doing as you say and not asking questions."

She looked at Grandmother, expecting a reaction, but Grandmother was just staring at Bloodroot as if he were an interesting creature.

There was a flicker of anger in Bloodroot's eyes. He must be used to having everyone do as he ordered, but he quickly plastered his charming smile on again, as if he were talking to an intelligent but naughty child. "In your human cultures, you have societies that do things differently from one another. The Dread Forest way does not follow the Redwood Forest way, nor should it. We simply are different, and that makes you uncomfortable. That is why your Grandmother thought it best to send Norzan back to his forest, when we could have healed him here," he added.

"I agreed that it was best to send him back to the Northwoods," Keelie said. "The home forest is the best place for an injured elf."

Bloodroot nodded. "That is what you think, Keliel. But how do you know he wouldn't have healed if he had stayed in the redwoods? You must open your mind to new things. Our way of life with our elves is symbiotic."

"I am open-minded, but I question your concept of living in a symbiotic relationship." She couldn't help but stare at Tavyn, whose eyes seem to drink her in like a double latte of tree shepherd. She turned to her grandmother. "Does

Dad know about this symbiotic lifestyle between the redwood elves and the trees?"

"I don't know." Grandmother stared blankly at Keelie. Something wasn't right with her.

To Keelie's relief, Sean came through the door. "I thought I saw someone walk in. Is everything okay?" He didn't seem pleased to see Tavyn's new look. Knot sat at Sean's feet, his tail twitching angrily.

Tavyn-Bloodroot stared back at Sean, and the possessed ranger breathed in deeply. His voice, still a mingle of woodsy tones and human language, came out in a rough growl. "Elf. You are strong." Bloodroot's eyes turned black, glowing like onyx with flashes of green fir.

"Thanks for waiting for me, you two." Risa's whine warbled in from the walkway outside. "If that had been Keelie, you would've waited for her." She came in, but stopped suddenly when she noticed Tavyn's changed appearance. "I have a salve for that."

Tavyn-Bloodroot's lecherous gaze fell upon Risa. "I've been observing you." He walked over to her and kissed her hand like they did in the old movies. He lifted his head and studied Risa like an artist. "You are a beauty."

She seemed confused, yet flattered. She let him hold her hand a moment longer, then withdrew it from his grasp.

Keelie noticed that Tavyn's nails were green. There was a lot of chlorophyll pumping through his body. Just a little made her sick. How was Tavyn staying alive? He must be drinking giant pots of coffee, the surefire cure for chlorophyll poisoning.

Tavyn-Bloodroot bowed to Risa, then to Keelie. "Until our next meeting, Lady Keliel. I hope you will expand your mind and consider all that I've said."

"I don't think I'll change my mind," she said, but she extended her hand to him and held his gaze as they shook.

He walked out the door, and moments later, Keelie felt a strong wave of green energy. Tavyn's body was traveling the sap with Bloodroot on board, and Wena's trunk vibrated as the Ancient's spirit rode her sap.

Kalix bowed to his guests. "I must bid you good night. My lady wife is unwell, and I must see that she rests." Kalix extended a hand toward Sariela, and she stood. She pushed past him and exited, leaving him to follow.

Keelie bowed her head to acknowledge his courtesy, because Grandmother's mind was apparently somewhere else. Keelie was getting really worried.

Risa glided over to Sean and leaned against him, her hand on his shoulder. "I'm so glad you're here. That was strange, even for them." Risa seemed to mean Keelie and her grandmother.

"Dad needs to know about this," Keelie said.

Grandmother shrugged. "Yes, I suppose he does. I'll talk to him tomorrow. I'm tired, and I need to be rested for rehearsal in the morning. I'd forgotten how much fun it is to recite Will's words. He was such a wonderful poet."

It bothered Keelie that Grandmother was putting the play ahead of the trees.

"You knew William Shakespeare?" Risa seemed in awe of Lady Keliatiel.

"Yes, I did." She smoothed a few strands of gray hair back from her forehead. "If you will excuse me, I must retire so I'll be ready for tomorrow. Lord Sean, you may see yourself out."

Sean moved away from Risa, who frowned when he did, and walked over to Keelie's side. He took her hand. "I'll be right outside if you need me."

"That's really not necessary, Sean," Grandmother said. "We are quite safe."

"Maybe not, but I'll feel better." Sean kissed Keelie on the forehead.

"It's going to be cold out there," Keelie said. "I hate for you to spend a miserable night because of us." Actually, she felt safer with him close by.

"I'm happy to help." Sean turned to Risa. "Good night, Risa," he said coolly. She glared at him. He saluted Knot. "Good night, Knot." The cat blinked cordially.

Sean stepped outside. Despite the danger, Keelie wanted to follow him and snag another kiss. It was wonderful being this close to him, but she was worried. What if she did age faster than him? Would he eventually go to Risa? Of course, if that happened, she'd be beyond caring. She had to live for today.

"Keelie, you and I must speak tomorrow," Grandmother said. "You'll find me at the Globe."

Well, good. Maybe they'd be able to discuss the strange situation here. Missing and injured tree shepherds, trees with delusions of world domination—what more could they have to discuss?

Grandmother glided to bed. She wasn't simply tired, Keelie knew. There was more going on, and after what happened to Norzan, Keelie thought she was right to be worried. She needed to talk to Dad. He needed to know about Tavyn-Bloodroot.

Risa went to bed, but Keelie stayed up, wondering if Laurie was spending the night somewhere else and if she should be worried. Laurie was with Scott, and it wasn't as if they were wandering around in the forest, even though they both had rose quartz charms.

She fixed herself a cup of tea, then went out to the bridge, dangling her feet over the edge and watching the fog-shrouded forest floor below. Nothing moved, although a small light glowed from one of the jouster's tents.

Keelie tried contacting Dad telepathically, but a strange voice answered.

*I'm here.*

Who was that? It was definitely not Dad.

*Where are you?* she asked.

*I'm in the forest.*

It didn't sound like Bloodroot's strong voice and personality. In fact, it didn't sound like a tree at all. *Who are you?*

*I am part of them, now.*

Dark green filled Keelie's mind. She could feel her feet growing into roots sinking deep into the Earth, and her head elongated, her arms transforming into branches. Her trunk hardened, and bark protected her.

Keelie felt pleasure as ocean mist rolled in and dampened

her roots. In the distance, she heard the echoes of a play being performed.

Gasping for air, Keelie awakened. Something hard had landed on her stomach. A loud purring brought her back to the moment. She opened her eyes. Knot was staring at her. Mist surrounded the tree house.

When had she gone to sleep? Her head ached as if she had an overdose of chlorophyll. Stumbling inside, she rubbed her cold hands together. Her nails were tinged green, the same color as the numbers on Laurie's travel alarm clock, which was glowing 3:00 AM.

Keelie really wanted to go to sleep. But wherever Laurie was, she had to find her. She needed to know that her friend was safe.

She walked to Grandmother's door on tiptoe. Grandmother was asleep, looking kind of small under the covers. A big part of Lady Keliatiel was her personality.

Keelie crept outside, then traveled the sap to Wena's base. Bromliel was standing guard, playing his Nintendo DS.

"Lady Keliel," he said, surprised.

"Where's Sean?"

Sean emerged from a nearby tent, dressed, but with his hair tousled from sleep. He looked adorable. His expression darkened when he noticed Keelie.

"What's wrong?"

"Laurie never came home. I thought I'd go look for her on the festival grounds. She might be at a party." Keelie tried to keep the worry out of her voice, but what was the point?

"I'll come with you." Sean nodded to Bromliel, who gave him the two-finger Boy Scout salute.

They walked toward the road, hearing the owls and night birds, and the crashing of small animals in the underbrush.

"Something is following us," Sean said quietly.

Not again. Keelie stopped, but he grabbed her arm and kept her moving. "You don't want to stop, Keelie. We'll look around when we get to the road."

The ferns moved to their left, and Keelie felt her heart thud against her ribs. "Did you bring a sword?"

"No. Nor a gun, nor a knife. Not even a spork," Sean said grimly. "How fast can you run?"

"Kind of fast. There were always girls who were faster. But I don't know about running through the woods at night. Isn't that how the guy with the chain saw catches you?"

"No chain saws here. It's probably just an animal."

She hoped it wasn't Peascod. She hadn't heard the familiar dissonant jangle that preceded his arrival.

"Right. I'm ready when you are."

Whatever was tailing them made a big clatter in the fallen branches of a small tree. Keelie took off at a sprint, with Sean right behind her. She dodged branches, jumped over small logs, and skirted big ferns. She tripped once, but Sean swept her up and carried her until they reached more level ground. Finally, they could see the road ahead. They put on a burst of speed, but whatever chased them was crashing through the underbrush, closer and closer. They hit the asphalt road just as the beast exploded from the ferns and small bushes. It rolled twice and then lay on its side, laughing.

"Coyote?" Keelie shrieked. Her fear ebbed to relief when she saw him.

"Fae prankster, you are dead." It was an empty threat, because Sean was on his knees, breathless.

"Why were you two sneaking around in the forest?" Coyote sat up, still laughing.

"We're going to look for Laurie," Keelie said between gulps of air. "She never came home."

"She's in the dwarf's RV with the human Scott," Coyote said. "They got lost in the mist on the beach and ended up farther away than they expected. The dwarf went to pick them up, and then it was too late to go through the forest."

"Well, she could have called me," Keelie said, grumpy. "Of course, I don't have a phone. So maybe she couldn't have."

A song drifted on the forest mist, and Keelie tried to hear it, but the melody was elusive. "What is that?"

Sean looked puzzled.

"Don't you hear that music? Someone is singing." It was a soprano voice, high and clear, and it sang of comfort and safety, as if every mother's lullaby were rolled into one beautiful and perfect melody.

"I don't hear it."

Keelie waded through ferns, heading up the hill toward the voice.

"That way is the Grove of the Ancients," Coyote noted. "I hear no song."

"Keelie, stop. We need to go home."

She heard Sean's words, but it was more important to go to Mother. Mother needed her and she would make her proud.

Coyote's voice sharpened. "Elf, grab her. Get her out of here."

Keelie protested as a strong form knocked her to her knees. She cried out, "Mother!" And then her breath was gone and she was being carried away from the beautiful song. She started to cry.

Coyote followed them for a few steps. Then he stopped, ears pricked up, and turned and raced away.

At seven thirty the next morning Keelie was sipping her fifth cup of coffee, but her headache still had not subsided. Last night seemed like a bad dream. She remembered traveling back up the sap with Sean, and Grandmother and Sariela putting her in bed, but her dreams were haunted by the song. It was not Mom who sang, but some dark, fearful thing. She had not slept well, waking up time and again, only to fall asleep and have the same dream and the melody that haunted her heart.

At least she didn't have to worry about Laurie, who'd been delivered bright and early by Sir Davey. Laurie was dressing for the festival, but first chance she had, Keelie planned to have a serious talk with her friend.

She sipped her coffee as Risa treated her cuts and scrapes with one of her salves, which actually made them feel better.

"She's not going to fall in love with her coffee cup, is she?" Sir Davey asked. He was resting on the couch. After traveling the sap for the first time, he was still recovering.

Risa gave him a dirty look. "I need to go check on my herbs."

"I needed to open Heartwood," Keelie said. The shop would be a full-time project through Sunday afternoon. Meanwhile, she desperately needed to reach Dad on Sir Davey's iPhone. She didn't dare say so aloud, however, with Kalix and Tavyn possibly within earshot.

"Well, I'm not looking forward to traveling the sap again," Sir Davey said. "It's unnatural for dwarves to fly. Just lower me on a rope."

"It'll be over in a second," Keelie assured him.

When they were walking to the festival grounds, Keelie told him about the Tavyn-Bloodroot possession.

"Sounds like dark Under-the-Hill magic, if you ask me," Sir Davey said gravely. He offered Keelie his iPhone and she eagerly dialed Dad's number, but there was no reception.

Keelie had already tried her telepathic link with Dad, but her head pounded painfully with each effort. Knot stayed with them, and they glimpsed Coyote watching them through the trees.

The familiar routine of setting up for a day of business was comforting. Heartwood was the one normal thing in her life right now. She was plugging in the coffeemaker when Risa floated into Heartwood. "I've made five sales already," Risa sang out cheerily.

Keelie stared at her.

Risa flinched. "What is wrong with you? You're still green."

"Tree shepherditis. The green lingers. Why are you so cheery?" The cheeriness made her teeth grate, but Keelie didn't say so.

"I like working with the humans. I think of myself as an elven fairy godmother, here to brighten their day with my beauty and my knowledge of the Earth. Who knows? I may do what the tree shepherds can't." She skipped out to her cart, where Laurie was already looking over her wares. Laurie was wearing one of the gorgeous Francesca gowns that she'd bought at the Wildewood Faire, which still made Keelie jealous.

Keelie imagined Risa selling her products on the Home Shopping Network and cringed. She would probably be a hit, and romantic havoc would spread across the world.

Laurie finally came in, just as Keelie was pouring herself the first cup of coffee. She gaped. "Your skin is green!"

"Yeah, chlorophyll poisoning, like in the Wildewood," Keelie muttered. "What happened to you and Scott? I was so worried and went looking for you. Then Coyote told me you were at Sir Davey's."

"I'm sorry, but there was no way to let you know," Laurie said earnestly. "You know the phone problem. Still friends?"

"Of course." They hugged, and Keelie was suddenly happy to just get to spend time with Laurie.

"So what's new at Heartwood?" Laurie started investigating the shop.

Knot hopped onto the table. He strolled over to Keelie,

and placed his paw on her hand. There was a tiny spark of fairy magic, like the ember in a fire beginning to flame. Keelie closed her eyes and focused. She could feel the fairy magic within her growing stronger, dispelling the green tree magic within and bringing balance.

Keelie opened her eyes and looked down at her nails— the green tinge was receding. "Thanks, Knot. I could have used you last night. I hope the Queen's Alehouse was fun. Coyote would have had fun, too, but he was busy saving my life. Like a guardian does, you know?"

The paw on her hand suddenly sprang claws, pinning her to the counter.

"Okay. Point taken. Lots of sharp little points taken. I'm grateful." The headache still lingered, but Keelie could deal. She'd just drink coffee all day. After Knot released her, she dug around in the first aid kit for little bandages to cover the punctures he'd left on the back of her hand.

"Wow. You're getting better at this," Laurie said.

Risa nodded. "Impressive." Knot jumped to the floor and flipped the tip of his tail as he walked. The elf girl's eyes radiated admiration. "He's so wonderful."

Laurie snorted. "He's cute for a cat. Very fluffy. But really, isn't this going a little too far?"

"You don't understand the path of true love," Risa said helplessly. "Knot is the beam of sunlight to my heart on a cold midwinter's day. He is the first bloom of spring in the garden of my love. He is the wind that blows the sails of my destiny. He has only to meow, and I will be there to do his bidding."

Keelie's headache was getting worse. Knot strutted across the floor, tail high in the air. He turned his head and meowed.

"No, I'm not giving you a treat," Keelie said.

"I'll bake you catnip oatmeal cookies," Risa promised. Knot's lips turned up, then he sprang away.

"You really are a love slave," Laurie said. "When is that charm going to fade?"

Risa sat down in one of Dad's fancy crystal-wrapped chairs. "No charm, and I build my potions to last."

"That's what happens when you mess with someone's love life," Keelie said. "The karma fairy came to see her. That's why she fell in love with a cat."

Laurie looked confused. "Is there such a thing as a karma fairy?"

"No. I'm just using it as a metaphor," Keelie said.

Risa's face became pinched and she wriggled uncomfortably in her chair. "I don't know. You never know with fairies."

Laurie stared at Risa. "I don't get why you would want to give a love potion to Sean, anyway. He's with Keelie."

"He's supposed to be with me," Risa snapped. "I was his betrothed."

"Oh, he dumped you." Laurie said.

"He didn't dump me, as you so crudely put it." Risa turned her head away. "We broke up because of someone else."

"I understand," Laurie said.

"What do you mean, you understand?" Keelie glared.

"She's feeling rejected," Laurie said to Keelie. "Put yourself in her position."

Risa turned around. "I am not feeling rejected."

"Quit trying to deny it. I see all the symptoms. Desperate for attention? Will get him back at any cost? I know, I've been there." Laurie sounded sympathetic.

"You have?" Risa said, surprise in her voice.

Keelie had never thought about this situation from Risa's perspective. She guessed it would've been embarrassing and it would've hurt to have your fiancé dump you for someone else. It's just that Keelie didn't want to see things from Risa's perspective. She was getting what she deserved. She'd fallen in love with a cat. Not even a real cat.

"So it's just going to be the two of us today?" Laurie changed the subject.

Keelie nodded. "I'm grateful for your help."

"If you get bored selling furniture, you can come help me," Risa offered. "I can give you a facial. Everyone will see how beautiful you are, and they're going to want to buy my products."

Laurie's eyes lit up. "Really?"

"You're leaving me for a facial?" Keelie muttered.

"Beauty is important," Risa said. "As I'm sure you'll discover some day."

Laurie grinned at Keelie. "Ouch."

Risa leaned closer to the table and scooted her chair up. She gazed at Laurie. "You and this Scott, is this a new relationship? Tell me all about it. Do you feel about him as I do about Knot?"

Laurie shrugged. "I don't know about this Knot thing, but I think Scott and I are interested in one another. We walked on the beach. We talked about elves, and we talked about Keelie, too. We're bonding because of you," Laurie said, aiming a big smile at her friend.

Keelie slammed her coffee cup down. "What do you mean, you talked about me?"

"You and your tree weirdness." Laurie didn't seem concerned by her friend's anger.

"It was the same way in the Dread Forest," Risa confided. "Trees walking around. Unicorns coming out of the roots of a tree, and then that little seedling growing into a huge tree. Don't get me started on the Earth magic and the fairy stuff."

Keelie had heard enough. If Laurie and Risa wanted to bond, fine. Keelie rose from her chair. "Okay ladies, you can move your conversation to the Green Goddess Cart. I have a business to run." They left, unperturbed by Keelie shooing them away from her shop.

Moments later, Tavyn stopped by. His skin was a normal elf color. "We've found evidence of the Redwood Tree Shepherd," he said.

"Where?"

"Deep in a grove of hemlock. Bloodroot is investigating with Bella Matera."

Tavyn didn't show any sign of ill effects from tree possession, but Keelie still treated him as if Bloodroot was listening. She didn't trust him.

"Do you mind if I ask you a question?"

The elf ranger smiled, his normal, handsome face friendly as if yesterday's frightening encounter had never happened.

"Ask away," he said.

"Do you often let Bloodroot take over your body?"

"Only when he needs to go out in the human world. He's been doing research. Sometimes we go to Los Angeles or San Francisco. It's an honor to be of service to him."

Keelie couldn't imagine Bloodroot in a large city, or what that would do to his elf host. It had taken Risa and Sean a whole day to recover from the trip to Los Angeles.

"Normally he wants to go to the library, but now that we have an Internet connection, he doesn't go into the city anymore," Tavyn added.

Keelie's head reeled. How advanced were the Ancients if they could use the Internet? And how did Tavyn survive being possessed, anyway? He either had powerful magic protecting him, or he was a zombie elf.

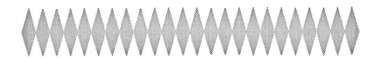

# eighteen

The sky was darkening when Keelie finished securing the shop for the day. After hours of talking to customers and arranging furniture shipments, she just wanted to crawl under the counter and snooze. Too bad Dad hadn't sent down any beds to sell.

The sound of laughter and applause drifted toward her, meaning that the evening performance was underway. Keelie wanted to head in the opposite direction, but Grandmother was there and she'd said that they needed to talk.

You bet they needed to talk. Keelie had a thing or two to say to her grandmother. Working in Heartwood alone was exhausting, and though they were supposed to be here to find Viran and help the trees, they had made little progress. The trees here were so powerful and scary that Keelie thought they needed more help than just one old lady elf and one half-elf teenager.

Keelie had known that the redwoods were different from other forests—more intelligent, more evolved. But she was shocked at the elves who allowed tree spirits to take them over as if they were puppets. She wondered if the Redwood Tree Shepherd had simply abandoned his post. Did tree shepherds ever ditch a job?

If even Grandmother was falling under their enthralling influence, as seemed to be the case, Viran could have fallen sway to their powerful magic.

She had to talk to Dad. She tried the elven cell phone again, but couldn't connect. With all the massive trees around, the tree-powered elven phone should work better than ever, but she couldn't even get a signal. Disgusted, Keelie headed toward the Globe. Maybe someone there would lend her a phone.

A jangle disrupted the air, except it didn't sound as sinister as it normally did. Keelie stopped at the entrance to the theater, where several smaller redwoods grew close together. She searched for Peascod, and drew in a breath when she saw him hobbling along the edge of the theater to a back exit. Relief rose in her as he kept moving.

From here, she could see the stage. The nearby trees' faces were out, lips repeating the lines they heard Hermia and Lysander speak.

"The trees really like Shakespeare." Coyote was sitting at her feet.

She jumped, then ran her fingers through her hair, trying to pretend that she hadn't been frightened. "What are you doing here?" The sneaky fairy was too quiet. She wondered how much he overheard when he skulked around.

"I'm observing."

"I thought you were supposed to protect me."

"Yes." He looked up at her with golden-amber eyes. "I am doing so this very moment."

Grandmother walked stiffly on stage. She had on her pearl-bedecked red wig, which made her look like the real Queen Elizabeth, but the attitude was all she really needed. Keelie noticed that Tavyn was sitting in the audience.

"My, my. She looks the part. I've been watching her. She enjoys being amongst actors." Coyote grinned, showing sharp teeth. "Humans."

"My grandmother enjoys ruling, even if it's just pretending to be in charge of humans. She should have been a queen."

"Perhaps once she was. Have you asked her?"

Startled, Keelie looked down at the fairy. "No. Should I?"

Coyote grinned up at her. "She likes to walk and talk to the trees, especially the ones named Bella and Bloodroot." He lifted his pointed nose in the air and sniffed. "Be careful, Keliel. Something moves in the forest."

Like Keelie needed to be told that. It was time to figure out the problem here, so that she could at least still enjoy her time in California. She wanted time for Sean, and time to hang out with Laurie.

Master Oswald walked out onto the stage in ridiculously stuffed pumpkin pants and a doublet with a peascod belly that made him look like a heavy-duty beer drinker. Grandmother said that the outfit was all the rage in 1680, but it was just silly.

"Lords, Ladies, Good Gentles all. It is my honor to present to you, Her Majesty the Queen."

Coyote tilted his head, bright eyes taking in everything.

A sharp pain hacked through Keelie's head.

*I'm close by. Watch out, tree shepherdess. Beware.*

Cold green energy filled Keelie. She scanned the trees. The voice had to be coming from them. Keelie's eyes locked with her Grandmother's. She had stopped in mid-wave, her made-up face even more pale than usual.

Grandmother must have heard the voice, too. She must have felt the same brief headache. Something or someone was threatening one of them.

Keelie closed her eyes. She didn't want to lose the connection.

Cold green filled her mind. Then she felt a caress of dark magic. It was like the seductive dark power that had flowed into her from the book she'd used in the Dread Forest, as if something was delving into her mind and her magic. Time to put up the barriers. She dug out the rose quartz that she'd shoved into her pocket.

Keelie imagined her feet like roots, seeking the power of the Earth. The raw Earth magic surged through her, casting out the invasive darkness. She opened her eyes just in time to see Grandmother crumple onto the stage.

She jumped up, ready to run to her, but tripped when her gown became snagged. She twisted to release the fabric. Coyote had her dress clenched in his teeth.

"Let go. I need to go to her."

He held on, backing away a step, pulling her with him.

She swatted at him. "Stupid fairy. She's in trouble. I have to go to her."

Knot came running to Keelie's side, hissing, his fur poofed out.

Coyote released her. "You can go now, but stay with Knot."

Keelie ran, Knot racing ahead of her, ears flat to his skull.

Costumed actors and townspeople blocked Keelie's view of Grandmother. She pushed her way into the crowd, jostling elbows and using her hips to shove people aside.

"Call 911," Master Oswald shouted.

911? The human emergency responders would discover that she wasn't human. Grandmother had to be okay. Keelie shoved her way to a clear spot, then dove between legs, dropping to the ground beside Grandmother. She lay pale and still, her red wig askew.

Knot raced in and hopped onto Grandmother's stiff bejeweled bodice. She coughed from the impact of the large orange tabby hitting her sternum, then she wheezed and her eyelids fluttered.

She was alive!

Knot started to lick her eyebrows.

"Get that cat off of her," someone from the crowd shouted.

Keelie wrapped her hands around Grandmother's scrawny old-lady-elf shoulders covered in stiff quilted sleeves. She pulled on her fairy magic, energy from the Earth, and the power of the fir trees around them. She envisioned light, heat, and green all swirling together.

"Come on, you've got to get up," she whispered into the pointed ear hidden by the soft, silvery hair that the wig had exposed. "Who else knows what I've done wrong? You've got to be awake to tell me how superior you are."

A mist gathered on the stage as the trees in spirit form hovered, watching. After a moment, the fog was so thick Keelie could only see the legs of the crowd around her. She envisioned a tornado of power above her, then tried to drive the magic and energy into Grandmother. It started down, then deflected, as if Grandmother had put up a shield to defend herself from Keelie's healing. Keelie stared down at the unconscious woman in the outlandish costume. What had Grandmother done? Was she wearing a charm against fae magic?

Master Oswald's deep bass boomed over the muffled and confused conversation. "Ladies and gentlemen, stay where you are. This fog is normal for our area. It will soon dissipate."

A musical voice spoke in Keelie's mind. *What is wrong, child?*

Keelie shivered as Bella Matera's voice seemed to pour into her ears like honey.

*My Grandmother…* Keelie couldn't finish the thought.

*Let me help you.* A powerful surge of buzzing green magic filled Keelie. It combined with the Earth magic she had summoned, twining like two layers that first stood apart, then slowly melted together.

Magic couldn't be seen by humans, but if they had fairy blood in them, they might have seen a blanket of golden-green gossamer drift from Keelie to cover Grandmother.

Keelie looked up in the fog and could see Bella's wraith-like form. Just as swiftly as it had floated in, the fog cleared.

*Your Grandmother will be fine. It would do her some good to come stay with me.* Bella's voice faded, as did the green of the magic gossamer blanket.

Suddenly Keelie could once again hear people talking around her, as if they'd been muted before. And close by, a distinct lick, lick, lick.

Knot had resumed administering his personal form of first aid. Grandmother's eyebrows were tilted at forty-five degree angles. It gave Grandmother a very alien look, like something from Star Trek. Too bad Risa wasn't here to witness Knot's healing treatment.

Grandmother moaned and her grip tightened around Keelie's hand. Knot's tail swished back and forth, and then he jumped off of Grandmother's chest. Relief flooded Keelie. One: Grandmother was coming round. Two: Knot had vamoosed.

"Help me up, Keliel," Grandmother said, her voice groggy. Her eyes opened, and Keelie suppressed a gasp. The whites of her eyes were green. Was she possessed, or was it chlorophyll poisoning?

"My head hurts," Grandmother said. She didn't sound possessed, just frail.

"No kidding," Keelie said. "I think you're going to need some coffee."

Master Oswald bent down on one knee. "My Queen, do you need a healer? Mayhap we need to take thee to a hospital?"

Grandmother rose to a sitting position and tucked her dress around her. The regal appearance was ruined by her designer eyebrows. Relieved that her grandmother was okay, Keelie bit down on her lips to keep a giggle from escaping.

"I will be fine," Grandmother said, pulling her hand out of Master Oswald's with a sour look. "I need to go back to my cabin and rest. I think I must have become dehydrated."

Tavyn and several of the elven rangers appeared. Keelie studied Tavyn as he helped Grandmother to her feet.

"You should go back to the tree house. I can't take you, but I'll bring your truck around," he said. His eyes were no longer that bright shade of green. If Bloodroot was here, he was not in Tavyn.

"I appreciate that," Grandmother murmured. "Keelie, the keys are in my purse." She motioned toward a velvet pouch which dangled from her waist by a golden cord.

Sean arrived, no doubt summoned by one of his men. Risa and Laurie came with him.

"What happened?" Sean asked.

"Grandmother collapsed. I'm going to take her back to

Wena, to the house." Keelie explained. She gave Tavyn the keys.

Risa walked forward and looped her arm through Sean's. "I guess you're going to have to stay with her tonight, Keelie. That's too bad—you're going to miss the bonfire on the beach."

"What bonfire on the beach?" Keelie asked.

Sean glared at Risa. "I'll stay with you, Keelie."

"Oh, you can't miss the bonfire," Risa said. "Your jousters are looking forward to you being there. Your idea to plan fun outings as a group is so terrific, and I'm sure it will help with camaraderie."

Sean never talked to Keelie about his jousters or the problems he was having. Their conversations were always interrupted by elves, cats, and other people. They were pulled in many directions, and none of the interruptions pushed them toward each other.

"Keelie, I need you," Grandmother said. Case in point, as Mom would have said.

"I have to go." Keelie said. "I wish I could stay."

"I'll go with you," Sean insisted.

Keelie glanced over his shoulder. His men had gathered. She shook her head. "Stay with your men. Maybe you can stop by later before you go to sleep. I wish you'd told me about the bonfire."

"You mean instead of sharing it with Risa?" He grinned and turned to the elf girl, who was smiling at them expectantly. "Who told you about the bonfire? Was it Bromliel?"

Risa stomped her foot, whirled and walked away.

"I didn't tell you because I forgot, Keelie. Somehow other things come to mind when we're together." He lifted Keelie's hand to his lips. "I'll be there tonight. Can we take a walk alone?"

Keelie smiled. "Yes." She imagined walking alone with Sean, undisturbed. No fairy trickster coyotes to chase them through the woods, no needy grandparent or duties to perform. They would talk. She could tell him about being a tree shepherd, and he could talk about what it was like training his jousters. And they could discuss their past, and their future.

Tavyn strode forward. "Keelie, your truck's parked outside." He handed her the keys.

Keelie walked past Risa as she helped Grandmother toward the exit. She leaned close to the elf girl. "Watch out for the sea lions. I hear they love redheads."

"We're not going to the tree house," Grandmother announced as they climbed into Dad's battered truck. "We need to go deep into the Redwood Forest."

"No we don't. We're going to the elven village. You need to rest. You passed out."

"Do not contradict me." Grandmother put on her stern Lady-of-the-Forest voice.

"We're going home," Keelie said matter-of-factly. "You need to rest. There is no way I'm going to let you go into the forest tonight."

"I told Bella Matera that we'd meet her there."

"If Dad were here, he'd tell you the same thing." Keelie was tired of putting the trees' needs ahead of her health and safety, and the health and safety of those that she loved. If she didn't take care of Grandmother and herself, then there would be no one to take care of the trees.

"I am here on a mission, as are you. If we hide in the elven village, we may doom this forest." Grandmother frowned. "You have taken risks before, Keelie. What makes you cautious now? We must go."

"Maybe it's just scarier in this place," Keelie snorted. "I can't believe you still want to go into that forest! Can you tell me what happened on that stage? Whose voice was that? And why couldn't my fairy magic heal you?"

Grandmother's expression softened. "You summoned fae magic to help me? Oh my dear." She touched Keelie's face with her hand. "Thank you. It didn't work because I was shielding against the tree magic, and yours was too similar."

"So you're afraid of Bloodroot, too," Keelie said.

Grandmother leaned her head to one side. "I felt someone calling me. He needed me. He was asking for help. He also warned me of danger."

"I heard the same voice," Keelie said. "But I was able to block it."

Grandmother looked interested. "How do you do that?"

"I use a combination of Earth and fairy magic."

"Then I cannot wield it."

"Maybe not the fairy magic, but you can talk to Sir Davey. I use rose quartz to call on Earth magic. It helps block out the trees."

Sighing, Grandmother looked out the passenger-side window, then turned her head. "The trees still need me. I feel needed here. These past few months with Zeke taking over the forest, I've felt useless."

Keelie was silent. Her grandmother *had* seemed lost since Dad had taken over the Dread Forest. "If you're going to help the trees, you have to find the balance," she said finally. That was the key to the Dread Forest. It was finding a balance between the light and the dark.

Keelie watched Grandmother out of the corner of her eye as the old woman sank deeper into the seat cushion. She seemed so fragile. Keelie didn't know if Grandmother was strong enough to deal with the trees. If she still couldn't reach Dad, she'd have to talk to Sir Davey. If nothing else, she'd find a crystal so that Grandmother could use earth magic as a barrier against the tree magic.

She parked the truck, and was grateful to see Kalix waiting for them. He carried Grandmother to Wena. Sariela and Keelie helped Grandmother to bed, and there was no more talk about going into the forest. Reason had won the night.

Keelie sat down in the dark. She had to think things through. All of this had started with the Redwood Tree Shepherd, who was still missing. The elves had asked for help in locating him, but they were the strangest elves Keelie had ever met. Granted, she didn't know too many of them. Then there were the Ancients—who were totally different from the old trees she knew in the Dread Forest. Keelie didn't trust Bloodroot. He gave her the creeps, the way he took over Tavyn's willing body. It seemed the two were up to something. And Bella Matera said she had come to save

Grandmother when she was injured, but still, something was off about Bella Matera.

What she couldn't forget was the voice warning her to beware. Beware of what? And where did Coyote fit into all of this?

There was only one course of action: she would have to go into the forest, to the hemlocks where Tavyn reported that the tree shepherd had been seen, and find Viran herself. It would be the only way to stop all this craziness. Keelie so desperately wanted it all to be over. She wanted to get to know Sean better, and to run the shop and make Dad proud of her. It would be wonderful to hang out with Laurie more.

Knot meowed, startling her.

"Yeah, I know it's dark. I needed to think without distractions."

Loud purrs filled the air.

There went the end of the quiet. Keelie walked into the kitchen and grabbed the tea kettle. The kitchen clock read 11:00—she had been sitting in the dark a long time. She was lighting one of the honeycomb candles when a figure entered the room.

"Is that you, Sean?" He had been planning to escort Risa and Laurie back to the tree house, and if Keelie could ditch the girls, then she would have the time she wanted with Sean. Maybe he could help her decide what to do.

"It is not Sean." It was a woodsy voice, rough along the edges.

Keelie turned and stared into the bright green eyes of

Tavyn, except this time she knew it wasn't Tavyn she was talking to. It was Bloodroot.

"What do you want?" Too bad this was Tavyn's own house. In old legends, fairies, vampires, and other magical creatures could not enter a house without being invited.

Tavyn-Bloodroot leaned against the doorjamb. "Why are you so negative about me, Keelie?"

Better to have it out in the open. "I don't trust you."

"Considering the company you keep, my feelings are hurt."

"What company?" Keelie didn't really want to argue with Tavyn-Bloodroot.

"A coyote. Garbage-eating fae."

Knot came and sat down between Keelie's legs. He turned his big kitty full moon gaze up at Tavyn-Bloodroot.

"And this one? Really, if the court were to send a guardian to protect their little prodigy, then they should've sent a knight."

"I don't know what you're talking about."

"I think you do."

"No, I don't."

"I want to talk to you, Keliel. How does a half-human, half-elf girl with a minute drop of fairy blood wield so much power? How were you able to tap into that power plant and restore the Wildewood?"

Keelie hadn't tapped into the power plant. She'd tapped into the wild Earth magic that flowed under the forest, magic that had surged through the nearby power plant and knocked it offline. But she wasn't about to reveal that. He'd probably twist the knowledge for his own dark purpose.

Tavyn-Bloodroot's eyes glowed. "I want to know." He reached-out and pulled Keelie to him. He pressed his lips against hers, and Keelie pulled back. She was ready to kick him in the privates when something yowled like a primordial feline, harkening back to the days of the saber-tooth tiger.

Knot had attached himself to Tavyn's shin and was hanging on for dear life. The bright green light disappeared from Tavyn's eyes and a cloud flowed out from him.

Bloodroot's wraithlike shape floated out of the tree house and ascended into Wena's canopy. "We'll talk again tomorrow, Keliel."

Trying not to act afraid, but on the inside quivering with fear, Keelie raised a fist in the air. "You bet we will, Bloodroot."

Tavyn stared into Keelie's eyes. A smile formed on his face. It wasn't a friendly smile, either.

"So, it seems the chameleon shows his true colors," said a familiar voice on the edge of the platform. It was Coyote. How had he gotten up in the tree? "I've been tracking you."

The sound of voices echoed through the forest. Tavyn turned to face Coyote. "You'll have to catch me first." He disappeared, traveling the sap to the base of the tree.

Coyote leaped off the platform, plunging for several feet before reappearing in the shape of a crow. He swooped out of sight.

The voices below grew excited. "Hey, Tavyn."

"Where's he going?"

"What is that thing?"

Knot sat on Keelie's foot. She looked down at him. "Do you have any idea what is going on around here?"

Knot jumped off the platform, vanishing with a green glow, a sign that he was traveling the sap. Keelie jumped into the sap after him and rode down, unsurprised that the cat already knew how to do it himself. At the base, she discovered Sean, Risa, and Laurie.

Risa came running up to them. "There's my Knotsie Wotsie." She wobbled to the left. "Whoops. We had some mead tonight around the bonfire, it was really great." Then the elf girl burped and collapsed against Keelie. She was like a lead weight.

A giggling Laurie helped Keelie with Risa. "We need to get her in bed."

Risa looked up. "I have sand in my shoes."

It stung to know that Laurie and Scott and Sean and Risa had been out on the beach together, like two couples double-dating, even if there had been a big crowd there. She'd been stuck here with Tavyn-Bloodroot.

Sean stepped closer. "Where did Tavyn go in such a hurry?"

Knot growled.

Keelie shrugged. "The farther away, the better."

Scott looked up at the building above them. "How do we get up there? There's no elevator or ladder."

Keelie saw that he was tightly gripping the rose quartz

she'd given him earlier. The Dread was certainly working around here.

Sean regarded her with a slow, appraising glance. "What's going on, Keelie?' He stepped closer to her, hovering. "I can't protect you if you don't trust me." He lowered his head until it was level with hers. He smelled like bonfire smoke.

"Tavyn came to see me. Then he ran off, and Coyote chased him."

Sean stared at her. "Your lips are green."

"He kissed me. He's seriously bent, Sean. Bloodroot was riding him."

Sean swore. "Which way did they go?"

Scott pointed in the direction of the Grove of Ancients. "That way."

"He thinks I tapped into the power plant to save the Wildewood and wants to know how I did it."

A sharp pain pierced her skull.

*Beware, Tree Shepherdess.*

Keelie immediately blocked the voice, but this time it was with her fairy magic. She had felt it surge through her before she had a chance to stop it.

The pain and the voice were gone.

Sean searched the woods with his gaze. "Something is contacting you, isn't it?" He looked down at her.

Voices exploded in anger. Risa had ridden the sap to the tree house already, but Laurie and Scott were arguing nearby.

"I can't believe you're asking me." Laurie's voice rose.

"Come on, Laurie. I never told you I felt that way about you," Scott said in a low tone.

"You ask her yourself, you cretin. You creep. You two-timer."

"What's wrong?" Keelie asked. Normally she wouldn't disturb a private conversation, but there was a lot at stake tonight.

Laurie dashed past Keelie and ran to the edge of the clearing. "I never want to see him again."

Luminous fog had drifted in while they'd spoken. Keelie turned to Scott. "Okay, what did you do?"

"Why does it have to be my fault?" Scott looked miserable. His shoulders sagged. "I just asked Laurie if she could ask Risa if she liked me."

Keelie looked down at Knot and sighed. "The forest is full of trees smarter than me, and I'm stuck with Captain Clueless."

Knot's eyes gleamed and he laughed, fangs showing.

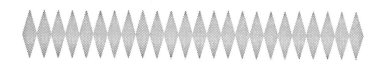

# nineteen

Keelie wanted to smack Scott on the back of the head. "You are such an insensitive idiot. She likes you. You took her for a walk on the beach—that's practically a date. And then you ask about Risa."

"Hey, I didn't lead Laurie on. Did I, Sean?"

Sean shrugged. "You're on your own, and so's Laurie, except she's going to get lost in the woods."

Keelie looked out into the darkness. "We need to go after her. We can't let her wander around the woods by herself."

"You're right," Scott said. "I'll go." He held up the rose quartz.

"You can't go alone. You'll end up lost or worse," Sean said. "I'll come too."

*The Grove*... the voice in Keelie's head reminded her of the dangers out there. A shiver shot down her back. "No time to lose." She headed toward the Grove.

Sean started after her. "Do you think Risa and your grandmother will be all right here?" He glanced back toward the treetop village.

"They're both asleep." Scott jogged beside them. "I'll grab some flashlights out of the truck. Laurie couldn't have gone far."

Keelie hoped he was right. She called on the tree spirts, but there was no answer. Puzzled, she called again, cautiously opening herself to the redwoods. Lancing pain made her reel.

Sean caught her. "What's wrong?"

"My head," she gasped, and suddenly the hot needle of agony was gone, replaced by cool green. Her vision was blurry. She thought she could see a yarnlike thread of warm green overlaid in the air, heading into the forest. It pulsed weakly, like a low-watt bulb, but Keelie felt a rush of love from the redwoods toward the source. The thread looped around the trees, fading as it went deeper in the woods.

"What about me?" Scott asked. "I think we should all stick together. These woods are beautiful during the day, but at night, they're spooky. I swear sometimes I see ghosts walking around, and it's really terrifying deeper in the forest."

A thick mist was rolling in from the sea. Sean and Keelie

stuck close together, with Scott following behind. She could hardly see him.

"Laurie, where are you? I'm an idiot!" Scott shouted.

Sean touched his pointed ears and looked pained. "You don't have to scream."

Keelie reached out to Bella Matera. *I need to find my friend, a human girl. She's lost here.*

There was no answer.

She saw the shape of the trees floating in the mist, silently watching them. Maybe they couldn't hear Keelie when they took on spirit form. The last thing she wanted to do was open herself magically to the trees. She didn't want Bloodroot in her head. But what if Laurie was in danger? Keelie dropped her magical barriers again.

*Ancient Ones, I need your help. Can you hear me?*

Silence. But at least the pain didn't return.

Sean stopped suddenly, and Keelie bumped into him. He bent down, then turned to silently give her Laurie's gray hoodie.

Keelie's heart sank. It was no help to know she'd been right. Laurie was in danger.

"She was wearing that." Scott's voice trembled. He turned to shout her name again, but Keelie grabbed his arm.

"Don't. Maybe we don't need to let anyone know we're here." Keelie saw Sean nod at her words. He was taking this very seriously.

"What about Laurie? She needs to know we're looking for her." Scott took a few steps toward the foggy hill, then anxiously returned.

"Two people went through here." Sean was crouched by a broken fern, pointing toward the ground.

Two people. Someone had Laurie.

A voice rang out in Keelie's mind. *Beware, Tree Shepherdess.*

Keelie grabbed Sean's sleeve. He put an arm around her waist.

"Beware of what?" she asked aloud, her voice echoing against the wall of mist. Again, there was only silence in the forest.

"It's that voice again. It keeps saying 'Beware, tree shepherdess.' Beware of what?"

*I will show you.*

Pain blossomed in her head as Keelie began seeing a scene. It was as if she was watching through someone else's eyes. Her hands were wrinkled and spotted with dark circles. She leaned on a staff carved from a redwood branch. Her legs ached. Her back hurt when she moved, yet she loved walking among the Ancients.

She was deep in the forest and stood before a tall tree with dark red roots almost the color of blood. Bloodroot. He pushed his face out of the trunk, and his eyes were green, bright green. *Good day, Shepherd.*

"G'day, Bloodroot. May you grow many rings today."

In her vision, Keelie walked deeper in the forest, leaving Bloodroot behind. Her bones ached with each step, and she felt as old as the forest. Yet the trees, far older than she, were tall and strong. Their minds sharp and their wisdom deep, like their roots in the Earth. Her time had come.

Soon, Keelie was deep in the forest, deeper than where the rangers, the protectors, dwelled. There, growing underneath the canopy, were the misty forms of small trees. Bella Matera watched over her treelings protectively. There was strong magic in this forest. The little ones were the future, and they would have to be protected. Keelie didn't know if she had the strength left to do so. She needed help.

She felt herself being whooshed back into her body.

Sean grabbed her hand and steadied her. "Are you okay?"

She flexed her knees. They didn't ache. Her back was strong and young. "I was inside someone else's body. I think maybe the Redwood Tree Shepherd's body. I felt so old, so helpless."

"Did you guys hear that?" Scott's face was turned toward the Grove of Ancients. "It sounded like a girl."

"Stick close to me. We're all hearing things," Sean said. "This mist is very strange. I'm glad we don't have this in the Dread Forest."

"Me, too."

Somewhere near her right, she heard a small meow. "Sean, did you hear Knot?"

"Maybe I did."

He shone the flashlight in the mist, but the light reflected back at them.

A voice spoke softly to their left. "If you keep walking that way, you're going to fall off the cliff."

Sean stopped. He pointed the flashlight toward the voice. "Who said that? Are the trees talking to me?"

"I know he's pretty, I know he's chivalrous, but he's missing some smarts, isn't he?"

Keelie knew that voice. "Sean, lower your flashlight. It's Coyote."

He did, and Coyote stepped out of the fog, his eyes glinting mischievously.

"Troublemaker," Sean said. "Have you seen Laurie, the human girl?"

"Glad to see you, too. So your Laurie is gone?" Coyote lifted his nose high. "The forest is filled with players tonight."

"What do you mean, 'players'? If you know where she is, you'd better tell us." Keelie tried to read his expression, but she wasn't used to reading canine expressions. Or maybe Knot just made his intentions clearer.

"We've lost Scott," Sean's quiet voice interrupted. His flashlight beam bounced off the mist. No Scott.

"They're safe for now," Coyote said. "But as you say, they too could take a tumble into the ocean. The cold ocean on a dark night, a high cliff, a shoreline piled with sharp rocks." The coyote shivered. "It has all the elements of a drama. Likely even a tragedy."

"Quit Spielberg-Shakespearing on me. Did you see Scott leave?" Keelie demanded.

Coyote sighed. "Follow me." He looked back at Sean. "Shine the light on my tail. I spent all day grooming it, but I'm afraid I missed some tangles."

"It looks great," Keelie said through her teeth. "Can you move it? We need to find Scott and Laurie."

They trudged through the undergrowth, following Coyote's illuminated tail. Keelie hung onto Sean's arm in the dark fog.

Scott's voice rang eerily through the fog. "Laurie, Sean, Keelie?" Sometimes it sounded as if he were right next to her. Then as if he was far off.

But there was no sound of Laurie. Nothing. Keelie was worried for her friend. Laurie had lived through the Wildewood incident, when they'd been chased by rampaging trees, but what if she encountered Tavyn, with Bloodroot along for the ride?

They forged ahead, and she was glad she wasn't alone this time. She had Sean and Coyote, although she still wasn't sure about Coyote. She wondered about the little meow she'd heard. Was Knot out here with them?

Coyote stopped. "Someone other than your friends and Tavyn is wandering the woods tonight. This place is like Los Angeles. I thought people came up here for rest and relaxation."

"Yeah, well, you're hiking a forest in the middle of the night with a tree shepherd, what did you expect? For us, the trees are a crowd." Keelie shivered. It was getting colder. She put on Laurie's hoodie, wondering if her friend was freezing under a tree.

"At least we're not dealing with goblins." Coyote's ears twitched nervously.

Sean whirled around. "Goblins? Don't even speak of it. They're supposed to all be dead."

"Dead, oh no. They're real, and they're thriving in the urban areas," Coyote said.

"The tree at the mall, he said something about gobblers. Do you think he meant goblins?" Keelie asked. She remembered reading about goblins in the Compendium. She turned to Coyote. "Are there goblins in the Redwood Forest?"

Tilting his head to the right, Coyote grinned at her. "Maybe yes. Maybe no."

"None of your games. A simple yes or no." Keelie was impatient.

"It's a little bit more complicated than that." Coyote sat down. "Would you like my suggestion?"

"Tell us what you know about the goblins." Sean sounded fierce. He reached out and grabbed Coyote by the scruff of his neck.

Whoa. Sean was usually calm and in charge. Keelie gestured for him to calm down. She wasn't sure if Coyote could be hurt, but a normal coyote would have been squealing and snarling long before now.

"Let him go, Sean."

"We can't let him get away with these outrageous comments, Keelie." Sean glared down at the coyote, who whined and tried to look pitiful. "If the goblins have come up from underground, humans are in extreme danger. The elves have long feared that the goblins would one day return. Lord Elianard thinks that humans make it easy for them, and if they return, more powerful, more able to wield magic—they would soon rule the Earth, above and below ground, over humans, over elves, and over the fae."

Keelie thought that Lord Elianard was always quick to blame humans for everything, but the haughty elf was the most venerated Lore Master of the North American elven clans.

Coyote nodded. "Goblins hate the Shining Ones, even more than they hate elves."

Cold fear sliced through Keelie. She'd never heard about a goblin threat.

"We need to think this through," she said. "Right now, we're in an ancient forest, lost in the fog, trying to find two people. That has to be our priority. We'll figure out this goblin-threat stuff later."

"So, tell your boyfriend to let me go." Coyote lifted his upper lip and showed teeth to Sean. Sean lifted Coyote by the scruff, paws dangling, off the ground.

Keelie stepped close, exasperated. She had to try to maintain control over the situation. "Everybody stay calm. Coyote, answer our question—are there goblins here? Then Sean will let you go. And then you're going to help us find Laurie and Scott."

Coyote's tail went all limp and he lifted a shoulder in a twisted shrug. "Okay."

Keelie figured this was an example of having to be dominant. She was the Coyote Whisperer. Maybe it would work on Knot—she could try to be the Freaky Fairy Kitty Whisperer.

Coyote's words brought her back with a snap. "What I know is ... there once was a goblin here, but he didn't leave this forest. I feel an essence of darkness."

"Essence of darkness?" Keelie had never heard of that. "Like a goblin?"

"If something with dark magic dies—if an evil creature dies—then its essence might remain, corrupting the place of its death."

"It's like a curse, isn't it?" Keelie said. Her voice lowered. "A goblin curse." It had to be connected to this forest's weirdness, but she didn't have time to sit and think it through.

"Yes." Coyote wriggled in Sean's arms. "Now tell him to put me down."

"Not yet." Her eyes met Sean's, and as if they had a psychic connection, he lifted Coyote a few more inches off the ground.

The fairy creature howled, his voice echoing through the forest. "Not fair."

"Where are Laurie and Scott?" Keelie demanded.

"Put me down and I'll help you find them."

"And you're going to stick close to me, Coyote, because you know a whole lot more than you're telling."

The coyote grinned, which was unfortunate, because it showed off his teeth, long and sharp. Sean lowered him to the forest floor. He yipped and leaped as if he'd fooled them. Sean's hand clamped back down on his neck.

Keelie smiled grimly and did her best impersonation of her grandmother's stern voice. "Behave."

Coyote looked up with wet eyes, his lower lip trembling. "And that won't work on me."

A woman's voice called from far off. "Knot, my love

where are you? Oh, darling, don't leave me. I don't think my heart can take it."

Sean looked over at Keelie. "That's Risa. What is she doing in the forest?"

"She's searching for Knot." Keelie was going to kick Risa on the butt.

"And Knot is following Tavyn. What are you going to do, Keelie?" Coyote asked. "Go after Laurie, help Risa?" He laughed again. "And do you know where your grandmother is?"

Her heart sank as she realized that she had no way of knowing how to find her grandmother if she too, was lost in the Redwood Forest.

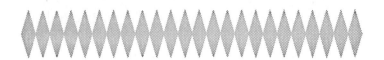

# twenty

"Is my grandmother out here? Is she in danger?"

"In this forest? Every second." Coyote sniffed the air. "I picked up the scent of the girl named Laurie on the western edge of the forest, near the beach."

If Coyote was telling the truth, at least Keelie wouldn't have to worry about her anymore. But Scott would still be missing, and maybe Grandmother, too.

"Sean, we're going to have to split up. Can you get Laurie to Sir Davey's RV?"

"I won't leave you here."

"Knot, where are you, my love?" Risa's voice came from farther north.

"I can't leave Risa to wander alone in the woods, either," Keelie said. "If she catches up with Knot, and he's after Tavyn, she's in great danger."

"It's true." Coyote spoke quickly. "Risa's love potion is like a magical GPS. She's compelled to seek her beloved, and it will lead her right to him."

Sean and Keelie locked eyes. "I'll find Laurie and get her to safety, then come right back for you," Sean said. "We'll find them, Keelie." He started to back away, then stopped and pulled Keelie to him, kissing her hard on the lips. He smiled as he released her.

The coyote's jaw dropped open in surprise. "My, my. I think our elf is thawing a bit here."

Despite the cold mist surrounding them, Keelie felt warm inside.

"Swear to me that you'll watch over her." Sean gestured with his head toward Keelie.

Coyote snarled. "Don't tell me my duties, elf boy."

Sean glared at him and stalked off into the forest.

Keelie sat at the base of the tree, wishing this were a regular forest. She could usually take comfort from talking to the trees, but not in this place. Feeling a surge of fairy magic, she looked around for its source. There were no fae here except for Coyote. And herself, of course.

Coyote came to her side and butted his head against her shoulder. She reached up to scratch his ears.

She felt itchy, and at the same time heard the jangle of

Peascod's hat. Her heart pounded against her rib cage when he hobbled into view from behind a hemlock tree. A harlequin-patterned mask covered his face, but from within the nimbus of his brown eyes, flames seem to flicker behind the pupils. Coyote growled as the jester walked closer to them, his gaze holding Keelie's.

She was trapped, held spellbound by his probing stare.

"Do you want to know the future?" His voice was scratchy, as if he'd been yelling.

Coyote's growl echoed through the trees, a spectral rumble that made chills go up and down Keelie's spine. If she hadn't known he was on her side, she would have been terrified. He snarled at the jester. "Fool, your lord has no sway in this forest."

Keelie wondered who Peascod's "lord" was. Someone even scarier, that was for sure. She did not want to meet him.

Peascod ignored Coyote and held out a glass sphere. A light from within glowed brightly, revealing Sean standing atop a snow-capped mountain, his green cloak billowing around him. "Look inside to see your future, Keliel."

Producing two more crystal balls, he started juggling all three high into the air. Keelie held her breath, afraid they would go soaring into the night sky never to return, like dreams taking flight in the middle of the night. Mesmerized, she slowly walked toward the glittering spheres. She had to know what her future held.

She wanted to touch them, to look at the wonder and secrets hidden deep in the center. When Peascod stopped juggling, she reached out a hand. But as she stepped forward,

Coyote gripped the back of her hoodie with his teeth and tugged her backwards. She reached around, trying to make him let go.

"Look again, Keliel."

The sound of Peascod's voice brought her attention back to the promises of the future held within the glass. He slowly moved his hand, and the image of Sean in the green cloak disappeared into that of a dark rider, whose cloak flowed around him like raven's wings.

Keelie stopped. Cold apprehension slid over her as a premonition prickled up her spine. She would meet the dark rider.

This jolted her back to reality. Keelie quickly reached down and touched the Earth, pulling up a current of magic. Suddenly, Knot appeared and ran directly between Keelie and Peascod. He meowed angrily.

The scary jester narrowed his eyes. He started juggling again, tossing the crystal balls into the air in ever-increasing arcs. She watched as they ascended into the night sky, toward the stars. When Peascod reached out to catch the balls, his hat jangled. It made Keelie feel as if someone's fingernail was raking down a chalkboard inside her head. The glass balls clacked against one another as he caught them. Keelie was afraid they would shatter.

Peascod bowed gracefully and then righted himself, as if he was performing in front of an admiring audience at the festival. Menace filled his eyes. "Magic is loose in the world, my dear Keliel."

"I am not your dear Keliel." She glowered at him.

"We are not so different."

Keelie didn't look away from him, even though every instinct in her body told her to do so. Jesters liked to taunt and tease. Maybe this was what Peascod was doing to her. Playing with her, like Knot played with a *feithid daoine.*

Peascod drew nearer to her, and a coldness wrapped all around her. Knot hissed and stepped closer, acting like a feline shield.

Peascod glared, but then he turned his head toward the forest. His eyes dilated, and Keelie thought she saw an eerie silver flicker in his pupils.

"Knot, where are you?" It was Risa again. Keelie never thought the day would arrive when she would be glad to see the elf girl.

"We'll meet again one day, Keliel Katharine Heartwood, with no guardians to protect you." Peascod smiled wickedly. His outline wavered, and she watched in horrified wonder as he seemed to melt into the forest floor.

He was gone. Relief washed over Keelie. She knew he'd spoken the truth. She would meet him again—it was a certainty that seemed as real as anything her new life had brought her.

Knot meowed angrily and hissed, tail bushed out. Next to him was Coyote, hunched and snarling. They did not like the jester, and for once Keelie agreed with them.

Keelie heard Risa coming closer. "Oh Knotsie Wotsie. My love, I hear you. Where are you?"

"Risa, over here." Keelie called. She held the flashlight up to act as a beacon for the lost elf girl.

Knot sniffed at the spot where the jester had vanished, then scratched at the soil and squatted over it. A moment later, Coyote sniffed where Knot had been and lifted his leg.

"No kidding. I kind of understand the urge," Keelie muttered. She was still shaking a little. Coyote just looked at her, then bolted into the forest.

There was a crackle of sticks and the movement of bushes on the ground. Risa stumbled into the clearing. She was covered in mud and had sticks poking up at odd angles in her hair. Her eyes immediately focused on Knot. She dropped to her knees. "Oh my love, I thought you were in danger."

"What the hell happened to you?" Keelie felt a rush of adrenaline and fear. "You look like Zombie Apocalypse Barbie."

Risa ignored her and rubbed Knot's ears. Knot drooled.

Keelie squatted and stared at Risa. "Tell me what happened."

"Sir Davey came by to check on your grandmother," Risa said distractedly. "He said he had something that might help her with the tree magic. When I went to tell her, she wasn't in her room. Sir Davey told me to stay because he was going to contact the ranger elves to help search for Lady Keliatiel, but I had to find Knot. I knew he was in danger."

"Search? You mean you didn't find her?"

"She's missing, but don't worry. Lady Keliatiel can take care of herself." Risa rubbed Knot's tummy. "I was frantic to find Knot. I couldn't stay in the house knowing he was in danger." Risa's face shone with love as she gazed at the cat.

Keelie gritted her teeth in frustration. "So who exactly is looking for my grandmother?"

Knot turned his head to look at Keelie, and for a moment Keelie thought she saw a flash of tenderness in the cat's eyes. He immediately wrapped his paws around her jean-clad legs and bit her.

Keelie shook her leg and lifted it, sending the cat flying toward the bushes.

Risa rose. "What did you do?" she shrieked.

"He's fine. See?"

A purring Knot strode back to Keelie and rubbed up against her ankle. Risa's face looked haunted. Tears streamed down her face.

"Knot and I have a complicated relationship," Keelie said. "I'll explain later, but now I need for you to tell me what happened before Grandmother disappeared. Did you hear any strange noises?"

Risa straightened her shoulders, her face stiff with concentration as she thought back. "The night was windy, and I heard the tapping of the branches at the window and this beautiful music."

"Harp music?"

"No, a song. It was lovely."

Keelie's skin grew clammy with fear. Now she knew who had her grandmother. Bella Matera. But why? Closing her eyes, Keelie opened up her telepathic communication.

*Bella Matera.*

Nothing.

*Where is my grandmother?*

Her head exploded with a sound that seemed to come from the trees. Keelie placed her hands over her ears, attempting to stop the spine-shattering noise. She stumbled, her equilibrium became distorted, and the world began to spin.

Risa reached out to steady her. "What's wrong?"

"The trees," Keelie gasped. "They're screaming, and I can't get them out of my head."

Risa held onto her. "Focus. Concentrate. Call upon your Earth magic."

Keelie sent a tendril of power into the Earth and touched cold, oily darkness. She yanked backed her power, nauseous. "I can't use it. The soil is polluted with dark magic."

"Here?" Risa stared at the ground, and at the normal-looking silhouettes of the ferns and bushes. "I knew there was something creepy about this place. But wait—you've used dark magic before. Why can't you use it now? Turn it to your purpose."

Yes. The dark magic within Keelie pulsed like a beating heart, a wild animal that had been caged and was waiting for its moment of sweet freedom. What would happen if she loosed it?

"I can't." Keelie said. There were consequences to using dark magic.

"You can. You can control it." Suddenly Risa fell to her knees. "My head. I think the trees are banging on my skull."

Keelie's thoughts seemed to skip, missing pieces, as if the trees were distorting her mind. She'd never experienced trees talking to anyone but tree shepherds, or trying to hurt people, but these were Ancients. Their store of knowledge was over two thousand years old. She had nothing to use against it.

Something heavy, fat, and fuzzy landed on her foot.

"Yeow fae meowgic."

Risa leaped up, staring at Knot. "He talked."

Keelie removed her hands from her ears and dropped to her knees. The world spun super-fast, faster than any ride she'd ever been on at a theme park. She must be hitting Super G. She raised her arms, fighting the centrifugal push. The dark fae magic within her, unleashed, glittered gold. Like an uncaged cheetah, it raced through her. A comet of magic flowed through her hands and spiraled into the sky, illuminating the forest around them in an eerie red light.

Keelie fell face-forward into the dirt.

"Keelie!" She heard the shout but couldn't make out the voice. Her nose scraped against a piece of bark as she remembered that Knot and Coyote had polluted the soil even more than the dark fae. She forced herself to roll over.

Something cold and heavy was walking on her forehead. A soothing purring filled her ears and embraced her mind. She heard the "lick, lick, lick" noise as something warm and wet sandpapered her eyebrows.

"Should he be doing that?" a female voice said. It sounded like Laurie.

"I think it's a good look for her," another feminine voice answered. That had to be Risa.

Keelie opened her eyes and stared into Knot's green gaze. He placed his paw on her forehead and licked his leg.

"Get off of me, you beast."

"See, she doesn't appreciate everything he does for her." Risa said.

Knot jumped off Keelie. His purr remained nearby.

"I don't know," Laurie said. "I mean, I think this intense love you have for him might require therapy, Risa. Or an antidote."

Keelie sat up. Her head still felt fragile, like an eggshell. "What happened? Laurie, where's Sean?"

"He found me," Laurie replied. "But then we got separated in the fog. I heard you screaming."

"The trees attacked us with some type of sonar, I think. I don't know how they did it, but it—"

"It gave us vertigo," Risa interjected. "And then we couldn't think. You couldn't tap into your tree magic, Keelie, but you found some way around it."

"How do you know that?" Keelie asked.

"Anyone who has taken Elianard's classes knows about the ancient powers of the trees. Plus, I use green magic, too." Risa pushed her hair back from her shoulder. "You're not the only elf with magic. Why do you think my family is the gardener of the Dread Forest? My pumpkins are famous."

Knot turned his face away and tried to look innocent. Keelie figured he'd been up to pumpkin mischief. Typical.

Her head throbbed, reminding her of their situation. "Have you seen my grandmother?" she asked Laurie.

"No, sorry. I was heading back to the festival grounds, because I thought Sir Davey could help me. But Sean found me. He said Scott is missing." Laurie looked as confused as Keelie felt.

"The trees are playing us," Keelie said. "Somehow they're the cause of this mayhem. But why? I think they want my grandmother to help them. They must have her."

Risa looked shocked. "How could you think that Lady Keliatiel would possibly agree to get involved in any shady dealings?"

"No, I think she's the victim here." Keelie rubbed her hands up and down her face. She had to concentrate. That's what Dad would tell her to do. Leave this elven circus of emotions for later. "First, we need to find my grandmother. I think she's in danger."

"How are we going to do that? So far, the trees are out-smarting us." Risa looked around at the tall shapes of the tree trunks as if they could hear her, which, of course, they could.

Laurie nodded. "I mean, from what I understand, these guys are like the PhDs of trees. What do they want?"

"Good question. I think it's time we found out." Keelie started walking toward the Grove of the Ancients, where the song had come from. Knot hurried to her side, leaving Laurie and Risa to catch up.

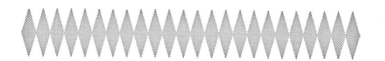

# twenty-one

Keelie shone the flashlight into the mist. They'd been walking for what seemed like forever, but there was no sign of Grandmother. She hoped they would run into Sean. Even Knot seemed frustrated.

Risa stopped. "I think we're going in a circle. That tree looks familiar."

"They all look the same to me," Laurie said. She sagged to the ground.

Keelie's heart pounded. Risa was right. "If we keep walking, eventually the sun will come up and we'll know which direction to go. At least to get out of the woods." Meanwhile, Grandmother was in danger.

"Where are we?" Risa asked.

"I don't know." Keelie said. "I thought we were heading toward the Grove of the Ancients, but we should have been there by now."

Laurie shivered. "I don't want to go there." She crossed her hands over chest.

"Use your rose quartz. I think we should go this way." Keelie shone her flashlight down a path with branches intertwining like a woodland arbor, then flipped the beam up. She couldn't even see the top of the canopy.

Bloodroot's voice drifted in her mind. *Are you sure this is the right way?*

*You have my grandmother, and I want her back.*

Knot forged ahead.

Keelie closed her mind. She knew she was on the right path. She could feel a thread of dark magic. A very powerful source of dark magic, and different from the dark fae magic that she'd felt around Peascod.

"It's this way. Follow me."

Laurie looked very afraid. "Why do you always have to go walking into creepy forests in the middle of the night? It's like a repeating plot line from a B horror movie."

"It's not a repeating plot line. I'm a tree shepherd, and helping forests in need, even in the middle of the night, is what I do. I don't have a choice."

Risa lifted her hands in frustration. "Will you two shut up?"

There was a loud snap, and Tavyn stepped out from behind the trunk of a giant Redwood.

"Allow me to escort you."

Risa shrieked, and Laurie stumbled backwards.

Keelie stood firmly in the middle of the path. "We don't need your help." She put her hands on her hips. Tree shepherds came to a bad end in this forest, and she was sure that Tavyn was involved.

Laurie leaned close to Keelie. "Are you crazy? He's a ranger elf. He can get us out of here."

"Yes, but he's also possessed by a tree."

"I didn't know trees could possess people. I thought he had a bad spray tan."

"I didn't know either, until I came to the redwoods. The Ancients are different." Keelie had been possessed by a tree in the Wildewood Forest, but that had just been for a second.

"Will you two shut up?" Tavyn shouted.

Keelie could feel the power of the Earth beneath her. She felt her fairy and tree magic swirling together like a whirlpool, stretching her skin from inside. But her dark fae magic hadn't been added to the blend. As long as she kept control of it, the trees wouldn't be able to draw on it.

Tavyn glared at Keelie. He thrust his head forward, sniffing. "I feel your power. You're so strong." He circled her. "The goblins know about you. Herne wants you for himself. They've known about you since your birth. They've been looking for one like you for two hundred years, ever since their seer predicted that a half-elven, half-human child would be born with the magic of the fae." He smiled, showing green teeth. "But we found you first."

Keelie swallowed, trying to process all that he'd said. "I've never heard about a prophecy." And what or who was Herne?

"The elves didn't know about the prophecy, but the goblins did." Bloodroot's voice had taken over Tavyn's. It was deep and woodsy.

"So, I'm just a half-human, half-elven girl. I don't have any great power. What use am I to the goblins?" Keelie thought that the less she did with goblins, the better. She shivered.

"You can wield power that the fairies and elves only dream about," Tavyn-Bloodroot replied. "You can change the shape of the natural world."

"Oh please. If I could do that, would I be here talking to you?"

A ghostly tree shape formed in the air and floated in front of them. "You're wanted now."

Tavyn-Bloodroot frowned. "We're on our way." He motioned to Keelie. "Follow me."

"What if we don't come with you?"

"You want to see your grandmother again. So follow me."

There was a muffled cry from nearby.

Tavyn-Bloodroot nodded. "To ensure your cooperation, and Knot's, we have something that belongs to you."

A wooden cage was lowered from the tops of the trees. Inside was a wild-eyed Scott.

Risa and Laurie gasped.

Scott saw Keelie and grabbed the bars of the cage. "Keelie,

get me out of here. I lost that pink rock you gave me. Hurry, you've got to do something. The trees are going to eat me."

"Stay calm, Scott," Keelie called up to him. But like a yo-yo, the wooden cage was yanked back up into the tree canopy.

"Okay, we'll follow you." Keelie detached one of the rose quartz charms that she wore on her belt loop. "But give him one of these, okay?"

"Of course. I figured you would see it my way." Tavyn-Bloodroot took the little charm and put it in his pocket.

Laurie glared at the tree-possessed elf ranger. "You'd better not hurt him."

"My dear, we are trees, not humans like you. Humans are the hurtful ones. We just want to make sure that your kind do not cause further destruction. We're the injured parties here."

Scott's screams echoed through the night forest.

Laurie looked up. "Can we get one of those to him? I know just how he feels."

"Me, too," Keelie said. She wished Ariel were here. A hawk would be able to fly the charm right to Scott. She looked down at Knot and held out another charm. "Can you get this rose quartz to him? Mr. Greenteeth doesn't seem to have any intention of giving it to him." She thought she'd made too many charms, but at this rate she'd be out soon.

Knot took the key ring with the pink stone hanging from it and clawed his way up the bark of the nearby redwood. I hope those claws hurt, Keelie thought, but she didn't dare say it in tree speak or Knot would be swatted down by a branch.

Tavyn-Bloodroot glared at the cat fast disappearing up the tree. "Come on, then." He marched up the gradual slope, going through the great ferns and brush that covered the green hill. The girls struggled after him until they reached the top and saw a clearing, surrounded by the tallest trees Keelie had ever seen.

"The Grove of the Ancients," she said aloud. She could sense that this was the source of the thread of dark magic.

Then she noticed Grandmother. Lady Keliatiel was sitting on a log in the center of the meadow with a very old man, who was wizened and wrinkled with age and holding a carved staff. He looked like a petrified wizard. It had to be the Redwood Tree Shepherd.

Keelie raced forward. "Grandmother, are you okay? We've been looking for you."

Her grandmother didn't seem to hear her. She and Viran appeared to be in a trance. At that moment, a clear bubble formed around them and they rose into the air, vanishing into the tree canopy.

Tavyn-Bloodroot leaned close. "She can't hear you. She's in her own world, lost in time."

"What have you done to her?" Keelie wondered how she could get Grandmother and the old tree shepherd back to the ground safely.

"She's in a kind of stasis, based on an elven charm that we have adapted to our own use. Tree shepherds are a constant source of magic, but your power exceeds our dreams."

Now she knew why they wanted her here. "So you just want to use us as batteries? For what?"

"To protect the forest from humans. Humans have outstripped your tree shepherd skills. But we've discovered a way to keep them out. We need to control the Dread."

"But the dark magic I feel here is not the Dread," Keelie said. "What you're doing is wrong. I will never help you."

"That's what we thought." Tavyn-Bloodroot nodded as if she'd confirmed it.

Suddenly, there were loud screams. Keelie looked behind her and saw Laurie and Risa ascending in a wooden cage. They were next to Scott, whose cage now dangled above her as well, transported there by the trees. He had the rose quartz, but there was no sign of Knot.

"If you want your friends to survive, I think you will cooperate."

Keelie had to find a way out of this. Sean and Coyote were somewhere out there, and Knot was somewhere up in the trees. She wished she could communicate with them.

Tavyn-Bloodroot turned to her. His eyes were bright green, but ringed with gold. Keelie recognized the sign of fairy magic. Dark fairy magic.

He leaned closer to her. "The elf jouster will not save you, nor will the fae creatures."

Tavyn-Bloodroot could read her mind. Keelie stared into his green-veined eyes. Focus. Concentrate. The trees had used a disorientation spell, based on sound waves. She pulled up her barriers against the trees, then pushed Tavyn-Bloodroot out of her mind. Maybe if she concentrated on something that she found irritating, she could telepathically send it to Tavyn.

She thought about nails raking down a chalkboard. Laurie had done it at Baywood Academy.

Tavyn-Bloodroot stumbled back, holding his head.

Around the cages that held Laurie, Scott, and Risa, misty forms floated and circled. Then Keelie heard the sound of children laughing. Totally not what she had expected.

She looked around. The largest tree in the Grove stood in front of her, and growing between its roots were small treelings. It was the nursery she'd seen in her dream. Keelie heard the beautiful music, the lilting melody that had haunted her from the night she'd first arrived.

But the taint of goblin magic was getting stronger; Keelie located its source. It was the treeling nursery. And pushing her face out of the massive trunk was none other than Bella Matera, the Mother Tree.

"Hello, Keelie. I'm glad you could come and meet my babies." Bella Matera pushed her whole body out of the trunk. No longer a part of the tree, she was in her spirit form, as were the little treelings, which had come down to dance and spin around their mother. Tavyn-Bloodroot pushed Keelie closer to Bella.

Bella clasped her elegant, treelike hands together. "Aren't they beautiful? They will survive no matter what. I have seen to it."

"What are you doing?" Keelie asked. "You're growing them in soil tainted with dark magic. What will it do to their roots?"

"It will make them stronger. They have to be strong to survive today. Do you know how many children I have lost over the past millennia? My heart has been broken thousands of times—whenever I hear a tree being cut down for lumber. Now they will strengthen, while the Dread keeps humans away."

"There has to be a better way."

"If there is, I haven't found one in two thousand years." Bella's voice sparked with anger. "When the goblin died at my roots, we drank in his blood. We tapped into the dark magic, and I found a new way to strengthen my young."

"I've never heard of trees using blood for power. You're the Ancients—you can't do this. Did you kill the goblin?"

"He had lost his way. He was sick, and going to die anyway. The elves killed him to keep him from revealing the Grove and their village."

"The elves killed a goblin here. Why didn't they tell me?" Keelie thought guiltily of the Red Cap she'd killed, but he'd attacked the people and forest around the High Mountain Faire. She'd done it to protect them ... but how was that different from what they'd done here?

"We call it survival." Bella Matera's face hovered inches from Keelie's. She turned her head toward the cages. "There is another here with green magic flowing through her veins. She can understand me." She pointed to the cages with her ghostly branches. "Release the elf girl and bring her to me."

The cages lowered. Tavyn-Bloodroot pulled Risa out and dragged her over to the queen tree's spirit.

Stubborn and haughty, Risa held her head high.

Bella examined her. "Her power is nothing near the strength of Keliel's, but there is a different kind of magic. A fertile power of the Earth. We can take it to feed my little ones."

"I'm with Keelie. I'm not going to help you." Risa lifted her chin.

Tavyn-Bloodroot slapped Risa across the face and she fell to the ground, angry red welts on her skin. "You will do as our queen commands."

"Leave her alone," Keelie shouted.

Tavyn-Bloodroot glared at her. "Why?"

"Because she's in love with my cat, and she's covered my butt on more than one occasion, and I guess that makes her my friend. Something you wouldn't understand since you've sucked up so much dark power that it's made you unbalanced. Can't you see what Bella is doing is wrong?"

"Do not talk to me about what is wrong. You were glad when dark magic restored your hawk's sight and helped you to make things right in your forest. We're only doing what is right in our forest." Tavyn-Bloodroot turned his attention back to Risa.

"Dark magic is only helpful when it restores balance," Keelie said. "Killing another creature is not restoring balance. Draining the magic of the tree shepherd is not restoring the balance. It's evil and it's wrong, and you and the other redwoods will pay the price."

"Yes, we will pay the price, but our treelings will stand a chance in this world, and we'll be able to protect ourselves from humans. You say killing another creature is wrong? How about the humans who tear us down, to be used for their comfort?"

Keelie stared at him. "Don't you know the karma fairy always finds you?"

He looked alarmed. "What karma fairy?"

Keelie shifted her gaze to Risa, who looked puzzled for a second, then nodded.

"I should know," Risa said. "The karma fairy paid me a visit. Why do you think I'm in love with a cat?"

"See?" Keelie shrugged innocently. "She tried to give my boyfriend Sean a love potion."

"Then I drank it instead because of a mix-up," Risa added.

Tavyn-Bloodroot narrowed his eyes. "You're in love with a cat because you made a stupid mistake."

"Why do you think there was such a mistake? It was because of the karma fairy. She's really good friends with Keelie." Risa nodded toward Keelie.

"There is nothing in the lore about a karma fairy. Why haven't we heard about it?" Tavyn-Bloodroot looked at Keelie for the answer.

"I don't know. I didn't know I was part of a goblin prophecy, either." That was certainly true.

A sharp pain erupted in Keelie's head. She winced.

*You're here, Tree Shepherdess. I tried to warn you away.* The voice seemed sad. Keelie kept her eye on Tavyn-Bloodroot to make sure he couldn't pick up on her telepathic communication.

"Why does Bella not know about this karma fairy? I

must ask her." Tavyn-Bloodroot walked toward Bella, who was back in her dark nursery.

If all the bad guys were present, then there was only one person her painful caller could be. Keelie sent a thought out. *You must be Viran, the Redwood Tree Shepherd.*

*I am he.*

*Bella and Bloodroot have taken my friends and me prisoner. They have my grandmother, too. How do I stop them?*

*I have no answer for you, Keliel of the Dread Forest. I am fading and cannot help you. I sought only to warn you. Too late, too late.* His voice seemed weaker, then vanished.

She looked at Risa, who was staring, frightened, at the treelings and their spectral mother. Somewhere above them, Grandmother floated, stuck in a tea party that would end when the trees were ready to drain her, and Keelie would be next. No help was coming.

She'd have to rescue everyone herself.

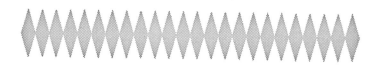

# twenty-two

Assess the situation. That was what her phys ed teacher had taught them when they did "summer survival" at Baywood Academy. Then, it had been about what to do if your surf board got pulled out too far or if someone tried to mug you. Now, Keelie considered this to be "summer survival" gone way bad.

She didn't know how to stop a redwood forest gone amuck. In the Wildewood, the trees had been angry and looking for vengeance, but these trees were polluted with dark magic, infested with the taint of a goblin's blood. They would kill.

Keelie felt alone and powerless. Her dark power was

dancing on the edge of her control, ready to erupt again. Control. Balance. Focus. That must be her mantra.

She remembered the calm charm that she'd used on Knot and Laurie. It had worked on them, but would it work on herself? She envisioned bright sunlight, to counteract the darkness of the forest, and felt the magic slowly grow within her. She said the words of the charm silently to herself. For a moment nothing changed ... she could hear Bella Matera laughing at Tavyn-Bloodroot, and felt his anger lash out like a knife.

Then the magic bubbled up, filling her, settling into every corner of her being.

Keelie saw that with Bella distracted, the treeling spirits were scooting over to Risa, drawn to her energy. She leaned close to the elf girl. "You've got that Mother Goddess thing going on. See if you can use your charm to bring the tree-lings under your spell."

Risa looked at the silvery, mistlike tree children. "They frighten me. My vegetables do not have spirits that dance around. I have no wish to befriend them."

"Try anyway." Keelie wondered if booting Risa's curvy backside would help. It would certainly make Keelie feel better.

"You are very harsh." Tears slid down Risa's face. "And to think that once I thought you and I could be friends."

"Yeah? When was that?" Keelie pressed her lips together. Great. "Antagonize your fellow hostages" was probably not in any rescue guide.

The tree-spirit children were watching them as if they

were interesting creatures. They'd probably never even seen elves, except for Tavyn.

"Risa, sing them a song or something. Do you sing to your radishes and pumpkins? Whatever you do to them, do it now for these tree spirits."

The elf girl tossed her head, but the mist had done a number on her hair and the sodden red curls drooped on her shoulders. She sighed, then began to sing. Her voice rose, and Keelie felt power in it, a green, vibrant glow that seemed surprisingly familiar. It was a lot like her own magic.

She watched as one by one the treelings drew closer, relaxed and fascinated by Risa's song.

Keelie wondered what she was going to do to the treelings once she had them. If they had dark magic flowing through their roots and rings, she didn't know if there was a way to counteract it. And she didn't want to hurt them. They were just babies.

It came to her. Fairy magic. She had been using it all along to balance the earth and tree magic, so she should be able to do it with the treelings. But she had no idea how she could do it without Bella or Bloodroot finding out.

Tavyn-Bloodroot strode over. "What are you doing? What magic is this?"

Bella Matera drifted after him. "Growing magic. More useful even than I'd thought."

Risa glared at Keelie. "Thanks a lot. Now I'll be nursemaid to the evil trees."

"My children are not evil," Bella snapped. She stared hard at Risa, and the girl's eyes went blank.

Keelie felt deflated. This was a big step backward—and she may have gotten Risa killed. But they were probably all doomed. Tavyn would never allow Scott and Laurie to go free to tell anyone about what had happened here. Panic overwhelmed her. Bella and Bloodroot were too powerful.

She searched her mind frantically for any scrap of knowledge that would help, regretting not studying the Compendium more. The only spell she remembered, other than the calm charm, was a hay-fever charm. Not too useful here. At least, if she died, Elianard would never learn what a slacker she was.

Keelie eyed the little treelings. Maybe she could use the hay-fever charm after all. It was a desperate idea, but she was definitely desperate.

She reached down and yanked out a hunk of moss.

Tavyn-Bloodroot noticed her movement. "What are you doing?"

"Nothing. I'm adjusting the bandage on my ankle. It itches." She tightened her fist.

"Don't be clever, Keliel, or your friends will pay."

Above them, the cages spun like tops, and Scott and Laurie yelled.

"Stop it. They're not hurting anyone." Keelie couldn't bear to hear her friends' terrified cries.

Bella Matera floated closer. "There is no such thing as a karma fairy. I've searched the root archives." She glanced at Keelie. "Do not be so quick to trick."

Tavyn-Bloodroot glared at Keelie. She gave him twinkle fingers and a little grin. *Gotcha.*

Meanwhile, the treeling spirits had drifted away from Risa and begun a dance, swirling in a mist-filled circle. They reminded Keelie of ghostly children playing "Ring Around the Rosie." She squeezed the moss in her hand, hoping it would do as a substitute for meadow grass. She summoned the memory of Mr. Heidelman mowing his grass at midnight. Now she just had to keep that image close by as she worked the next bit. Instead of curing hay fever, she had to reverse the spell to inflict it. Talk about bad karma.

Keelie leaned close to Risa, who now had a thread of drool hanging from her lip. Too bad she couldn't keep her like this. She shrugged and reached into the Earth, feeling for the Under-the-Hill that had to be here, as it did under every forest.

She prodded deep until she felt a stirring of the golden magic that signaled fae dwellings. It was frustrating, and it took too long, like using a metal detector on the beach. She kept an eye on Tavyn and Bella Matera as she searched, hoping they would not be able to feel the fae magic. At last, she sensed it—small, cold, dusty places, long-abandoned, but still sparking with fae energy. She pulled a strand of it, yanking hard until it came loose and she could wrap it around Risa.

The minute the strand touched Risa, it dissolved into golden sparkles that disappeared into her flesh. Risa blinked twice as her eyes refocused. She ran the back of her hand over her mouth. "Ugh. What happened?"

"You got whammied. Feeling okay?"

Risa nodded. "You brought me back?"

Keelie shrugged. "I have an idea that might get us out of here, but I need your help," she whispered.

"What do you want me to do?"

"See if you can attract the treelings to you again."

"You brought me back. You could have just left me like that forever." Risa was smiling at her. "You know, if you hadn't stolen Sean and possessed the heart of my beloved Knot, I think we could've been good friends."

"Don't flatter yourself." Keelie said. She smiled inwardly.

Risa concentrated again on the treelings. Soon the scent of cinnamon—elf magic—floated in the air, and the treelings stopped dancing and hovered in the dark meadow, watching Risa. She seemed to shimmer with pulsing energy as she smiled and lifted her hands. "Hello, little ones." Her voice was like chimes.

The misty little forms floated back toward Risa. They were small, like wispy clouds on a spring day. One of them giggled innocently, but still, Keelie detected an undercurrent of darkness. They began swirling around Risa.

Keelie closed her eyes, tapping into the green tree magic around her. She focused on Bella Matera's children. They were so small, but already she sensed that the darkness had intertwined itself into them on the cellular level. This dark magic was different than she'd experienced in the Dread Forest—it reminded her of what she'd felt in the mall parking lot in L.A. when she'd driven past the SUV. She wondered if it had been full of goblins.

Keelie lifted her eyes. Bella and Tavyn-Bloodroot had been conferring on the other side of the clearing, but now came toward them, drawn by the dancing children. Her heart raced. "Hurry, Risa."

The little trees swirled faster around Risa. Green energy flowed from the elf girl, and her eyes were glazed as if she was in a trance.

The time had come to use the hay-fever charm.

Keelie forced herself to recall the sound of Mr. Heidelman's lawn mower at midnight and the scent of freshly mown grass wafting through her window. She tightened her hand around the bits of moss.

She had to reach the goblin magic directly. With her tree sense, Keelie looked into the treelings' slender trunks. Their cellulose was green, but slotted with oozy, oily tissue. Their mitochondria were polluted with dark magic. Keelie had to eradicate it, like chemo to a cancer cell, but first she had to use the charm.

She reached down to the line of fae energy she'd tapped earlier, and combined it with the tree magic she'd pulled from the trees around her. She combined the two, twisting the magics tightly until bright golden sparkles formed within her. The power exploded, surging through her.

Keelie opened her eyes to see her hands and arms glowing with golden iridescence. The moss she'd torn floated in midair before her.

"Children," Keelie's voice was loamy and commanding. Grandmother would be pleased.

The treelings stopped spinning. Risa collapsed as she released them to Keelie's care.

Keelie blew, and the floating moss raced toward the treel-ings like poisonous darts, each greeny bit hitting a treeling spirit. The treeling cloud-forms screamed in pain and raced back to their tree bodies, the saplings in the protected glade.

Bella shrieked. "My babies!"

"No!" Tavyn-Bloodroot shouted. "Stop!" He ran toward Keelie, but a big orange object landed heavily on him, hiss-ing, and started biting and scratching.

*Knot.*

Tavyn-Bloodroot tore the cat from his face and threw him to the side. Knot hit hard against the trunk of a tree and slid bonelessly to the ground.

The sound of voices came from the forest, and Tavyn-Bloodroot drew a sword and raced toward it.

Risa lifted her head and stretched her arms out to Knot. "Beloved." She dragged herself over to the motionless, furry lump.

Keelie wanted to run to him, too, but she couldn't stop now. She had to pull the dark goblin essence out of the little treelings before the elder spirits could stop her.

Golden light surrounded each small tree. Keelie held out her hand and let the magic flow freely. Like water from an overturned bucket, the golden cloud shimmered out in a wide, uncontrolled arc.

Bella began manically spinning around Keelie. She sang a beautiful melody about the stars; Keelie suddenly felt sleepy, but Bella Matera's song was too frantic and she was able to shake it off.

Then, an ear-splitting howl shattered the hypnotic feeling. Coyote was beside Keelie. He howled again, a long, wavering note.

Bella shrieked in anger. "Your grandmother is dead, tree shepherd. Dead!" She reached upward and Keelie saw that the bubble with Grandmother and Viran was moving back and forth among the sharp upper branches of the trees. Grandmother seemed alert now, and her face was contorted with fear. Viran was on all fours, screaming down at them, although no sound escaped the bubble. She could see his mouth form a word over and over.

Bella would make the bubble burst and they would fall to their deaths, and it would be Keelie's fault. But would Grandmother want her to risk the forest to save her? Keelie looked at the treeling spirits, each still encased in fae magic. The magic was doing its work, and Bella Matera now swooped among them, anguish on her face.

From within her mind, she heard a voice, not the Redwood Tree Shepherd's voice, but another, familiar one.

*Keelie, I'm coming. Stay strong.*

It was Sean. He was speaking to her telepathically.

*Focus, Keelie. Stay focused. I'll take care of Tavyn.*

The sound of clashing swords came from the west. Keelie cleared her mind and tried to focus once more on the trees, but now she could hear Grandmother's shrieks and cries for help.

Wait a minute. Grandmother wouldn't scream in fear.

Her eyes met Coyote's, and he grinned at her, tongue lolling, before leaping into the air. As he arced through space he dissolved, and Keelie saw a great crow flap its way up in a spiraling climb.

Bella saw him too and screamed "No," calling on the trees of the Grove. Branches lashed at Coyote, trying to knock the crow from the air, but he dodged them, intent on the bubble and its frantic captives. He flew above it, and then dove down and through the bubble.

Time stopped for a second as Keelie saw the sphere vanish. The crow flapped between two trees and circled back. No falling bodies, no screaming victims. It had been an illusion.

Her head felt clear now, and she turned her attention to the little trees that now reached branches out toward their mother. Black wisps floated from their trunks as Keelie pushed more fairy magic into them. She had to pull as much of the taint out of them as possible, but she could only do so much with her magic.

She closed her eyes. She envisioned their rings, then down to the cellular level. Most of the treelings were clean now, but there were some who remained tainted with darkness. The treelings with the goblin blood would have to be watched carefully over their lifetime, or at least until a cure could be found.

When Keelie opened her eyes, Bella, still in spirit form, was floating above her treelings, weeping.

Coyote, back in coyote form, touched his nose to her hand. "Now would be a good time to save your grandmother and Viran."

"Where are they?" Keelie asked. "Take me to them."

"Follow me." Coyote guided Keelie to a giant redwood with blood-red roots and a blood-red trunk. The ground beneath it glowed faintly blue, with the remains of the elemental that Bloodroot had sent to find the missing tree shepherd.

Bloodroot's tree. She should've known. Keelie pressed her hand against the bark. It hummed with dark energy, and more.

*Keliel. You have come, my child.* It was Viran, the tree shepherd. He was inside the tree. How was that possible?

Across the path, another tree hummed with similar energy. Keelie placed her hands on its trunk. *Grandmother?*

*Keelie, keep your hands against the bark. Then we can join forces to break through the binding sap.*

Keelie didn't know if she had the energy or magical resources left to break Grandmother and Viran free, but she pressed her hands into the trunk. She felt a doorway open to Grandmother, whose strong will and magic were so powerful.

A loud crack ripped through the air. Keelie covered her ears as sound waves pulsed around her. Coyote howled.

A green shimmer surrounded the tree, and Grandmother stepped out of the crack, pulp clinging to her hair and clothes.

She brushed herself off as she rushed to Bloodroot's trunk. "We need to help Viran."

Bella Matera screamed, and the ground and trees trembled with the aftershock of her rage. She was seconds away.

With their hands on the trunk of the mighty redwood, Grandmother and Keelie joined magical energy. It felt strange to allow Grandmother to pull on her power. Keelie felt her remaining magic tug through her hands and into the redwood's tainted roots. The magic rose through the bark. Sensing a line of Earth energy, she added it to the power Grandmother wielded. All around the tree, dirt spewed into the air like geysers.

"Stop." Bella flew at them, but they ignored her. Without the tree shepherds' magic to draw upon, her power had faded.

Another loud crack tore Keelie's ears, and she covered them. At least this time she'd known what to expect.

Grandmother stepped back.

Green and yellow energy glowed around Bloodroot's trunk. Emerald lights sparkled and a wizened man, with silver hair, staggered out clutching a staff and covered in redwood pulp. Keelie recognized him as the wizard from her dreams, and as the man in the bubble with Grandmother. Viran, the Redwood Tree Shepherd.

"Thank you, my dears." He bowed his head to them.

Bella floated over to Keelie, who stared at her warily, wondering what she would do next. She didn't know if she had it in her to fight anymore.

Grandmother struggled to her feet, and Keelie let Viran lean on her shoulder. Bella zoomed around in front of them, blocking their way.

"You can't take him. His magic belongs to me."

"Stay away from my grandchild." Grandmother stepped forward, confronting her.

"Grandmother, be careful. She's still plenty strong."

Grandmother held out her hands and green magic floated upwards from her palms. "I send you back to your tree and there bind you, Bella. Walk no more."

Bella's face lengthened with dismay and she started to fade, but she pulled on her power and returned. "None but the Redwood Tree Shepherd can do that, and I've taken his power. You are no longer lady of any forest. Your words have no power, here."

"You have a new tree shepherd now, Bella." Viran's voice was strong, but he leaned more on Keelie as if the effort of speaking had drained him of his last bit of energy. "Can you not feel it?"

"That is not possible." Bella frowned as she glared at Viran. "You are our shepherd. You have always been our shepherd."

"My body is worn out. My time is ended," Viran said. He turned to Grandmother. "Lady Keliatiel, I grant you my place, my power. By the Great Sylvus, so be it."

Grandmother stood taller and bowed her head to him. Around them, trees murmured their greetings to their new shepherdess.

Keelie could feel more of Viran's life force ebbing away. She knew no healing spells to help a dying tree shepherd. She remembered a passage about the Great Sylvus, and the covenant formed between shepherds and forests. She knew what she had to do. She said the words:

*"Hear the Lore of Old, formed in the days of stars and moon, When forests slept in the Mother's womb, And*

*the Great Sylvus called upon his shepherds, To guard the*
*flock of wood and green."*

Grandmother smiled. "Elianard will be pleased."

Keelie grinned back. Warmth and loved filled her as Grandmother reached out to grasp Keelie's hand, and together they joined their green magic and pushed Bella's protesting spirit back into her trunk.

"My babies, who will watch my babies?" Bella's face appeared on her trunk.

Sympathy for the tree filled Keelie. Bella had witnessed the death of so many of her children in the forest.

"I will," Grandmother said.

"I will help." Keelie added.

Viran lifted his staff. "Sleep, Bella."

The tree closed her eyes and her face faded back into the coarse bark of the redwood.

Viran leaned against Keelie. "My time is short."

Just then, Coyote rushed toward Keelie. Behind him, Tavyn-Bloodroot screamed in outrage and rushed toward Grandmother, Keelie, and Viran, his sword raised. Sean leaped into the clearing after him and attacked. Tavyn-Bloodroot whirled, clashing his sword against Sean's. Grandmother hurried Keelie and Viran to the other side of Bloodroot's massive trunk. Keelie pushed Grandmother's hands away, anxious to see. Sean fought hard, but his sword seemed to have no effect on the tree-possessed elf.

Tavyn-Bloodroot knocked Sean's sword aside and pinned him to another tree with one arm. He laughed like a cartoon villain about to deliver an evil monologue. "Do you think you can hurt me, elf?"

A blast erupted like lightning from inside Tavyn-Bloodroot. The impact sent Sean stumbling back.

The skin over Tavyn's face split in two, and dark green light tinged in purple and red spilled out. Sean reached out and tore at Tavyn's face, pulling the skin from the features that pushed out from below the flesh.

The creature underneath was humanoid, with long pointed ears that arced behind his head and long, greasy dreadlocks. His eyes were bright green, the pupils vertical slits that glowed with malevolence. Even his skin was vile—mottled green and gray, with splatters of red.

Although she'd never seen one, Keelie knew she stood before a goblin.

"I thought you guys were gone," she whispered. She'd had dreams about creatures like this, but she thought they were the boogeyman.

Tavyn whirled upon Sean, whose sword was at the ready once more. "Elf cannot kill elf, Sean-Niriel's-son. The price is high for those who do."

"You are no elf."

That was the truth. Keelie stared at the goblin. He was like a Red Cap on steroids.

Tavyn laughed. "I am half elf. Let me make a long family saga short: I'm the half-elf, half-goblin son of Kalix's sister. Kalix raised me as his own, but he is the one who slew my goblin father, he whose blood nourishes the roots of the

Ancients. Kalix knew I was part goblin, but I hid my true nature from him."

Viran frowned. "I told Kalix nothing good ever came of helping a goblin."

Tavyn hissed. "You're dying, old man, and because of your advice, my father is dead. But his intent lives on in the trees. You couldn't stop that, tree shepherd."

Sean was nodding grimly. "I will let you live, goblin, but never come near Keelie again."

"I promise. I'll be a good goblin and leave your girl-friend, alone." He laughed. "Good goblin."

Tavyn turned to Grandmother, who was staring in disbelief at the creature in front of her. "You thought Bloodroot possessed Tavyn. It was the other way around. I took over Bloodroot."

Then Tavyn's bitter gaze focused on Keelie. "We have a lot in common, you and I, Keliel."

"I have nothing in common with you." She was disgusted by Tavyn. He'd been such a handsome young elf, but his true nature was repellent.

"You and I both lost a parent, and we are both half-breeds. We have the blood of the dark fae singing within us, and we both can control Earth magic." Tavyn grinned at Keelie. "You and I are going to make a wonderful pair." He made a gesture and suddenly he was Tavyn the elf again, although his long hair was still in dreads.

Sean moved forward. Tavyn spun around and pointed a finger. "Better keep an eye on your lovely Keelie. The goblins know her name."

Tavyn laughed again and began to spin. Dirt flew everywhere, spraying them with rocks and debris. In seconds, Tavyn was gone. A hole in the earth was all that remained. From deep inside came the jangle of Peascod's jester hat, and dark laughter. Was the creepy jester a goblin, too? That would explain a lot.

Chills consumed Keelie. She knew this wouldn't be the last time she saw Tavyn, and she wondered what his relationship was with Peascod. She didn't want to see either of them ever again.

A tree spirit drifted over, and Keelie realized that it was Bloodroot. Without the goblins' influence he seemed stern, but somehow kindly. His tree-face eyes were gray, no longer the brilliant green of the goblin's poisoned sap. He hovered near Viran. Viran closed his eyes. Keelie knew the two were talking in tree speak, but she couldn't hear their words.

The Redwood Tree Shepherd nodded. "It is time, Keliatiel."

"What's going on?" Keelie asked.

Grandmother closed her eyes. Green magic flowed through her body, and when she reopened her eyes, they were a supernaturally bright green.

"Are you both in agreement?" she asked.

"Yes, my lady." Viran straightened.

The tree spirit Bloodroot bowed. *Yes, shepherdess.*

"We must wait until Lord Zekeliel comes, and then we shall perform the ceremony."

"Dad's coming?" Keelie asked.

"It's going to be okay, Keelie." Grandmother said reassuringly. She stepped closer to Viran, and he leaned on her. "I've summoned your father. The trees are no longer blocking us."

The Redwood Tree Shepherd placed his gnarled hand on Keelie's shoulder. "It is my time to fade, child. Bloodroot has requested an Involucrum: a binding of shepherd and tree. My spirit will live on with the tree. We will become as one, and I will be able to guide the new treelings. So, in a way, I will still be here. You and your father will help me make the transition."

"But you can't fade. I just found you." Tears brimmed in Keelie's eyes, making everything blurry.

"You have saved me, child."

"Keelie," a soft voice said from below. It was Coyote. He pointed his sharp nose toward the clearing behind them.

Risa was carrying Knot in her arms. His head was pressed against her chest, his legs dangled, and his tail hung limp. She clutched him tightly to her chest. "Keelie, what are we going to do?"

"Knot?" The tears that had blurred Keelie's eyes now flowed down her cheeks. She couldn't lose him. He was gross and obnoxious and she loved him so much. She couldn't live without him. Her throat burned and her heart ached with such deep pain that she feared taking her next breath. How could she live without Knot?

Keelie reached out to Risa. "May I hold him?"

Wetness shimmered in Risa's eyes. She sobbed and held Knot's body closer.

"He was my guardian." Keelie just wanted to say good-bye.

Risa nodded and gently kissed Knot on the top of his furry head. "Good night, my sweet prince." She laid the cat in Keelie's arms.

Keelie pressed his solid weight close to her chest. This was where he belonged, next to her heart. "How am I going to live without you?" She bent down closer to him and whispered in his ear, so only she and he knew the words she said. "I love you."

Risa sobbed.

Keelie's hot tears fell on Knot's thick orange fur. She reached up to smooth them away—and felt the purring. She saw his paws squeeze into little biscuits, and his tail twitch upward.

"I should drop you on your pumpkin-colored head," Keelie hissed in his ear. "You faker." She looked up at Risa, who was staring at her, startled. "He's going to be fine." She didn't know whether to be relieved or angry at Knot's play-acting.

"How can you be so cold-hearted? You saw how he was thrown up against that tree." Risa's eyes were wide.

Knot reached up and swatted Keelie on the cheek, then twisted in her grasp and sprang away.

"You rotten cat," she called after him.

He ran over to Risa and launched himself onto her leg, sinking his claws deep into her skin. "Ow!" The elf girl shook her leg. Knot released his claws and bolted away, as if he had fleas dancing in his fur.

Keelie placed her elbow on Risa's shoulder. "I think he's warming up to you. He's showing you some affection."

"That's affection?" Risa rubbed her injured leg. "He's never hurt me before."

"Hard to explain about fae cats."

Sean was lowering Scott and Laurie's cages. They argued all the way down.

"You led me to believe that you cared," Laurie shouted.

"I did not. I wanted to get to know Risa. She's hot."

"And what am I?"

"You're not my type. You're into shopping and yourself."

"I am not."

"That's all you talked about on the beach—yourself."

"Ahh!" Laurie's outraged yell echoed from the trees.

"True love?" Sean cocked an eyebrow at Keelie.

She stared dubiously at the bickering couple. "Not on a dare."

Sean was about to say more, but Grandmother called for Keelie's help. He smiled. "Later," he said softly.

It was all the promise she needed.

Keelie dressed in her green robes and raised the hood over her head. She dreaded the Involucrum. Dad had arrived last night, and today, at dawn, Viran would bind his spirit with Bloodroot. Viran had chosen a destiny that would allow him to continue in the forest.

Dad and Grandmother were waiting for her by Wena's roots. The tree shepherds would perform the ceremony alone, without any of the other elves.

She traveled the sap to the bottom.

Grandmother and Dad wore green robes also, except theirs were embroidered with gold-and-silver trees. Viran wore a plain white robe and leaned on his staff. He looked like a medieval monk ready to go to prayers.

He held out his elbow. "I would be honored if you would accompany me to the Grove of the Ancients."

Keelie blinked several times in an attempt to stop the tears from flowing. "I would be honored."

She accepted his outstretched elbow. It was still dawn and foggy, with the briny scent of the ocean in the air. The trees, in spirit form, drifted along with them.

Silence accompanied their reverent walk to the Grove of the Ancients. There, trees as tall as the sky reached for the heavens, visible now in the dim early morning light. Keelie sensed their great power and wisdom. She was awed as she gazed upwards.

Viran leaned closer to her. "The trees say they can hear the stars sing to the Earth." The elder elf looked up. "I look forward to hearing the stars sing to the Earth." He smiled at her and patted her hand.

"I'm sure it will be beautiful." Keelie blinked back tears. She saw the distinctive red bark of Bloodroot, now streaked with gold.

Viran winked and grinned mischievously. She felt sad

that she hadn't had the opportunity to get to know him. She would've learned a lot from him. Maybe she still could.

A tall tree spirit walked forward. "I am Hurus." A long gossamer beard hung from his chin. "We're honored, tree shepherds, that you will help our shepherd and brother find peace in the binding of souls."

Dad and Grandmother bowed their heads. "It is our honor, Hurus."

"May the Great Sylvus be with you." Bloodroot drifted forward and bowed his head.

The sleeves of Dad's robe billowed in the cool breeze as he held out his hand. Keelie left Viran to stand by her father and grandmother, and Viran and Bloodroot walked to the center of the Grove. Hurus moved to the southern point of the circle, and Dad took the north. Grandmother stood to the east of the two in the center, and Keelie walked slowly to the last place, on the west.

As they stood in the four cardinal directions, faint gold light was beginning to illuminate the east. Clouds seemed to be dipped in pink, as if some supernatural being had finger painted in the sky. The pale rays seemed to create a celestial crown over Grandmother's hooded head.

Viran faced Bloodroot's spirit.

Dad's voice boomed as he spoke, lifting his arms to the sky. "May our brothers, tree and shepherd, become as one. May their unified wisdom guide this forest. May the Great Sylvus bring his blessings upon them."

The wind began to blow, and the green magic of the trees flowed across the ground, then surrounded them. The entire forest was present, great trees and small. Grandmother raised her arms, and Keelie did as well, as did the tall tree spirit and Dad. Keelie felt the sizzle of green magic spark from hand to hand until Bloodroot and Viran were in a circle of green power that pulsed with the heart of the ancient forest.

For the first time, Keelie could hear the redwoods in her head. The chiming voices of the tree spirits joined in song, a harmony of celebration for their brother the tree shepherd. Keelie wanted to be a part of this song forever. She felt herself lean into it, letting her magical essence open fully. Across from her, Grandmother made a motion, and the song abruptly vanished. She saw Grandmother exchange a look with Dad.

Now she knew what the tree shepherds meant to their forests. Keelie shivered with pride in her father, as well as with reverence and sadness as she watched Viran's body fade away until there was nothing but a bright light.

As the sun climbed higher in the sky, the light of Viran's spirit melded with Bloodroot's, and Keelie could see both of them, one superimposed on the other. Grandmother stepped aside to let them drift to Bloodroot's tree and enter into it. Bloodroot went first, and then Viran. As Viran's spirit entered the tree, he turned and touched his chest, then pointed at the tree shepherds. A spark flew from his fingertip as he faded, forever marking the bark in the exact spot where a human heart would be.

The other tree spirits faded as the sun's rays touched the treetops, chasing the sea mist in the forest below. Around them, a mantle of green and a sense of peace filled the Grove of the Ancients. Birds sang and flitted and swooped.

Keelie lowered her hood and lifted her face to the sun's warmth.

Dad walked over to her, a big grin on his face. "Time to go, kiddo."

"So that's it? That's an Involucrum? I sort of expected something bigger," Keelie lied. It had been profoundly awesome.

"Like what?" Dad asked.

"I don't know. Something with more fireworks."

Dad tousled her curls. "The Great Sylvus likes to keep things simple."

Grandmother blinked several times and held her head high as she joined them. "I agree. Keeping to the basics keeps everything closer to the heart."

A surprised Keelie looked toward her grandmother. When had she become so philosophical?

Grandmother caught Keelie's gaze and sniffed, suddenly remembering her true nature. "Zeke, I need to return to the village. I need my rest for the performance tonight." She lifted the hem of her robe and strode forward.

Dad arched a questioning eyebrow toward Keelie.

She shrugged. "The show must go on."

After breakfast, they walked to Heartwood to open up shop. Dad smoothed his hand over the counter as if greeting an old friend. Keelie knew he was sourcing the wood. Somewhere around here, Lord Elianard was in a meeting with the redwood elves, having a serious discussion about the use of magic and the aftermath of the goblin's taint. The appearance of goblins in the forest complicated the Lore Master's job. He'd have to update parts of the Compendium. Keelie groaned at the thought of all the studying she had yet to do.

"I heard you were doing well with the shop," Dad said. "I took a look at the books this morning. Very impressive." His hair was loosely tied in a ponytail now, out of the way, but still covering his pointed ear tips.

Keelie beamed as she tallied the sales numbers. She'd been wanting to demonstrate her efficiency at handling the business. "So am I good enough to get a bigger clothes allowance? They don't have a Francesca outlet here, but when we get to the High Mountain Faire, I'd love a new outfit. It's not too expensive."

"I know your definition of 'not too expensive' and I shudder at the thought, but we'll see."

"How was your meeting with Kalix?" Keelie looked up from the yellow pad. The elf ranger had defended his half-goblin nephew, saying that he'd only been thinking of the welfare of the trees. His aunt had done the same.

"Not good." Dad arched his eyebrow in irritation. "I have issued a warning to all elves around the world about Tavyn and the re-emergence of the goblins. Things are going to be different," he added sadly. "It's as if we've lost our innocence now that we know they are back. We're always going to have to be on guard. Always wondering if the goblins are planning something."

"Maybe it won't be as bad as you think," Keelie said. "At least the other elves are aware, and the clans are now communicating with one another."

Dad shrugged. "I don't know." He patted the counter with his right hand. "I have another meeting in an hour. I'm flummoxed by the way the redwood elves think about the world in general, but they like your grandmother. In fact, they love her as their new tree shepherd. Mother seems content, but I'm not so sure."

"Kalix and Sariela said that she could stay with them as long as she wants, but she's decided to build a new place for herself, closer to the Grove." Keelie wondered how Kalix and Sariela were going to live with the truth of what their nephew had done.

"She will adapt," Dad said. He sounded more hopeful than certain.

"I think the way a tree or a person thinks is related to where their roots are first planted." Keelie knew it was a lame saying, but she hoped Dad would get the general idea. Grandmother was happy being in the Redwood Forest. She was walking and talking with the Ancients and having a good time doing it. Keelie returned her attention to her yellow note pad and her numbers.

Dad kept hanging around, as if he had something to say but didn't know how to express it. Never a good sign. She ignored him until he cleared his throat. "Keelie."

"Yes, Dad?"

"It's going to take a while to straighten things out in the redwoods. It's good we have another week at the festival. You're going to need to continue to run Heartwood." He looked kind of worried about what her possible reaction might be to his next words. "By yourself."

That was it? She thought she was going to get a lecture about Sean.

"No problem, Dad. I've been doing it by myself all along. However, you're going to need to make some more baby blocks and dollhouses. We're out of stock."

He stared, open-mouthed, as if he couldn't believe what he was hearing. "I'm proud of you. I don't have time to make more blocks, though."

"They're our biggest impulse-seller. We need more."

"Maybe later." He looked outside, as if searching for a way to make an escape.

"Quit whining and get to work. I've got customers asking for the blocks, and my supplier is slacking."

He brushed a kiss across her forehead. "You are a hard taskmistress." Keelie grinned as he vanished into the rear of the shop to look for tools and scrap wood.

She put away her account book and pad and walked over to Tudor Turnings. Sean wouldn't be free until the evening because he was taking Earth magic classes with Sir Davey. All the jousters were taking emergency Earth magic lessons, to use when dealing with the goblins.

Keelie thought again of Tavyn, which in turn reminded her of Peascod. She shivered. She truly wished she'd never see them again.

Tudor Turnings was empty. The shop was crammed with fun furniture, the type of stuff that children loved, with odd knobs and painted faces inside of drawers. Scott was no-where to be seen. A strange smacky noise was coming from behind the counter. She hoped it wasn't a rat.

Keelie leaned over to investigate, then pulled quickly back.

Scott and Laurie were kissing, mouths glued to one an-other in an intense lip-lock. It looked as if Laurie was going to suck all of Scott's teeth out of his face.

Keelie backed away, then ran out of the shop.

As she rushed past Risa's Green Goddess cart, the elf girl called out, "Hey Keelie, do you think your friend Janice could ship me some herbs? Like real fast?"

Keelie stopped. Risa was holding two empty tea mugs in her hands.

"What herbs?" She looked at the jars of bath products, bottles of tinctures, and tins of salves in the cart. It was packed to the brim with Risa's fragrant herbal creations. "What do you possibly need that you can't get from your father back home?"

"Some lovewort flowers," Risa grinned mischievously and glanced over in the direction of Tudor Turnings.

"Lovewort flowers?" Keelie turned back and thought she heard more noisy kissing. She stared at the empty mugs. No wonder love was in the air.

Inside Heartwood, Dad was sorting through tools on the counter. He'd set out a saw and an old-fashioned drill bit. "Leave these here, Keelie. I have to be at a meeting in five minutes, but I'll return."

"Lord Zekeliel, may I prepare you a cup of tea? You can

drink it on your way to the meeting." Risa batted her eyelashes and smiled coyly.

"No tea for Dad. He's allergic." Keelie grabbed Dad by the elbow and nudged him along.

Dad laughed as Keelie guided him along the path to the Globe. "That was rude and unlike you, Keelie. I thought you liked Risa now."

"She's okay. But Dad, promise me, whatever you do, don't drink anything she gives you."

The last thing Keelie needed was a stepmother.

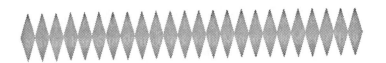

# epilogue

The following week, Keelie packed up the last remaining items in the shop. She looked forward to returning to her home forest—even if it was only for a couple of days. She'd been summoned to the Northwoods, and Sean would be going with her.

Knot was sleeping on an empty shelf, using the Compendium as a pillow. He smelled like mead, probably because he spent all of his spare time at the Queen's Alehouse. Keelie yanked the book out from underneath him and smiled as his head hit the board with a loud thud. He rolled over with a snort.

It took two hands to hold the Compendium. Keelie had to admit she liked the old book. Lord Elianard had been right. She had learned a lot from it. The hay-fever and calm charms had come in handy, and the information about goblins would be useful. If she had to be totally honest, she must admit she liked reading it. It made her feel magically nerdy.

Grandmother and Risa entered the shop.

"Is he here?" Risa asked, tossing her curls.

Keelie knew she meant Knot. She pointed beneath the shelf. "He's sleeping. He had a few meads with the jousters."

"He'll be down at the stables at all hours now that he's hanging out with them," Risa said in a disapproving tone.

"We need to build up the Dread in the Redwood Forest to protect the new treelings," Grandmother announced. A few days as the Redwood Tree Shepherd and she was already barking out orders.

"There's no way I'm exposing myself to the redwoods like that," Keelie said. And she didn't have Alora to help her this time, either.

"Actually, I had another idea for protecting the forest," Risa said. She exchanged a look with Grandmother, who motioned for her to continue. Keelie didn't like the idea of these two in cahoots together.

"I think maybe a charm will do, instead."

"A charm?" Keelie stared at the elf girl.

"Yes," Grandmother said. "I would tap into the 'nature' around here and you would create that calm charm, like you did for Laurie." Risa nodded in agreement.

"Are you kidding me?" Keelie said. "I can't put a calm charm on the entire Redwood Forest."

"No, we'd just do it at the park entrance."

Then Keelie understood. If she tied the charm to the park entrance sign, then people would feel calm and happy entering the park. Happy people love redwoods. Happy redwoods would mean happy treelings, growing up without ever plotting evil deeds.

She lifted the Compendium. "Ladies, let's get to work."

At the Redwood Park entrance sign, Keelie held up the elven charm book. Risa stood to the left, and Grandmother stood to the right. Beams of sunlight shone down through storm clouds onto the sign, and the tall Ancients around them made the afternoon silence seem almost holy.

Knot balanced atop the wooden sign like a tourist kitty waiting for someone to take his picture. The only thing missing was Smokey the Bear to pose with him.

"Get off of there." Keelie gestured at him. He ignored her and washed his tail.

"Leave him, he looks cute," Risa insisted. Keelie wondered if the elf girl would ever be totally rid of the love potion in her system.

Grandmother lifted her hands in exasperation. "Just get on with it."

Pulling on a thread of Earth magic, Keelie summoned the fairy power that lay beneath their feet. She held the magics until she felt Grandmother's power surround them, then wove the three magics together. Risa added her green garden magic, as well.

Keelie closed her eyes and spoke the elven words to the calm charm. She thought about families coming to the forest, filled with love and reverence for the redwoods and wanting to protect them. "People will love the redwoods," she said aloud. "They will protect them. "

The strands of their magical energies glowed strongly as they surrounded the sign. Gold, silver, dark green, bright green, and—pumpkin orange?

A loud purring interrupted them. Keelie opened her eyes.

Orange cat hair floated in a shaft of sunlight. Grandmother swatted it away from her nose. "Cats!"

"I wonder if it's going to work," Risa said.

Grandmother looked pensive. "Of course it will."

Keelie stared at Knot, who stared back impassively. Had no one else seen the pumpkin-orange energy?

A hybrid minivan pulled up in front of the sign and parked. A family of five jumped out. The mom and dad and their three kids looked stressed. They rushed to the sign.

"These are some big trees, Doris. I'll bet they'd make a lot of patio furniture." Dad looked at the two boys and the three of them laughed.

Grandmother groaned. "Let's go. I can't stand it."

Risa looked shocked. "Do they really think of furniture when first they see these trees?"

The mother motioned for the kids and husband to hurry. "Come on, let's get a picture and get a move on. I want to get to the All You Can Eat buffet in Juliet City."

By the time they reached the sign, Grandmother had

spoken a hiding spell to make the three of them invisible. Handy, thought Keelie. Gotta learn to do that one.

She turned to look at the family, which had suddenly grown quiet. Smiles draped their faces. Everyone was gazing up at the tall redwoods. The dad looked at the mom. "I thought it would be good for the kids to see these ancient trees."

"They're so beautiful," the mother said, with awe in her voice. "Majestic. They should be protected, always."

The kids were smiling. "Can we hike? I want a book that identifies all the trees."

"I want to be a forest ranger when I grow up," the little girl said. "I want to take care of these trees forever."

The dad nodded. "What a great idea. Come on, kids."

As the family walked away, pointing out the wonders in the forest, Grandmother nodded with satisfaction. "Job well done, ladies."

Only Keelie overhead the dad say, "I think we need to get a cat."

"Cats are wonderful creatures," the mother said dreamily.

"Let's get two," the little boy said.

"Of course," their father agreed.

The kids shouted with happiness.

Grandmother led the way through the forest, with Risa and Keelie behind her. Bounding back and forth through the ferns in front of them was a very self-satisfied Knot.

## About Gillian Summers

A forest dweller, Gillian was raised by gypsies at a Renaissance Faire. She likes knitting, hot soup, and costumes, and adores oatmeal—especially in the form of cookies. She loathes concrete, but tolerates it if it means attending a science fiction convention. She's an obsessive collector of beads, recipes, knitting needles, and tarot cards, and admits to reading *InStyle* Magazine. You can find her in her north Georgia cabin, where she lives with her large, friendly dogs and obnoxious cats, and at www.gilliansummers.com.

*Watch for Book II*
*of the Scions of Shadow Trilogy.*

# FAIRE FOLK TRILOGY
## BOOKS 1, 2 & 3 OF THE FAIRE FOLK SAGA

### The Tree Shepherd's Daughter
978-0-7387-1081-5 • 336 pp. • US $9.95

After her mother dies, fifteen-year-old Keelie Heartwood suddenly finds herself reenacting the Dark Ages at a Colorado renaissance festival with her nomadic father—an L.A. girl's worst nightmare! Even weirder, Keelie realizes that she can see fairies and communicate with trees. Coping with her new identity brings Keelie face-to-face with a community of elves, guarded secrets, and the threat of disaster.

### Into the Wildewood
978-0-7387-1332-8 • 312 pp. • US $9.95

Finally getting to know her dad has been cool. But camping out in a homemade gingerbread RV while acting out the sixteenth century? Not so fab. Actually, life for Keelie is less than enchanting. Fairies appearing in the oddest places. That vain and nasty elf-girl Elia. And why hasn't Sean, the hot elf who kissed her, called? Keelie is pretty sure that things couldn't get any stranger—until a unicorn shows up!

### The Secret of the Dread Forest
978-0-7387-1411-0 • 288 pp. • US $9.95

Keelie's "real" friends are gone, her dad is busy being Lord of the Forest, and her budding romance with the hunky Sean is dashed. Except for her impossible cat Knot, and Alora, a bratty little princess tree, Keelie has no one to hang with—except her frenemy, the elf-girl Elia. Meanwhile, an age-old rift among the elves reaches a dangerous climax. The fate of the Dread Forest—and of all who dwell within it—lies in Keelie's hands.

www.fluxnow.com    available at your favorite bookstore    1.877.639.9753    flux